COERCION

Also by Tim Tigner

Flash

Betrayal

COERCION

A THRILLER

TIM TIGNER

This is a work of fiction. Names, characters, organizations, places, events, and incidents are either products of the author's imagination or are used fictitiously.

Published by Thomas & Mercer, Seattle

www.apub.com

ISBN-13: 9781503944367
ISBN-10: 1503944360

Cover design by Chelsea Wirtz

Printed in the United States of America

This novel is dedicated to my beloved wife Elena, whose support and sacrifices made it possible.

CAST OF CHARACTERS

Alex Ferris: International Private Investigator.
Andrey Demerko: Chief of Staff for Minister Sugurov.
Anna Zaitseva: Doctor at Academic City Hospital.
Elaine Evans: Engineer at United Electronics.
Frank Ferris: Alex's fraternal twin brother.
Igor Stepashin: KGB Head of the Guards Directorate.
Jason Stormer: Head of Stormer & Associates.
Knyaz AG: Karpov's company.
Knyaz: Name for Karpov's inner circle.
Kostya Zaitsev: Anna's brother (deceased).
Leo Antsiferov: Deputy Minister of Foreign Affairs.
Luda Orlova: Senior Accountant at SibOil.
Maximov: KGB Major and Aide to Karpov.
Mikhail Sergeyevich Gorbachev: President of USSR.
Pavel Sugurov: Minister of Foreign Affairs.
Professor Petrov: Anna's patient.
Sergey Shipilov: KGB Agent working for Yarik.
Vasily Karpov: KGB Head of Industrial Security.
Victor Titov: Deep-cover KGB mole. Karpov's son.
Vova: Male nurse at Academic City Hospital.
Yarik: KGB Head of the Executive Action Directorate.

"We had no idea the Soviets were ripping off our technology so skillfully, so comprehensively, so effectively, right under our noses."

—*Richard N. Perle, Assistant Secretary of Defense*

PROLOGUE

KGB Research Facility, Siberia, 1979

The door closed behind them with a hiss. General Vasily Karpov knew it was the hermetic seal, but he couldn't help feeling that the room was scolding him for what he was about to do.

He looked up at Yarik for support—the giant was a pro—but the steely stare coming back at him was somehow more disturbing than the images Karpov sought to drown out, and he looked away. Karpov appreciated Yarik's point of view and respected the enforcer's binary code of ethics, but as a chess grand master he had a hard time reducing things to a simple them-or-us. He wanted to do better.

In contrast, General Igor Stepashin's face showed a calm, supportive resolve. It meant little to Karpov. As a diplomat, Stepashin always showed the appropriate emotion. To know his true state of mind you had to look deep. Karpov chose not to look. This might be a classic moral conundrum, but it was hardly a dilemma. The needs of the many did outweigh the needs of the few.

As their country's future president, Karpov felt compelled to demonstrate leadership, to make a meaningful speech about posterity and sacrifice, but there was no room in that sterile corridor for such big words. Instead, he looked down at the detonator in his hand and thought about the future—first the country's, and then, with mixed feelings, his own. Murder changes a man . . .

He pressed the red button.

Karpov could not see or hear what happened on the other side of the laboratory door, but as the head of the KGB's Scientific and Technical Directorate, he knew how Noxin nerve gas worked. The moment he closed the door he found himself picturing the scene. It was as though he were still in the room. A part of his soul always would be.

He pictured the six scientists and engineers shaking hands and patting backs, congratulating each other on the successful completion and flawless presentation of the Peitho Pill. It was a feel-good moment, and they were justifiably proud, having dedicated eighteen months of their lives to secretly developing their general's audacious invention.

Then a whiff of gas turned their euphoria to hysteria, flooding their bodies with adrenaline as their limbic minds registered the alkaloid scent. But no act or agent could reverse the crushing hyperconstriction of their diaphragms. Their emptied lungs would never fill again. Noxin could not be denied.

Karpov bowed his head and clenched his eyes, but images of futile gasps and grimaced lips kept coming. He opened his eyes and tried to focus his mind on the cascading numbers of his digital watch. He had known all along that this day would come. Fifty-eight, fifty-nine, sixty—sixty seconds since detonation. No doubt they were frantically pumping each other's chests—desperate minds grasping at feeble straws. By now Kiril had paired up with Dima, Oleg with Anton, and Vanya with Mark. As professionals, they knew it was pointless, but as family men, what alternative did they have? They would keep at it until splintering ribs punctured starving lungs or exhaustion overtook them . . .

He kicked the corridor's stainless baseboard. "No matter. They're martyrs now, even if only we three will ever know." Yarik and Stepashin cocked their heads, but Karpov paid them no heed. He had not meant to think aloud.

It was true, he thought. The sacrifice those scientists were making here today gave him the exclusive use of the Peitho Pill and with it, the power to heal their ailing nation. The Soviet Union was in desperate need of a viable economic system, and Peitho empowered Karpov to create one. What were half a dozen lives in comparison?

Karpov stopped pacing the corridor and checked his watch again. It would take another ten minutes for the laboratory's advanced ventilation system to scrub the Noxin from the air. Then the three general officers could reenter, retrieve all the Peitho Pill materials, and replace them with ones from the Noxin nerve gas project. The cover-up would be as airtight as the laboratory, and Peitho would be theirs alone.

Stepashin interrupted the silence. "You've really outdone yourself, Karpov. You told us it was going to be huge, but the opportunities Peitho presents seem limitless. We'll be able to control anyone, get anything—"

"And do it secretly," Yarik interjected. "Wish I'd thought of it."

Karpov stopped pacing and looked up. If his friends were not distracted by sentiment . . . He felt the fire reigniting in his eyes, like the pilot light on a blast furnace. "I have the advantage of seeing a lot of gadget and gizmo proposals in the course of my job. One of them got me thinking. It was a special bomb, a bomb designed to blow up a car at the prompting of a radio signal. It was the size of a pea," he held up his thumb and index finger in the tiny sign, "small enough to slip into a car's gas tank. That was the mental trigger, the size of the thing. I reasoned that if you paired up one of its miniature radio receivers with a single drop of the lab's latest poison, you could then threaten to do the same thing to a person—terminate him at will, I mean."

A flash of understanding shot across Yarik's face. He'd always enjoyed an intuitive grasp of the military tactics. "But we won't use it for that, for termination, will we?"

"No, we won't. We're going to get creative . . ."

CHAPTER 1

Siberia, August 1990

A powerful gust of wind shook the helicopter and yanked Deputy Minister Leo Antsiferov out of his contemplative trance. As his sweaty hand clenched the bucking joystick, his eyes refocused their thousand-yard stare on the wild surroundings. The craggy peaks and crinkled slopes of the Siberian outback were breathtaking in the moonlight. Leo used to find peace while flying in conditions like these, but tonight his mind was as blustery as the weather. There were too many reminders.

First, there was his passenger, Andrey Demerko. Sitting down in the gunner's seat, Andrey was as perceptive as a man could be, yet ignorant as the rocks over which they flew. He had once been Leo's good friend—in fact Andrey still believed he was—but Leo was no friend to him, not really.

Then, there was the date. In three hours the sun would rise on the first anniversary of Leo's conscription. He found it hard to believe that only a year had passed since he was last a happy man, with a loving family, interesting work, and great prospects. Now he had dismal prospects, repulsive work, and an estranged wife. But little Georgy was still alive, so Leo had made a good trade.

He switched the helicopter's joystick to his left hand so he could wipe away tears with his right. Then he went back a year in his mind, playing over once again the dreadful night it all began, picking at the scab of a wound that would not heal.

♦ ♦ ♦

Leo remembered how peacefully that fateful evening had started. Only the thunderstorm raging outside hinted at the danger hidden within their Moscow apartment. Oxana was off visiting her sister; Maya and Georgy lay tucked in their beds, and his work was in order: *check, check, and check*. This combination gave Leo the ever-welcome opportunity to enjoy a good book the right way.

He grabbed a bottle of vodka from the freezer, *Crime and Punishment* from the bookshelf, and sank into his favorite leather armchair. These stolen hours and his children's loving smiles made Leo feel like the luckiest man alive.

He was deep into both the novel and the bottle when the phone finally disturbed his cherished reprieve. It was midnight. He set down Dostoyevsky and picked up the cordless receiver, answering without preamble: "How was your trip?"

"Listen to me very carefully." The voice was cold and computerized, its tone commanding. "Go to Maya's room."

Leo suffered a momentary mental delay something like a power glitch, then shock, fear, rage, and panic all ran their courses in a millisecond, jolting his synapses and neutralizing the vodka. He pulled the phone away from his ear, clutching it like a venomous snake while his mind and body accelerated to combat speed. He ran to the master bedroom and retrieved his handgun from the lockbox under the bed. The Makarov felt oddly heavy in his hand, reminding Leo that his days in uniform were well behind him now. He prayed his reflexes had not atrophied along with his muscles.

Leo arrived at the door to his daughter's room just twenty seconds after the phone's first ring. He found Maya peacefully asleep in her bed, but resisted the temptation to dismiss the caller outright. Instead, he stepped back to think. It wasn't easy with his heart playing timpani on his eardrums. There was no place in the room for an adult to hide, and the window was twelve stories up. It was a long shot, but Leo looked out anyway: nothing but the full moon above and the empty road below. He let out a deep breath and Maya stirred, causing the moonlight to dance in her hair. She looked like an angel with a halo of curly blond locks—Leo froze. Little Georgy also had curly blond hair, and his mother kept it a little too long, perhaps . . . No!

Leo ran to his boy's room and popped around the doorframe ready to fire. He found . . . nothing. Georgy, too, was quietly asleep in his bed.

Leo walked back to Maya's room and sat on the edge of her bed. Only practiced, diplomatic nerves kept him in check as he picked up the receiver again.

"I'm there."

"Good boy. Now, tell me today's pass codes for the Ministry mainframe."

The Ministry the caller referred to was Russia's Ministry of Foreign Affairs, where Leo was one of six deputy ministers. Handing over the computer pass codes would be like tipping Russia's hand at dozens of high-stakes international poker games. Other government organizations might have their books cooked for appearance's sake, but negotiators at the MFA had to know what was of true strategic importance to Russia, and what was propaganda.

"I can't do that."

The mechanical voice did not waver at the rebuff. "Of course you can, Leo. It is a simple choice, a trade really. You give me the codes, and I let your daughter live."

Leo's heart jumped back into his throat as the percussion recommenced in his ears. He threw down the phone and raced to the front door, his finger poised on the Makarov's trigger. All was quiet. He checked and double-checked the black-and-white screen of the intercom, unsure if he should trust the fuzzy image. The guard appeared to be at his post. Leo pushed the talk button. "Anything unusual to report, Arkady?"

"Nothing, sir."

"Thank you. Keep a watchful eye; I think something may be up."

"Yes, sir."

Enough with diplomacy. Leo returned to his daughter's room and picked up the receiver. Maya was still sleeping so he spoke softly, but firmly. "Go to hell!"

"No, Deputy Antsiferov, it is your daughter who is going to hell, and you are the one who is sending her there. Last chance, Leo. The codes. Do not make me do it."

The speaker sounded sober and sincere. Leo clenched his jaw. He was by his daughter's bed, gun in hand, guard at door. In all probability it was a Ministry security check—severe but not without precedent.

"No."

Three simple words followed, words that made it difficult for him to ask for anything ever again: "As you wish."

The scene that followed burned itself into Leo's retinas, and a year later he knew it would be there every time he closed his eyes for the rest of his life. Little Maya suddenly lifted her curly locks and opened her big blue eyes to look up at him with a scared look on her angelic face. She said, "Papa" in her sweet soprano, trembled as though possessed, and then she died.

Leo stared in disbelief. It was as though someone had turned out a light, Maya's light, the light of his life. His angel was dead.

Sometime later—whether seconds or hours he was not sure—Leo remembered the telephone. He peeled himself off his daughter's corpse and picked up the receiver.

"I'll get you! I'll get you if—"

"Listen, Leo. Listen." The mechanical voice cut him off with its icy command. "Go to Georgy's room."

CHAPTER 2

Siberia, August 1990

This is no time for self-pity, Leo thought. *You have a problem to solve.*

Problem to solve? More like disaster to avert. With one careless slip of the tongue, just a few superfluous words in a bar, he had set his friend Andrey up to receive a similar midnight call with an offer he couldn't refuse. Leo had to undo what he had done, and quickly. Each sweep of the helicopter's rotors brought Andrey that much closer to sharing his hell. The question was *how*.

Cruel coincidence had brought both Leo and Andrey to the same city and the same hotel on the same evening. Fate had picked up the job from there. Somewhere in the endless stream of vodka and war stories Leo had let it slip that he was piloting a helicopter to Novosibirsk early in the morning. Then, as if prompted by the Devil's own cue, Foreign Minister Sugurov had called his chief of staff: he needed Andrey in Moscow.

"We're in luck, sir. Leo is here with me, and he happens to be flying to Novosibirsk in a few hours. If I go with him, I can catch the early flight from there. That will get me to the Ministry by ten."

Leo had choked on his drink as he heard those words. That was six hours ago. He still tasted the vodka.

What Leo had not let slip was how or why he was flying. That story could never just slip out. The truth was, he had used rank, intimidation, and lies to gain the use of a military helicopter to smuggle a briefcase of God-knows-what to a dead-drop in Novosibirsk. He was playing messenger for his merciless masters.

Leo suspected that his masters had many clever ways of circumventing Soviet security, but he had few details on how they worked or even what they wanted, and he didn't care to speculate. As bad as his own situation was, the big picture was what haunted his dreams. In all likelihood, there were dozens if not hundreds of victims like him out there, a plague of conscripts secretly ravaging Russia—perhaps even the world. Who were they? What did their masters want? Where would it end?

His masters demanded absolute secrecy. They expected him to be alone that night in the helicopter. They would likely interpret Andrey's presence on this secret mission as an offensive maneuver, and then act accordingly.

Gazing through the helicopter windshield toward the black horizon, thinking about the void that occupied the place where his future had been, Leo found the courage to be honest with himself. He had gotten drunk and let his plans slip because subconsciously, he longed to share his burden.

Leo had kept his dreadful secret for a year, but he would not be able to hold it together for much longer. The stress of constantly deceiving everyone he loved and continually betraying everything he believed in was killing him. He had cancer of the soul. Ironically, in some regards it wasn't killing him fast enough. Not knowing who his masters were, what they had in mind, when they were watching him, or where this would lead, was literally driving him mad. He did not want to go out that way.

He needed to share his burden, to find a way out. Andrey Demerko was his best and only hope.

Andrey was the finest strategist Leo knew, and a powerful operative as well. Even with Andrey's help, however, he feared the situation was hopeless. Leo was no fool himself, and he couldn't even fathom how to begin to fight.

How do you attack an invisible enemy? Sure, he could try to uncover them, but how could he possibly avoid all the conscripted eyes and wary ears while scouring the darkness for his masters? How could he wipe them all out before they counterattacked? How do you thrust a sword when you don't know who is friend and who is foe? Where do you turn when you can't trust anybody? If they could reach a deputy minister, why not a minister? Why not a president? Gorbachev had a daughter. It was an agonizing situation for a soldier and a patriot to be in. He knew that the Devil was at work in his beloved country, and yet was powerless to fight.

The gamble Leo faced was whether Andrey would choose to look past Leo's traitorous acts to the coercion behind them and join Leo in the fight, or choose to follow protocol and have Leo arrested for treason.

Back in the bar Leo had been about to take that gamble when Foreign Minister Sugurov's call disrupted the collegial atmosphere, crumbling his will and providing a welcome chance to procrastinate.

Perhaps now was the time? They were still three hundred kilometers from Novosibirsk. It would normally take the Mi-28 only an hour to cover that distance at full throttle, but to avoid radar Leo was flying contour to the ground at low altitude so their flight time would be closer to ninety minutes. Would that be long enough?

His alternatives were very limited at this point. To save his friend, Leo had to find a way to make sure his masters did not see Andrey arrive with him. One option Leo had was to tell Andrey the truth, hoping to enlist his help but at least gaining enough understanding that he could then drop Andrey off somewhere before anyone saw them together. Alternatively, if Leo did not confide in Andrey, he would then have to contrive some inevitably far-fetched reason for getting his colleague out of the helicopter prior to reaching the airport. What could that possibly be? Leo started to brainstorm, but stopped himself abruptly. Who was he fooling? The time to talk had arrived.

Leo took a deep breath and began. "Andrey."

"Yeah."

"It's time I told you how Maya died."

For a second there was a silence as, Leo assumed, Andrey tried to digest the implication of what he had just heard. Then the world erupted around them.

An explosive crash somewhere behind them shook the helicopter violently before sending it into a plummeting spin. Time slowed down as Leo's mind raced and the rotors passed one by one. Had another aircraft hit them? Did a fuel leak catch fire? Were they fired upon? The helicopter was behaving as though the whole tail were gone. It was uncontrollable. He realized that at the moment the cause didn't really matter; the effect was all that counted.

As a veteran pilot, Leo knew that the only thing you could do without a tail was brace for impact. He thought of Oxana and Georgy, and how he loved them. He thought of Andrey and Sugurov, and how he had betrayed them. He thought of Maya, and how he would see her now. Strangely enough, it occurred to Leo that he was not scared. Perhaps he had no fear left for himself. Perhaps he just welcomed death. He closed his eyes, gritted his teeth, and thought about how sad it was for a man to go to his death knowing that he had failed.

CHAPTER 3

Three months later. Palo Alto, California, November 1990

Alex paused at the door to the hotel suite before knocking. He'd racked his brain to find a better path than this, one that didn't stray into a moral gray zone, but there simply wasn't one, and time was running out. He hoped that by leaving his gun at home, he would remain squarely on the side of the angels.

He rolled his broad shoulders and visualized his next moves. All three men were bigger, and two were pros. He was counting on solid preparation, superior training, the element of surprise, and perhaps an angel or two.

Alex scrunched his face a few times to relax his features. Then he smoothed his fake mustache, donned a smile, and knocked.

The peephole darkened and then the larger of the two bodyguards, the one Alex had nicknamed Big, opened the door wide. Big's three hundred pounds still blocked entry, but he wasn't acting hostile. They had come all the way from Colombia to visit Stanford on the invitation of the baseball team, and Alex was dressed in a Cardinal uniform, complete with cap and bat.

"I'm here to go over the schedule with Enrique, and answer any questions you might have. May I come in?"

Big stepped back, allowing Alex to pass. Beyond him in the large opening between the suite's sitting room and bedroom, Alex saw the second bodyguard. Ugly was sitting on Enrique's back as the prospective Cardinal knocked out push-ups. It was an impressive display of strength and a powerful indicator of personality, and it played right into Alex's hand.

As he brushed past Big, Alex used his left hand to discreetly plunge a tranquilizer dart into the bodyguard's left thigh while maintaining a friendly visage and warm eye contact with the others as they stood. Four quick but casual strides took him to within striking distance and exposed the rest of the bedroom. That was when his well-laid plan fell apart.

Two more men were standing there. Large men with thick forearms crossing broad chests. They too were Colombians, but they clearly weren't Enrique's friends, teammates, or domestic servants. These looked like his father's enforcers: rough, ready, and unreasonable.

But first things first. Alex brought his bat up and around and across Ugly's right wrist in a single sweep that carried all his momentum. As the crack of the bat and crunch of the bone gave voice to the violence of the blow and Ugly brought his good hand to his broken wrist, Alex used his left hand to pull a dart from the bandolier beneath his right sleeve and flick it forcefully into the wounded man's backside. Already leaning forward to clutch his wrist, Ugly nose-dived into the carpet as Enrique scurried behind Rough and Ready.

Outnumbered in close quarters, Alex knew that victory required speed, so he kept channeling his momentum. Accelerating the ash bat through a full arc, he launched it at Rough's forehead like a battering ram. As it flew he feigned a leap at Ready but spun instead, whipping another dart free in the process and sending it sailing toward Ready's center of mass before his foe could reorient. There was a crack and a curse, and Rough and Ready both dropped, leaving Enrique the last Colombian left standing.

"Sorry about your friends," Alex said. "But I really needed to get you alone. Sorry about this, too," he added, pulling another dart from his bandolier.

CHAPTER 4

Palo Alto, CAlifornia, 1980

"The Peregrine has hatched."

Victor had been just twenty-two when he heard those words for the second time. He was standing in a dimly lit, smoky room, watching horny fraternity guys make their last-ditch efforts to score liquor-loosened sorority girls while Pink Floyd blared numbingly in the background. Graduation was just twelve hours away.

A stunning coed with long blond hair walked through the crowd to Victor as though he were starring in a beer commercial. She put her arms around his neck, gave him a knockout smile, and started to dance without saying a word. It was the kind of sultry, undulating dance that called up images of Arabian nights and set your blood afire as your throat went dry. After a nice wide-eyed stare, Victor ripped his gaze from Blondie's cleavage and began to gyrate. She ran her tongue across her lips to focus his eyes and then mouthed the code in Russian.

Victor dropped his beer on the frat house floor as his mind balked beneath the weight of a dozen questions and the burden of things to come. She steadied him as his knees grew weak, while his erection stayed his bladder. Now he understood.

Once Victor stabilized, Blondie stepped back to scoff at him. Then she locked his eyes in a sober stare. "Remember, even at a party, you still serve *The Party*." Then she turned and dissolved into the crowd while reality closed around him like an iron fist. After years of establishing deep cover in the US, Victor was being activated.

He had come to the US five years earlier, a boy of seventeen. Once they implanted him with surgical precision, the KGB had withdrawn from Victor's life like a disease in remission. They wanted his roots to grow, wanted him to branch out, blend in, and develop. He sensed their presence from time to time—watching him, measuring him, judging his competency for things to come. It didn't really bother him. Life as a student had made his future with the KGB seem removed and abstract. He had put it out of his mind as something distant and foreign, like the threat of lung cancer to someone lighting a cigarette.

Victor knew that his college years in America were one long job interview, a KGB test. Now that he was graduating, it appeared the results were in. How had he scored? That was no simple question. Oh, his grades were great, and his student leadership outstanding, but Victor was never sure what the men in Moscow were really looking for. The price of failure, on the other hand, was crystal clear. He supposed they wanted it that way.

At least reacting to activation did not require much effort on his part. There were no bags to pack or bills to pay; they would take care of everything. Victor simply had to show up at the Air Canada desk, ready to go anywhere. He hoped Blondie would be accompanying him on the trip—a last-wish sort of thing—but it was not to be. Eight hours after graduation Victor found himself on the loneliest flight he ever took. Cyprus was a fine place to make a man disappear.

He landed on the Mediterranean island with a backpack over his shoulder and his heart on his sleeve. During disembarkation on the

Larnaca tarmac, Victor stepped back in the aircraft doorway so he could scan the waiting crowd while the other passengers descended the staircase. What was it going to be? Whom would they send? Would he ever leave this island?

A newspaper dipped, a perfectly coiffed head looked up, and piercing eyes arrested his gaze: *Father.*

Women flushed, men flinched, doors opened, doubts vanished—Vasily Karpov changed things just by walking into a room. The General's charisma had little effect on Victor, however. He was immune. All he ever felt was fear, the fear of letting the Great Man down. Was it a good sign that his father had come personally, or a bad one? Victor swallowed hard even as he drew his hand away from the ceramic knife in his sleeve.

Five minutes later, after a welcome as warm and tender as a court summons, Victor was sitting in silence in the passenger seat of a Mercedes. He was in the defendant's chair, about to be read his sentence. *Just get it over with.*

He worked hard not to fidget as his father exited west from the airport and accelerated toward the Troodos Mountains. Now that Victor knew he had a future, he was trying to take his mind off the fact that he was about to have it dictated to him. There was nothing on The General's face, no indication, good or bad, of things to come. If his father ever had a heart, he had lost it long ago.

They had driven a thousand vertical meters and were above the drifting mist when Karpov finally spoke. His words were the biggest surprise so far—yet but a subtle whiff of what was to come. "You're one of the few people on this planet who has lived in both superpowers, Victor. Tell me, which do you prefer?"

There was a loaded question. On the one hand, a KGB general was asking a deep-cover Soviet mole to choose between the US and the USSR. On the other hand, a father was asking his son if he would rather live in California or Siberia. Only one thing was certain: whether general or father, Vasily Karpov was all business. Victor would have to answer truthfully, defensibly, and quickly. He pictured the BMW he now drove—zero to sixty in under six seconds. Then he thought of the Lada he would have in Russia—zero to sixty only if he was lucky. And of course there was the food . . .

"You don't need to answer that," Karpov said, cracking what appeared to be a genuine smile. "Actually, if you set aside language and the proximity of relatives, there is only one honest answer to the question. The average American has ten times the purchasing power of the average Russian, and twenty times the choices. And then there's the weather. What I really want to ask you is this: Why? Why is that the case?"

Why indeed, Victor thought. Both the US and Russia were superpowers. The populations were roughly the same. The Soviet Union, with more than double America's landmass, had far more natural resources. Russia's population was better educated, its single-party government less encumbered. So what was it? Why would his father be asking . . . ? It took a couple of minutes, the hot and sweaty kind, but when he got it, Victor knew he had the right answer. But was it the correct one? "Bad management."

"Precisely."

Victor began to glow—for the first time in his life, he had said exactly the right thing to his father. And his father, for the first time since Victor had met him, seemed to be human. As it turned out, Karpov was just setting him up for the punt.

"We're going to change all that."

The words hit Victor with near-physical force, sending him reeling. Father was not one to fantasize or speculate.

Karpov pressed on. "Why is the Soviet Union considered a superpower?"

"The Red Army, our nuclear arsenal, the KGB . . ."

"Correct. Now a tougher question: Are those criteria still appropriate?"

"To determine if a country is a superpower?"

"Yes."

What did his father mean? By suggesting that military power was no longer appropriate, he was also implying that something had replaced it. What criterion could make a country more worthy of the superpower moniker than military might? Again, the lightbulb clicked on and the glow returned. "No. Now that nukes have leveled the field, *economic* power determines who rules."

"You're absolutely correct."

Another genuine smile. Victor braced himself for the next punt.

"When I was your age," Karpov continued, "I came to that same conclusion. For months it tormented my mind like a broken tooth. You see, Victor, for men like you and me, defining an issue is not enough. We have to solve it."

"How do you solve something like that?" Victor couldn't stop himself from asking.

Karpov's smile began to melt. "The same way you solve any other problem: by acting.

"I spent a couple of years planning, and then, for the last twenty years, I've implemented. Thus far, I have managed to get most of the pieces in place. A great chess match is about to begin, Victor: us against the world. And you know what? We're going to win."

Victor found his head spinning again, but his father pressed on. "We're going to win because we'll be the only ones who know the game is on. A decade from now, the Soviet Union will be an *economic* superpower, and I will be at the helm."

Karpov finally paused, allowing Victor to swallow the princely news. "Digestion will come later," he said, "meanwhile, let me paint the broad strokes.

"You are the fourth, and you will be the final person to know of my plan. As you might guess, Igor Stepashin and Yarik are the other two. The three of you will know the general plan, and everything about your own area of contribution, but for security reasons none of you will have all of the specifics. Those will be shared when the need arises."

Victor nodded.

"I call us the *Knyaz*."

"The Nobility?"

"We needed a name, and I liked the irony."

"A bastard and three orphans: nobility indeed."

"Yet destined to rule," Karpov replied, his tone making it clear that Victor was not to take this lightly.

"Why give us a name?"

"The moniker adds a layer of anonymity. Yarik, Stepashin, and I learned at a young age of the tremendous tactical advantage a group gains by working together when nobody knows that its members are connected. Deception is, after all, at the heart of all warfare."

Victor realized that his confusion was apparent when Karpov continued.

"For example, a key element of my plan has been to move the four of us through a series of positions that provide the Knyaz with strategic advantage. This was no small task, as the positions in question were all highly coveted. But, with the others working in the background to subtly promote the one while simultaneously sabotaging his likely competition—"

"The *four* of us," Victor interrupted. "Are you telling me that the five years I spent in the US were part of *your* plan, the master plan you developed during your Academy years—to take over the Soviet Union?"

"Yes, Victor. I am."

CHAPTER 5

Cyprus, 1980

Victor looked out the window toward the crude stone walls that divided the mountainside into arable plateaus, but did not see them. His thoughts were focused on the window of his mind. Only four people knew of his father's plan, and Victor was now one of them. Karpov was investing in him. Was it conceivable that respect would follow? For the second time in his life, he was learning that nothing was as it seemed, and he had the uneasy feeling that there was more to come.

He turned in the car seat to look at his father. "I thought you sent me to the US to get rid of me—like the affluent Americans who send their kids to boarding school."

Karpov did not have an answer ready for that one, so Victor enjoyed a moment's respite while his father composed his thoughts.

"Any man can be a father, Victor. Only I can do what our country needs me to do. Your compatriots' need for a founding father trumped your need for a paternalistic one."

"Is that why I didn't know your name, didn't know you were alive for the first sixteen years of my life? Is that—?"

"Victor. Now is not the time for this."

Would it ever be? "So, I'm to stay in the US?"

"Yes."

"Working for the KGB?"

"And the Knyaz."

"And what will my Knyaz job be?"

"One that parallels your KGB assignment."

"And that is?" *Here it comes.*

"Your job within the KGB Illegals Directorate will be running a group of agents whose task is to accumulate defense intelligence at the contractor level."

"You mean spying on missile manufacturers and counting tank orders?"

"Yes, but with a caveat. You will be working from the inside. Once the KGB sets you up undercover, I will require you to take their work a few steps further. Your Knyaz job will be identifying revolutionary new technologies—civilian technologies—while they're still in the developmental stage. You will be stealing them for the Soviet Union, and then sabotaging the American companies that invented them so we can beat them to market."

While those words hung in the air like cannonballs over Victor's head, Karpov pulled into the driveway of a rustic cliff-side cabin. The next time Victor took note of his surroundings, he was seated in a wooden armchair on the cabin's back terrace, looking out over fragrant coniferous hills toward the sparkling Mediterranean Sea. He had no recollection of how he had gotten there. His mind was awash in image and revelation.

Karpov took a seat next to him. He pulled two freshly cut cigars and a silver lighter from his breast pocket and raised his eyebrows. "Sometimes even Californians must yield to occasion."

Victor managed a weak smile.

Karpov lit his cigar and sat on the edge of his chair amidst a cloud of blue smoke while Victor slid all the way back in his, holding the arms as if bracing for impact. He wasn't ready to light up yet. "The KGB is asking you to assume a role, to play a game with the Americans. I'm making the game that much more interesting by asking you to do the same thing to the KGB. It's nothing traitorous, mind you. I'm not asking you to serve a different master—you'll still be working for the people of the Soviet Union—I'm just changing your management."

The lump in Victor's throat grew to choking size—assisted, perhaps, by the blue cloud—but still his father pressed on. He always pressed on.

"I've given you a glimpse of the tasks that lie ahead of you, now let me show you a couple of the tools. First the mundane." Karpov handed him a large envelope. "Congratulations, you've been accepted at Stanford. You're going to be an engineer."

"Stanford . . ." The word dissolved the lump in his throat like water on Alka-Seltzer. Victor instantly felt bubbly and refreshed. Staying on at Stanford sounded fantastic and he loved engineering. It felt odd to have his future dictated like a weather forecast, but as long as it called for sunny skies . . .

"Now the magical," Karpov said, placing a large syringe on the wooden arm of Victor's porch chair. Victor picked it up without comment. The syringe was not much bigger than the cigar in his hand. Instead of a needle, it ended in a tapered plastic tip that was reminiscent of the sharp end of a mechanical pencil.

"What you hold in your hand represents a decade of my life. It took me that long to become the head of the Scientific and Technical Directorate, but it was worth it to have this secretly developed."

"What is it?"

"I call my brainchild the *Peitho Pill* after the Greek goddess of coercion. It's what's going to make everything that I've told you possible. With Peitho in your pocket, you will be able to work both jobs, and perform remarkably at each. But I'm getting ahead of myself. Simply put, Peitho is the ultimate coercive tool."

As Karpov took a long pull on his Cuban, Victor found himself sliding forward in his chair.

"The syringe you're holding is specially designed to implant the capsule you see here." Karpov pointed to a vitamin-sized capsule at the base of the syringe's tip. "That capsule is Peitho. I had originally conceived of a device that could be slipped into someone's food, so we called the project the Peitho *Pill.* The engineers quickly concluded that an injectable capsule would work better, so the design changed, but the alliterative name stuck.

"In injectable form, you don't have to worry about how to get your target to swallow Peitho, and the capsule will stay in place until it's activated by radio transmission. It will sit harmlessly in place for years, rather than just a digestive cycle.

"Getting back to the design, the tapered tip punctures the skin of the buttocks like a regular needle, but then it stretches the skin, so the residual blemish is little worse than a mosquito bite."

"Why's the size of the blemish important?"

"Because we might not want the patient to know Peitho is there."

Victor decided he would chew on that piece of information for a while before questioning it further. There was a lot about this *coercive tool* that caught his interest. "What's the numbered ring above the taper for?"

"You rotate it to the approximate weight of the patient. It regulates the tip's length, so you always implant Peitho at the appropriate depth."

"It goes all the way down to ten kilos," Victor said, more to himself than to his father. Karpov didn't respond, and Victor wasn't sure he wanted him to.

Victor found himself as much intrigued by the Peitho Pill's engineering as the plans for its use. He took that as a good sign, considering Karpov's Stanford revelation. "So what's in the capsule?"

"Peitho contains a bicomponent acid, a poison, and a signal receiver."

"What's the poison?"

"It's a KGB concoction that's lethal within seconds, and leaves the same pathological markers as a heart attack."

"Yeah, but what happens when the autopsy uncovers the signal receiver?"

"That won't happen. When Peitho receives the activation signal, it mixes the two components of the acid, which then dissolves both the signal receiver and the capsule, releasing the poison into the bloodstream. The acid itself even breaks down into naturally occurring compounds. There's nothing suspicious left to find, and regardless, the coroner is not likely to cut open the buttocks of a heart attack victim."

Absolutely brilliant, Victor thought. His mind continued to work the concept while his father watched. Then he hit a snag. "Given the growing number of signals flying over the airwaves these days, what's to prevent a random transmission from activating the pill and killing the person we're exploiting?"

"Probability. Peitho codes are fourteen characters long, so the odds of randomly hitting on the correct code are thirty-six to the fourteenth power. I don't think they even have names for numbers that large. On top of that it has to be cleanly transmitted, meaning there's nothing else transmitted for three seconds before or after the correct code. Some nuclear launch sequences are less secure."

"Why wouldn't the victim just cut it out? That can't be any tougher than digging out a bullet, and Yarik seems to have that done all the time."

"Why not indeed? A brilliant engineer not much older than you solved that problem for me. He designed Peitho's coating to be photosensitive. Visible light, which surgeons would use during any conventional procedure, and intensive X-rays, which doctors would use to pinpoint or even accidentally discover Peitho, will dissolve the capsule instantly. To answer your question, the patient will die and Peitho will vanish before the doctor can get to it."

"So what do you do if—?"

"You find yourself on the wrong end of an implant? There are two potential solutions: either destroy every record of your fourteen-digit Peitho code, or have Peitho surgically removed using red light, as in a photographic darkroom. The buttocks are neither sensitive nor crucial, so precision isn't imperative. Look, Victor, don't worry too much about the details now. Yarik will take you through it all again *ad nauseam* this summer. My goal today is just to get you acquainted with Peitho. You're going to be working a lot together."

♦ ♦ ♦

Tomorrow night he and the goddess of persuasion had yet another date, and as much as he looked forward to that, it was tonight's adventure that really had Victor excited. Tonight would be the maiden voyage of his father's latest invention, Medusa. Tonight he was going to introduce her to an old friend.

CHAPTER 6

Palo Alto, California, November 1990

Alex cracked an ammonia capsule under his captive's nose.

Enrique coughed, opened his eyes, and immediately began studying his surroundings while trying to shake the fog from his head. He was seated in a wheelchair before a folding table that supported a pizza box, a couple bottles of water, a satellite phone, and a photograph. He tested his arms and legs and found them free to move, but remained sitting while studying the small, windowless room with its bare concrete floor and walls.

"It's a storage unit," Alex said, stepping forward from behind and taking a seat across the table from Enrique in a folding chair. "You feeling okay?"

"Been better, but yeah, I'm okay. What's going on?"

"I need your help."

"You have a funny way of asking."

"I couldn't think of a better way. I tried, but couldn't. Hungry? The pizza's not bad."

"Who the hell are you? You went through both my bodyguards and two of my father's best men faster than I can sprint to second base."

"I'm just a guy who needs your help."

"Help with what?"

Alex picked the photo up off the table and handed it to Enrique. "That's Tommy Chirico. He's eleven. He was kidnapped last week in Sabaneta. His parents hired me to get him home safely."

"I don't know anything about that."

"I know you don't. Your father might not know the specifics either. But you and I both know that nothing happens in Sabaneta without his blessing. So if he doesn't already know where Tommy is, he can find out in two minutes and fix it in five. I want you to call your father and ask him to have Tommy Chirico driven home. Preferably within the next five minutes."

"Or you'll kill me?"

"I'm not going to kill you. I'm not going to do anything to you. I'm not that kind of guy."

"I've seen some evidence to the contrary. As have four of my friends."

"A broken wrist and a concussion. That's what most northern boys call a hockey season. But seriously, think about how much easier it would have been for me to use a gun like Tommy's kidnappers did. Instead, I went in with a baseball bat and half a dozen tranquilizer darts."

Enrique didn't reply to that. He just stood up, slowly, testing Alex.

Alex didn't move. "But suppose I was?" Alex added. "Suppose I was the kind of guy who's holding little Tommy right now: violent, desperate, and cruel? Suppose your hands and feet had been bound to that chair for a week, and there was a burlap bag over your head? Suppose you were hungry enough to eat live bugs but half glad you were starving because you were so scared that every time you ate you shit your pants? Suppose you didn't know if you'd ever feel warm or safe or loved again? Tommy is only eleven years old. Make the call."

Enrique did.

And then they waited.

And then Alex's cell phone rang. But the call wasn't from Tommy's parents, telling him that their son was home. It was a different call altogether. And it had Alex running for his car.

CHAPTER 7

Novosibirsk, Russia

Karpov knew something was wrong the moment he popped into Nazarov's office on a surprise visit. Nazarov grew bug eyes on his paled face, jumped to his feet behind his big oak desk, and then tried to look calm. "Good morning, general."

Nazarov was the director of SibOil, which drilled one of Siberia's largest oil reserves. Since that oil reserve was the source of the Knyaz's financing, Karpov checked in whenever it was convenient. More often than not, he found work to do. Nazarov, like most communist bureaucrats, was more concerned with preserving his own privileged status than with promoting his business or protecting his people. Karpov had that very characteristic in mind when he put Nazarov in place: It maximized his control.

Walking across the office, Karpov paid the director no attention. Instead, he watched the woman Nazarov was speaking with as she turned to look over her shoulder. Her face flushed the moment she saw him, and she, too, scrambled to her feet.

Karpov had been affecting people that way for several years now. His progressive policies had turned around Siberian industry and made him the darling of the local press. Still, he had not gotten used to the stares.

He extended his hand. "Good morning. I don't believe we've met. I'm General Vasily Karpov."

"Orlova, Luda Orlova. I'm a senior accountant here at SibOil. It's a privilege to meet you, general."

"Tell me, Senior Accountant Luda Orlova, what you've done to put such a sour look on your director's face?"

"It seems we have an accounting discrepancy, general," Nazarov hastened to say.

"I'd like to hear Ms. Orlova tell me about it."

Luda lowered her eyes and then gave a glance over at Nazarov, who returned a single nod. "The Libyan Oil Company paid us twice for our shipment this month, ten million dollars instead of five. So I placed a call to the LOCo accounting to find out if they wanted us to refund the money or credit it to next month. When the operator asked who was calling, I said I was from SibOil, and she put me straight through to their president." She paused and looked up nervously for a second before returning her eyes to the floor. "Before I could say a word, LOCo's president began apologizing for the mistake. He said that his CFO had been in an automobile accident while he himself was out of town, and that the substitute accountant didn't know that half the money for SibOil was supposed to go to Knyaz."

Karpov canted his head and raised his eyebrows in query. *No wonder Nazarov looked pale*, he thought.

"I asked the president of LOCo why he would send half our money to a company named Knyaz, and he said, 'What do you mean why? That's what we've always done.' At that point, I didn't know what to think, and I didn't want to risk offending him, so I said, 'Is there anything I can do for you?' He said, 'Yes. Give Nazarov my apologies and tell him it won't happen again.'"

"And that's when you came to see the director?" Karpov asked.

"Yes." She hesitated, and then spoke the words that changed her stars. "While I was waiting for a break in his schedule I did some calculations."

Karpov watched from the corner of his eye as Nazarov squirmed his way from pale to red.

"We've been working with LOCo since we first started pumping oil. If they've been sending half our money to Knyaz all these years as their president said, then as of this month, Knyaz would have four hundred fifty-five million dollars of our money. Plus interest. I know that's a ridiculous idea, especially since all our oil is accounted for, but I wanted to be thorough."

Karpov flashed his eyes in admiration to soften her up. "So tell me, what do you think really happened?"

"I think LOCo has SibOil confused with another of its suppliers. Knyaz is also a Russian name, although I've never heard of them. Perhaps he thinks we're all the same."

"I'm sure you're right," Karpov said.

Luda continued. "But there is still the issue of the extra five million dollars. The daily interest alone is more than I earn in a year."

"Well, that will surely teach them not to make the same mistake twice. Tell me, where was your boss during all this?"

"Mr. Ivanov is at an accounting seminar in Moscow all week. I would normally have left this for him, Mr. Ivanov always deals with LOCo personally, but the overpayment was so large that, well . . ."

"You did the right thing. With LOCo informed, SibOil is now in the clear. Further activity by anyone but Ivanov can only make things worse. I suggest we agree to table this until he returns, or LOCo calls back. Agreed?"

"Agreed," both Luda and Nazarov answered.

"Excellent. Now if you'll excuse me, there's other business requiring my attention, so I'll leave you to your good work."

Out in the hallway Karpov rolled his eyes but then grinned. His system worked brilliantly in times like these. And there were always times like these in an operation as big as his.

The general managers like Nazarov, along with key accountants and engineers, bankers and lawyers, and the local Party leadership, were all discrete members of the Knyaz outer circle. Each knew about one of Karpov's trees, but none knew their tree was part of a forest. They thought of Karpov's setup as routine politics, as the I've-got-your-back-you've-got-mine scenario that worked behind the scenes of every powerful organization the world over. It was camouflaged compartmentalization, grand deception disguised as a common indiscretion, and it worked beautifully.

Back in his jeep, Karpov called Yarik.

"Go ahead," the giant answered.

"We've got a problem at SibOil. LOCo screwed up, and an eager accountant learned of the Knyaz payments. She even did the math and got a sense of the big picture."

"Stalin solution?" Yarik asked.

"Yes, no person, no problem. But no sport this time around, my friend. We need it to look accidental."

CHAPTER 8

Palo Alto, California

Alex sat stunned in his twin's kitchen, staring at the notebook, *the puzzler,* as Frank called it. He was staring, but no longer seeing. It had been sixteen hours since he received the mysterious call: "They're about to kill your brother."

He had raced to his brother's house only to find a smoking gun and a cooling corpse. Between that and the Colombian kidnapping, he had not slept in over forty-eight hours. The adrenaline had worn off, and caffeine no longer moved the needle. Part of his brain was aware that something had happened in the background, but it hadn't registered yet. He was still digesting the big news. This beautiful Palo Alto home was no longer his brother's house. It was his dead brother's house.

Frank was dead, presumably by his own hand, and Alex was now alone in the world.

Bang . . . bang . . . bang. There it was again. This time it registered. Someone was at the front door.

Alex slid *the puzzler* into a kitchen drawer, ran his hands vigorously through his thick brown hair, and then crossed the living room to the front door.

The peephole revealed a familiar pair of steely eyes. "Jason Stormer." It was a statement, a question, and the answer to an unpleasant surprise.

"It's been a while," Jason replied.

Jason and Alex had gone through Stanford together, and there had always been a chemical friction between them, despite or perhaps because of their many similarities. Jason and Frank, however, had hit it off through college and graduate school. Alex had not seen Jason since graduation, but Frank's occasional mention of his name still raised Alex's hackles.

"Yes, it has been a while." Alex wasn't sure what to say next. He wasn't the formal type, but *Frank's not here, he's dead* wasn't quite right either. He settled for "Come in."

Alex led Jason back to the kitchen, gestured to the chair across the table from the one he'd spent the night in, and sat.

"I'm terribly sorry," Jason said. "Your brother was as good a man as any I've ever known."

"How did you hear?" Alex asked, surprised. Had Frank been important enough that his death made the news? He'd been too absorbed in his *puzzler* analysis to think about turning on the TV.

It was Jason's turn to look surprised. "I thought you'd have figured that out by now, being a PI and all. Frank and I were supposed to meet here last night, but by the time I arrived from the airport, the ambulance was already loading."

Alex ignored the jibe. "You were supposed to meet Frank here last night?"

"I flew up special yesterday. At his request," Jason added.

"Why?"

"He didn't say, specifically. Just sent me an e-mail requesting an urgent meeting. You know I was consulting for him on the UE-2000, don't you?"

"He didn't mention it. But then, we didn't spend a lot of time on shoptalk."

Jason gave him a thin smile. "Yes, I suppose years of working for the State Department would condition anyone to keep the work-related chitchat to a minimum."

Alex wanted to be gracious, let bygones be bygones and all that, but he was grieving, exhausted, and Jason was still a master at getting under his skin. "Is there something I can do for you?"

"No. I just found myself drawn here on the way to the airport. Felt I should pay my respects. What happened, Alex?"

"The police say Frank shot himself . . . that his failure at work was too much for him to bear."

"And I gather by your tone that you have another idea?"

Alex did, in fact. The sleepless night had been a productive one. He thought he knew who killed Frank and why. But he wasn't inclined to discuss the results of his analysis with Jason. On the other hand, he was pleased to have another source of information at hand. "Do me a favor and forward me that e-mail?"

Jason returned a sideways glance. "The invitation from Frank? I doubt I still have it. I usually delete as I read unless they're technical. It was a simple 'I need to see you ASAP. Can you come by the house tomorrow evening?' "

"Was that unusual?"

"Not at all. Frank loved Friday-night brainstorming sessions: a couple guys, an old single malt, some fine cigars . . ."

Alex felt himself starting to tear up as he pictured many a similar session he had shared with Frank. He forced his thoughts back to business. "Tell me about the UE-2000, Jason. What's it worth?"

"Worth? Billions. Tens of billions. If it works."

And there it was: three commas' worth of motive, missed by the Palo Alto police. "What's so special about this aircraft engine?"

"You two really didn't talk shop, did you? The UE-2000 uses forty percent less fuel than anything else out there."

"So it's a big deal for aviation?"

"It's expected to revolutionize the industry, Alex."

"If it works."

"If it works."

"What's the secret?"

Jason hesitated.

"Don't for a second consider giving me a need-to-know line."

Jason smiled. "The design takes advantage of the extreme temperature differential between the outside air at high altitude and that inside the engine. It's analogous to the way a turbocharger gets more thrust by recycling exhaust, although completely different technically. And the efficiency is much greater.

"What do you think happened to your brother?"

"The evidence supporting suicide is considerable. Overwhelming, even. The forensic evidence makes it clear that Frank pulled the trigger himself without duress, and the circumstantial evidence supplies sufficient motive for him to do so. But I know Frank wasn't a quitter."

"People change. Stress changes them. Frank had the future of the world riding on his shoulders. When was the last time you saw your brother?"

"Christmas."

"That was just after he got the big promotion. I bet he was high as a kite then."

"He was. Thirty-two years old and the envy of the aviation industry. A modern-day da Vinci."

"Kind of makes you feel small by comparison, doesn't it? Not that anyone is comparing, of course. But you know, twins and all . . ."

"What's your point?"

"My point is that if you invert the high Frank was feeling at Christmas, then you'll have some idea of how low he's been the last six months or so. He was supposed to deliver the engine in July and premier it at the Paris Air Show. Now it's November, and the project is in worse shape than when he took over. We don't even have a projected launch date."

Alex kept his face neutral. He'd gather information now, and analyze it later. "What is it you do for United Electronics?"

"I'm an operations consultant." He pulled a business card from his breast pocket. "Have my own company."

Another similarity, damn it. "You do technical troubleshooting?"

"That's right."

"Can you be more specific?"

"Frank brought me on board about three months into his tenure to solve a problem he was having with software. I fixed it in less than twenty-four hours. Then there was a structural integrity issue, followed by a friction issue. It was one thing after another. Kind of like working with Edison on the lightbulb. Typical when technological leaps are involved."

"It doesn't sound like you're feeling suicidal, Jason."

Jason's face remained serene, but Alex knew he'd gotten to him.

"The difference between my responsibilities and Frank's was scope. I answered for specific issues. When I solved one, I got my reward, and got my ego charged. Frank answered for everything. His ego was banking on the supercharge he'd get when he eventually released the UE-2000 to production. But until that time, every day was a drain. Perhaps the latest progress report sucked the last of his reserves."

"That's exactly what the police said. So, do you expect to continue working for United Electronics?"

Jason shook his head. "The UE-2000 is only one of several projects I've got going. I don't need the work, so I'm not going to subject myself to the constant reminder of a lost friend.

"How about you, Alex? How's the inaugural year of International Private Investigations treating you?"

"No complaints."

"How many on your team?"

"Just me."

"Keep it simple. Good for you. Are you headed back to San Diego soon?"

"I think I'll stick around a while. Play a little game of cat and mouse."

Jason drew in his breath as though preparing a witty knock-yourself-out response, but then paused with a contemplative look on his face. After a moment he said, "That doesn't seem fair."

"What do you mean?"

"Well, if it wasn't suicide, then the murderer is very clever. And this clever murderer undoubtedly knows who you are."

"Agreed."

"You, on the other hand, have no clue as to his identity."

"So?"

"So, Alex, that makes you the mouse."

CHAPTER 9

Seattle, Washington

Victor used his night-vision goggles to survey the backyard. With the Davis house's grand old trees, thick grass, and gentle slope, poets might describe it as a good place to be a squirrel. With the house's fenceless yards, trusting neighbors, and darkened streets, Victor would describe it as the perfect place to be a spy. He returned the goggles to his bag and slipped out of the woods.

He found the patio door unlocked. This was a double bonus as it indicated that the alarm would also be unarmed. It just didn't get any easier than this. Victor had come equipped to handle locks and alarms, but he was pleased that those skills might not be required. Creative engineering, grand deception, blind extortion, those were his passions in life, and he enjoyed them much more than this risky business.

The sensor in his hand emitted a low, steady hum, indicating that the alarm was indeed inactive. Victor had learned that few Americans bothered to set their alarms at night. It was one more thing that made operating in the "land of the free" so easy. People were so trusting here, at least those from the middle and upper classes. The poor knew better.

They were still grounded in global reality. *It's a dog-eat-dog world, Dr. Davis, and you are about to feel the teeth.*

The Davises had extinguished the last light at their Seattle residence two hours earlier, just after ten. Victor had spent the intervening time studying the house layout, courtesy of the builder's marketing brochure, and rehearsing various contingency plans in his head. The former activity would enable him to navigate confidently in the dark. This was not crucial—he had identified the girl's room by the curtains—but he wanted to be thorough and preferred to walk around without the encumbrance of night-vision goggles. The latter activity was just a reflection of his meticulous personality. It only took one mistake . . .

The Davises owned a cocker spaniel named Taffy. They had brought her home for Clara's third birthday, and the two girls were now growing up together. Taffy was a friendly dog that slept on a bone-shaped pillow in the family room and would eat almost anything. She loved attention and was discouraged from barking. It was amazing what you could learn from kids.

Most mothers probably don't have the KGB in mind when teaching the don't-talk-to-strangers rule, but then, in his experience, most kids don't really learn it anyway. They certainly weren't the suspicious type in the Davises' stately neighborhood.

Victor stood beside the patio door with his back to the wall and pumped a syringe full of ketamine hydrochloride into a small beefsteak. Ketamine was primarily a veterinary anesthetic, but he rarely used it on animals. He tossed the steak through the patio door onto the kitchen floor and then slid it closed again.

Tonight's operation was part of an emergency stopgap measure and included a few new challenges, one of which was figuring out how to attract Taffy quietly if the muffled sound of the kitchen's sliding door was not enough. Victor was pleased with the creative solution he had devised. He would crack the door again and spray cow's blood from a perfume atomizer. He wasn't sure the scent would work as a lure, but he thought it was a cool idea and was looking forward to the experiment. Victor liked to expand his repertoire and refine his technique a bit more with each operation.

Taffy came zipping into the kitchen, ears flapping, a second after Victor closed the door. The steak had been enough; so much for tonight's experiment. She devoured the meat as though these midnight feedings were standard practice and then looked around for more to drop from the benevolent sky. She caught sight of Victor through the glass and shifted her tail wagging in his direction. Her tail got slower and slower as she begged, like a windup toy running out of juice. Two minutes later she was dreaming of bones. Five minutes after that, Victor completed the first of the night's surgical procedures. His plan was tracking like a Swiss watch.

With phase one complete, Victor extracted what looked like a large Mont Blanc fountain pen from his hip pack. This was Medusa. Medusa was a derivative of sea-snake venom that would instantly paralyze the average man for twenty to thirty seconds if sprayed on his face. Like the cow's blood atomizer, Victor did not expect to need the pen, but he wanted to be prepared for the unexpected. Meticulous.

Earlier in the week Victor had tried his father's latest concoction on himself to ensure that it really worked. He had stood before a mirror and a wall clock with a second hand and sprayed himself in the face. The instant the mist hit his nose he froze in place looking like a G.I. Joe action figure holding a can of mace. It felt like the nightmare in which you can't move, only it was real and therefore much more terrifying—like living rigor mortis. For his victims, it would be a preview of what was to come.

Victor had used Medusa for the first time the previous evening. Going in he'd been nervous, kind of like a first date but with the knowledge that if things did not go as expected, he would get more than a slap on the face. When the moment of truth came, however, Medusa had not let him down. In fact, she had lifted him up, way up. Medusa had transported him to a wonderland where he was omnipotent and the world was his for the taking. He was craving their next date.

Under Medusa's spell, Frank Ferris had stood there helplessly, horribly paralyzed while Victor placed the gun in his hand, brought it naturally to his temple, and pulled the trigger: fast, fulfilling, and forensically perfect.

Victor instantly began craving his next power rush the way a junkie craves his next hit. Before Frank Ferris, he had never given his power the ultimate exercise. Oh, he had led many victims in a dance around death's door, but he had never pushed one through from up close and personal before. The old rush, the Peitho rush, was great—having another man, a powerful, arrogant man, whimpering to you for mercy was the cat's meow—but this new rush, the Medusa rush, was the lion's roar.

The dog started snoring, bringing Victor back to the moment. It was time to create an agent.

The Davises' new home, with its quiet floorboards and wall-to-wall carpeting, aided his silent ascent up the stairs and down the hall to Clara's room. Once outside her door, Victor paused just long enough to douse a handkerchief with chloroform before entering. It would keep her asleep while he injected the ketamine.

Victor slipped into her bedroom and closed the door behind. Clara was about to experience every child's nightmare, but she would sleep through it. He hoped her parents would remain equally oblivious.

He was struck by how nice Clara's room was, so warm and cozy and full of knickknacks and toys. Russian children didn't have rooms like this. Heck, they were lucky to have a room at all. He certainly never had a room of his own. *Prissy bitch.*

Victor snarled as he laid the chloroform-soaked handkerchief over the six-year-old's nose and mouth. She did not so much as twitch. While he waited silently in the dark for the anesthetic to take hold, Victor thought about what it would be like to one day find himself at the other end of the Peitho syringe and totally within another man's power. Then he thought of his father, and realized he already was . . .

Holding a penlight in his teeth, Victor prepared a cocktail of antibiotics, anti-inflammatories, immunosuppressants, and numbing agents, filling a 10cc syringe with the contents of five different vials. Then he injected it into the gluteus maximus of his six-year-old victim. The cocktail would both mitigate Clara's immune reaction to the implant and chemically camouflage it from her senses.

With the preparatory injection complete, he withdrew a Peitho syringe from his pack with great satisfaction. His father's invention was as brilliant as they come, and Victor felt a touch of pride every time he used it.

He watched the second hand on Clara's Strawberry Shortcake clock make a full sweep before proceeding. He almost blushed while setting the needle depth for a twenty-kilo subject. All is fair in love and war, he mumbled, and plunged it into her pink flesh with a warrior's resolve.

He felt the plunger hit bottom. Dr. Davis was now his slave.

Victor withdrew the syringe beneath a compressed cotton ball and let out a sigh of relief. He maintained pressure on the site for two minutes to ensure hemostasis. Then he wiped it clean, applied a drop of skin sealant, and the cover-up was done. By morning, the injection site would look and feel no worse than a bug bite, and given the location, Clara would probably not notice it at all.

Victor packed up his supplies as carefully as an operating-room nurse. Aside from a satiated dog and a picture taped to the wall, he would leave no trace of his midnight visit. Meticulous.

As he slid the patio door shut behind him, Victor knew he had locked up another Knyaz victory. He knew he was the best, whether his father would acknowledge it or not.

The rising moon that greeted Victor reminded him of the next problem he had to tackle. His life was full of challenges—for a decade the stream had been unending—but this next one would be different. Victor was about to engage his first active opponent. The prospect thrilled him. He looked forward to finding a clever way of dealing with Alexander Temogen Ferris.

CHAPTER 10

Palo Alto, California

Alex watched the familiar ponytail bobbing beneath residential streetlamps as the jogger approached his position. As was her morning ritual, Elaine hopped the split-rail fence to enter the park before it opened. Normally she would knock out five kilometers on the hilly perimeter trail before either the sun or her daughter rose. But not today.

Moving silently to the spot he'd selected for the confrontation, Alex stepped onto the trail and raised his Glock.

A few seconds later Elaine Evans, senior engineer, single mother, and the woman Frank finally came to suspect as the saboteur, rounded the bend and staggered to a stop as her hands flew up in the universal sign of surrender.

"I saw what you did to the engine last night," Alex said, beckoning her off the trail toward a picnic table in a recessed clearing. "You're going to tell me why."

She was only about three yards away, close enough for him to read her expression even in the predawn light. It contained an odd mixture of shock, panic, and relief. That was much more encouraging than guile, indignation, and rage, but then she'd fooled Frank for months, so he wasn't going to take anything at face value.

"Who are you?" she asked, her voice cracking but her gaze unwavering.

"Alex Ferris," he said, emphasizing the last name.

"Frank's brother?"

He nodded, and then beckoned again with the gun.

Her shoulders telegraphed relief at the revelation of his identity. She complied with his request in silence, selecting the seat farthest from the trail without regard for the cluttering twigs or droppings.

"Why did you do it?" he repeated, still standing.

"Why are we here?" she countered. "Why didn't you just turn me in? If you really saw something."

Alex was ready for the question and willing to go along to secure her trust and cooperation. "Since he was twelve, my brother kept a special notebook on his nightstand he called *the puzzler*. Most nights before bed he'd jot down a question that perplexed him, and as often as not he'd awake with an answer. After he was killed, I turned to *the puzzler* for clues. The whole year was full of Q and A that I'm guessing will sound pretty familiar to you, things like: *Why does it crack? Temperature gradient. How to regenerate? Xenon gas.* For the last two months, however, the question remained the same, and the morning epiphany was always absent, that is until the morning he died. The question repeated some sixty times was 'Who?' What do you think the ultimate answer was?"

Her head slumped, but after a long pause she looked up and said, "Me."

"Elaine," Alex confirmed. "And then last night I saw you do something that looked like it would do more than just crack or degenerate some component. It looked like something that would have had Frank writing, *Why did it explode?*"

Elaine's face contorted with emotion. She repeated herself. "Why didn't you turn me in? Why are we here?"

"Two reasons. First, because everything I've learned about you tells me you have neither the temperament nor the motive for industrial espionage or violent behavior. And last night aside, I've seen nothing to make me think you're anything but a salt-of-the-earth Christian with a job she loves doing her best to raise a daughter on her own."

"And the second reason?"

"You had tears in your eyes last night. Twice you put down the wrench to wipe them away. I know spies, and spies don't cry.

"Also, I don't particularly care about the industrial espionage. What I do care about is finding the person who killed Frank, and I think you can help. I think you know who killed him. But I also think you're scared to death the same thing may happen to you. Or your daughter. You're being coerced, aren't you? They've threatened Kimberly?"

Elaine nodded once.

Alex waited.

"Who are you, Alex? I mean, what makes you think you can help me?"

It was a fair question, and hard to answer without knowing exactly who he was up against. "I'm not associated with any law-enforcement organization if that's what you mean. Until about six months ago, I worked for the government in intelligence operations. Before that I was a Special Forces soldier, a Green Beret. But now I'm on my own, a PI. So on the one hand, I'm just a guy. On the other hand, most generals will tell you there's no more powerful weapon in the world than a well-trained soldier. I'm very well trained, and I'm highly motivated, and I don't have to play by anybody's rules."

CHAPTER 11

Moscow, Russia

Russian Foreign Minister Sugurov found himself staring through the window of his lofty office, looking at nothing at all while nervously waiting for the crucial call. He was used to managing complex and unpredictable foreign operations. But this operation, while foreign, was entirely beyond the scope of his sanctioned duties. It was clandestine. Completely off the books. And the future of Russia depended on him and his deputy conducting it in absolute secrecy.

That was why they were using the American. Absolute secrecy.

Sugurov turned to reach for a cigarette, but his hand never made it to the pack. The distinctive *ri-ri-ring* of his private phone diverted his hand to the special black receiver instead. He looked at the gilded clock above his desk—a gift from Gorbachev himself to commemorate fifty years of distinguished service—and nodded. Seven p.m. in Moscow meant eight a.m. in California. Andrey was right on time.

The telltale *swish* came across the line as the scrambler engaged. Sugurov always found the sound comforting, although the news that followed often was not.

"I'm listening."

"Good evening, sir. Are we secure?"

"Good morning, Andrey. Yes, we are secure."

"It appears that all is going well. The kickoff went as scripted. There are still a lot of balls in the air, but I believe those balls will be landing as predicted."

"Is Alex's mind proving to be as sharp as you'd expected, his demeanor as unflappable?"

"The latter was the wild card, of course. Grief fractures some, but Alex became laser focused on finding his brother's killer. I predict that he will be heading to Russia within a week."

"Excellent. However, if for some reason it begins to look like Alex will take much longer than that, you'll need to find a way to nudge him along."

"Is it that urgent, that . . . bad, sir?"

"Yes, I'm afraid it is. Gorbachev is losing power by the hour. Perestroika is a beautiful plan, but a long-term one. Long-term plans do not bode well for politicians in years when it's hard to buy bread and sausage. You—and Alex—have simply got to come through. Quickly."

"Understood."

"One more thing. You've done a fine job of leading Alex to the water, Andrey, and I admire the way you got him to dive right in. But keep in mind that Alex has no idea he's swimming in a shark tank. For that matter, even we don't know who lies beneath or how deep the currents flow. So bear in mind that no matter how good you think Alex Ferris may be, he will be killed without your help."

"You can count on me, sir, to the end."

CHAPTER 12

Palo Alto, California

The sky was growing lighter, and woodland creatures were starting to stir, but the sun had not yet peeked over the horizon as Alex studied Elaine's face from across the picnic table. He had taken a chance and laid it all on the line. Now it was her turn.

"They'll kill my daughter," she said. "They'll kill her, just like that." She tried to snap her fingers but there was no pop. "Please, please . . . help me." Her last words were a whispered sob.

It was a promising start, but it was also exactly what someone trying to play him would do. Someone had fooled Frank, and now Frank was dead. Alex sat down across from her with his gun hand below the table but his finger on the trigger. "They did kill my brother, so I will finish them. And I will help you. Are you afraid someone is watching you now?"

"I . . . I don't know. I never know. They seem to know everything. At first I thought you were one of them."

"Who are they? Who is doing this to you, to Kimberly?"

Elaine trembled at the mention of her daughter's name. "I don't know.

They do everything through phone calls and faxes. The voice is always the same, but I'm sure it's disguised."

"Tell me everything from the beginning."

Elaine nodded slowly and then took a couple introspective breaths to compose herself. Alex waited patiently, actively listening to the woods around for sounds of disturbance while noting that a glimmer of hope had crept into Elaine's swollen eyes.

"It started a year and a half ago, July 5, 1989 to be exact. I got a call early in the morning. The voice told me that MiMi, my mother, was not doing well, that I should go to her room. MiMi, you see, had been living with us ever since my father died. I went to see her, but she said she felt fine. Then the voice ordered me to look at her bottom. I almost hung up at that point, thinking it was just a very sick prank caller. But there was something about his voice—I didn't dare defy.

"I found what looked like a nasty bug bite. Then the voice said Kimberly wasn't doing well, either. I checked her and saw that she had the same bite as MiMi. 'What is it?' I screamed into the telephone. The answer nearly gave me a heart attack. 'Poison,' he replied, 'a very deadly poison. But don't worry; it's also a very special poison. It only activates if I tell it to.'

"I stood there for a minute, certain that I was dreaming because something like this could not happen in real life. But of course it was happening. 'Oh please, no, don't do it,' I begged. Then he said, 'I won't. But here's what you're going to do for me . . .'

"There was nothing I wouldn't have done. You understand, don't you?"

Alex nodded somberly, urging her to continue.

"But now, now things are escalating. As you noted, now people could get killed. It didn't start like that. At first he just had me bring him plans and progress reports for the UE-2000."

"You've met him? You know his name? You've seen his face?"

"No, oh no." Elaine shook her head and then raised it from her hands. She still looked pitiful, frightened, drained, but there was also hope in the corners of her eyes. "He concocted a different elaborate setup each time there was an exchange. He usually used a kid off the street. It was like living in a spy movie. That first time he had me leave the envelope in my shopping cart at the grocery store after I'd loaded my car. As I was driving away a kid came up on a skateboard, took the envelope, and disappeared behind the store. Then a couple of days later, I got pictures in the mail, frames of a video showing me leaving the envelope. He wanted to let me know he had me in more ways than one."

"Was that all you did, deliver plans?"

"No. After New Year's it got much worse."

"After New Year's? That was when Frank took over."

"You're right, it was." She grimaced and met his eye momentarily, obviously remembering that he, too, had suffered. "That was when the voice told me we were starting Phase Two.

"I tried to get out then." She gave him a guilty look. "I told him I had done enough, that he should get someone else. He told me to forget about that. He said that I was his bitch, and that if I tried to deny him, he would kill MiMi, then and there. He said that if I tried to leave him, it would happen immediately, before I could even hang up the phone. 'Tell me you're my bitch! Tell me now, or it's bye-bye MiMi.' He seemed almost excited at the prospect.

"Of course I did as he asked. Thereafter at the end of every conversation he would ask me, 'Who are you?' and I would have to answer, 'I'm your bitch.'" Elaine paused to wipe her eyes. "Silly as it may sound, his base language shook me. He was always very polite, even gentlemanly, except when he was making threats. I felt like I was dealing with a split personality, and that made it even scarier."

"It's a common technique. Keeps you off balance and makes you want to please the good guy. Same psychology as good cop bad cop. Sorry to interrupt. You were telling me about Phase Two."

"Instead of just stealing secrets, he started having me sabotage the project as well, in lots of different ways. He would give me a computer virus to plant, or a list of slightly altered blueprint specifications to switch for the real ones, or a coating that I was to spray on certain parts. But this last time—" Her voice cracked. "This last time . . . well you were right. It wasn't just sabotage. It will explode. At a demonstration. I could be responsible for, for the unthinkable."

Alex was sold. He wanted to reach across the table and take her hands to offer comfort, but the picture of Frank's bloodied corpse cautioned him to keep his heart in check. "We'll figure this out. We'll find a way to keep everyone safe. Of course, the best way for me to do that, to end this, is to catch him. Tell me, how did he give those parts to you?"

"I would usually just find them on the driver's seat of my car, with instructions. If no parts or tools were required, he would just fax me instructions at home."

"How did you inform him that you had completed an assignment?"

"He always just knew."

"Have you told anyone?"

"I wanted to, longed to, but I couldn't endanger MiMi and Kimberly. I forgot to tell you, from time to time he'd leave pictures hidden in different places in our home—in the medicine chest, on cereal boxes, even in my wallet—pictures of dead little girls with phrases typed below like, 'Don't even think about it,' or 'Mommy dialed 9-1-1.'"

"What made you so sure he wasn't bluffing?"

"The confidence in his voice for starters. The wound was real. The concept seemed plausible. He seemed perfectly willing to demonstrate on MiMi if I wanted to call his bluff. Even if he was bluffing about the poison, I figured he could just come back and kidnap Kimberly another time to get what he wanted. The only thing I could do to guarantee Kimberly's safety was to do what he asked. Of course, as time went by, I realized that I was only renting her safety. I once asked him when it would all be over, and he said the poison would lose its potency in ten years. At first it seemed like an unbearably long time. But once I thought about it, I realized that Kimberly will only be fourteen then, just starting her life. It gave me hope."

"Why didn't you have MiMi and Kimberly checked out by a doctor?"

"He warned me against that. Said the Peitho Pills were booby-trapped, that medical tampering would kill them. He specifically stressed that X-rays focused on her bottom would activate the poison and kill them immediately, right there on the table."

"Peitho Pills?" Alex asked.

"That's what he said. I tried looking Peitho Pill up everywhere, thinking he'd finally screwed up and I'd be able to find a cure. Eventually I concluded that it's just a nickname. Peitho, by the way, was the Greek goddess of persuasion."

"That's fitting. I'll check with a former colleague, see if the government has ever heard of it."

Elaine nodded.

Alex changed gears. "According to my research your mother passed away four months ago."

"Yes. But that was natural causes. She was seventy-three and diabetic."

"You don't think—"

"No. He called me the day after. Said he was not the cause. Told me I had to have her cremated."

"Did you?"

"Yes. It was what she wanted anyway."

Damn. This guy was covering all his bases. "Are you the only person at UE in his power?"

"I'm not sure, but I think not. He once said, 'Others are taking care of that.'"

"Any idea who those others are?"

"For a while I tried to guess, looking at people's eyes and using my intuition. I didn't get anywhere and found the process maddening, so I put it out of my mind."

The next question was going to be tough, but Alex had to ask it. "Do you think Frank was working for them, too?"

"Heavens, no. He was the one they were working against. Frank kept finding ingenious ways to counteract all the sabotage they had me do; it was driving them crazy."

A wave of pride swept over Alex, and he felt himself starting to tear up, so he pressed on. "Them?"

"I say 'them' because he always said 'we.' But I only ever had contact with one guy."

"Do you have any idea who he is?"

"No. But I think I know who he works for."

Alex's heart missed a beat. He raised his eyebrows rather than asking the question as he clenched the edge of the picnic table.

"About two months ago I got an extra page attached to a fax from him, by mistake I'm sure. It mentioned Irkutsk Motorworks."

"As in Irkutsk, Russia?"

"Yes. I only know that because they're in the industry." Elaine squinted. "How do you know that?"

"My mother was Russian. *Ya mnogo znayu pro Rosseyou*. Do they make engines for military aircraft?"

"No. I'm pretty sure they just do passenger and cargo models."

"Did you keep the fax?"

"It made me nervous having it around. I was afraid he would find it, so after a couple of nervous days, I burned it."

"Damn. Was the Irkutsk Motorworks fax in English?"

"Yes, it was. Unfortunately, it was just the last page of the fax, so there were only two lines."

Alex held his breath.

"I'll never forget them." She smiled for the first time. "'This last series of mishaps should ensure that Irkutsk Motorworks beats United Electronics to market by at least twelve months. I'm working to widen the gap even further.' It was signed with what I assume was an acronym, a word spelled B-U-K-T-O-P."

CHAPTER 13

Palo Alto, California

"I can tell by your expression that BUKTOP means something to you," Elaine said.

Alex nodded. "Those letters read differently in the Cyrillic alphabet. To a Russian, BUKTOP is VICTOR. It's a signature."

"Do you know whose?"

"No. And it's a common first name, so it will be useless at this stage of the investigation, especially since Victor is here. But that really doesn't matter. What matters is that we know who Victor is working for. Irkutsk Motorworks was the name I needed."

"But Irkutsk is halfway around the world in the middle of nowhere."

"More than half if you fly the usual way. Irkutsk is further east of Moscow than New York is of San Francisco."

"Fly? You're not really thinking about going to Irkutsk, are you?"

"I'm going wherever it takes. I've always gone—in the Special Forces, the CIA, and as a PI. If it were China, I might think twice. But in this case, I'll fit in almost as well as I do here. I speak the language fluently, and the Soviet Union was the focus of much of my government work."

This revelation seemed to give Elaine pause. "That's quite a coincidence."

Alex thought so, too, but didn't want to go there now. "You were due for some good luck."

She smiled weakly, her mind already elsewhere. Gone were the tears. Analytics had replace emotions. Her engineering mind had kicked in, and she was running permutations. He let her run with them.

"What am I supposed to do?" she finally asked. "You were right. The UE-2000 will explode today. But what you don't know is that there's going to be a demonstration today. There will be onlookers who could get seriously injured or even killed. I can't cross the line from saboteur to murderer, not now that you've put hope on the horizon. But if I don't cross that line, my daughter . . ." She didn't finish. The emotions were back.

"You can do what I did early this morning when I found my car wired to explode."

"Your what!"

Alex didn't elaborate. "You can interrupt the circuit, so to speak. Leave the sabotage in place so Victor can't say you didn't do your job, but arrange things so that the UE-2000 fails to function for some other reason. You said Victor always knows what's going on, that you never need to report. That means he'll know you did as asked, and you'll be safe. You just need to ensure that when the other engineers investigate the cause of that failure, they find and fix your sabotage as well."

She thought about that for a moment while nodding appreciatively. "That takes care of today. What about tomorrow?"

"Let me take care of tomorrow."

"How are you going to do that? The car bomb changes everything. That means they're on to you. Watching you. Going to Irkutsk would be like walking into a propeller blade."

"I'll just make sure they're neither watching nor expecting me."

"And how will you do that?"

"They made that part easy. All I have to do is die."

CHAPTER 14

Palo Alto, California

"The authorities have just released the name of a man killed earlier this evening when his car exploded in a Bay Area driveway. He is Alexander Ferris of San Diego, California. This is not the first time tragedy has struck the Ferris family. Investigators found that the powerful incendiary device used tonight is reminiscent of the terrorist bomb that killed his parents seventeen years ago in Rome, opening speculation about the origin of the crime. Given that this follows on the heels of his brother's recent—."

Victor turned off the car radio. *At last.* For some inexplicable reason, the bomb had not gone off the first time Alex drove the car. Victor had planned to go back tonight to check his work, but now that would not be necessary. Whatever jiggled out of place must have jiggled back in. *Better late than never.*

Victor pulled his BMW into the Shell station that housed his favorite phone booth. It was the old-fashioned kind, the type you could step inside and shut the door. It was practically his second office. Eager to share his latest victory, he began dialing a long series of codes from memory. Halfway through he stopped and looked out into the fog. He had it again, the strange feeling that he was being watched.

Victor did a careful three-hundred-sixty-degree survey around the Shell station and the surrounding streets. He was looking for whatever had caused a blip on his radar, but he saw nothing. Things had been going wrong for Victor lately, and it was beginning to play with his mind. *This was no time to get paranoid. Get* paranoid? He had *been* paranoid for a decade. Paranoia was what kept him out of an American jail, or worse, much worse, the KGB's infamous Lubyanka.

He shook his head and finished the sequence. Then he covered the mouthpiece with a scrambler.

"Yarik."

"It's Victor calling. You can call off your men at the airports. Alex is dead."

Yarik grunted in disappointment. "I was looking forward to meeting him. The file you faxed over was quite enticing. Never had the chance to play with a Green Beret before."

"It was a long shot anyway. Just being meticulous. It is a pity that he'll never know the pleasure of your company. Some people are just born lucky."

"Don't suppose you used one of my special condoms?"

"You're a funny man, Yarik. No, I arranged a barbecue. You know how Americans love those."

"With C4 briquettes?"

"Best thing when you want your cooking well done."

"Isn't that likely to get the police involved?"

"Sure, but with his brother just ten days cold, I figured the best thing to do on this one was to hide in plain sight. The C4 makes it look like a terrorist hit, so the local cops will assume it's revenge for something Alex did in the CIA and gladly write it off as being out of their jurisdiction. Meanwhile the CIA won't care since he's retired."

"Sounds good to me."

Victor put down the phone and found himself in an unexpectedly reflective mood. It was sad that he should find it easier to talk to a professional assassin than to his own father. Actually, he found it easier to talk to just about anyone than his father. With Karpov, Victor felt as though he was always on trial, always a defendant with something to prove. Soon, however, he would deliver American industry on a silver platter. Then Karpov would finally accept him, embrace him, and Victor would live within the glow he had experienced when his father first revealed his plans. A smile grew on his face as the melancholy vanished. *Meanwhile, you've got another call to make . . .*

CHAPTER 15

Moscow, Russia

Sugurov was pacing his office when the call came through. What was happening to him? He wasn't the nervous type. The Cuban Missile Crisis, the War in Afghanistan, decades of conflict in the Caucuses, none had shaken him. Why should this one be different? The answer was obvious, but not comforting. This time he was fighting an invisible enemy, indigenous terrorists whose numbers were not counted, whose objectives were not clear, and whose tactics were not known.

Ri-ri-ring . . . swish.

"I'm listening."

"Good evening, sir. Are we secure?"

"Good morning. Yes, we are secure."

"Alex just bought a ticket to Irkutsk using the name Grekov."

"Grekov?"

"Yes, Alexander Grekov. Apparently he still has a Soviet passport from his CIA days."

"Why Irkutsk? Does he think that's where they're based?"

“Apparently. I’m afraid I have not been able to learn any more than that yet. Clearly it is my top priority.”

“You’ve booked yourself on the same flight, I assume?”

“Of course. We’ll be passing through Moscow Sheremetyevo tomorrow.”

“Good to know. Anything else?”

“Yes. Victor put a bomb under Alex’s car. I disarmed it—pulled the detonator cap out so it would look accidental if Victor went back. He didn’t, but then Alex also found it so my actions may have confused him. Regardless, Alex eventually went on to detonate the bomb himself in order to make it look like he was dead. Then he used a police contact to get his name leaked to the press. Victor fell for it. I just heard him call in the news.”

“Whom did he call?”

“I couldn’t tell. I only heard his end of the conversation and unfortunately I couldn’t see or hear what number he entered. He always uses relay codes and a mouthpiece scrambler.”

“You think this will give Alex the freedom he needs to figure this out?”

“For as long as it lasts. Sir, I was thinking, it’s not too late to go to Gorbachev with what we know.”

“We’ve been over that, Andrey. Without knowing who they are, it’s simply too risky. Once Ferris figures that out, then maybe.”

“Gorbachev has resources we don’t,” Andrey said.

“Exactly. He’ll want to use them. He’ll confide in the men he trusts. Just like you and I would have confided in Leo. But they got to Leo, so surely they’ve gotten to others in high places. Perhaps dozens of others. No, we’ve got to take them out covertly, before they know we’ve learned of their existence. If we panic them, they may act rashly and create more chaos than the current government could possibly survive. So you stick with Alex, Andrey. You keep him on track and out of trouble.”

“You can count on me, sir.”

“We all are.”

PART II

CHAPTER 16

Novosibirsk, Siberia

Yarik looked at his watch and saw that he had just enough time for a quick hit before catching the early flight from Novosibirsk to Irkutsk for Karpov's nine-o'clock meeting. His tight schedule meant that there was no time for artistry—just a quick "accidental" neck snap. That was a shame. As far as Yarik was concerned, straightforward hits were for Cretans and Goombahs. He would make up for that regression this afternoon. He would get creative with the engineer from Irkutsk Motorworks he suspected of slipping secrets to his Mongolian mistress.

He scanned Luda Orlova's courtyard for activity. There was none. The street sweepers and dog walkers had not yet emerged. Yarik pulled his fur cap down snugly on his big, bald dome and walked briskly from the car to entrance number four. He suffered from the fact that his appearance, while a valuable asset most of the time, was a liability whenever anonymity was required. Nobody ever forgot how Yarik looked. At times like these, his only option was to avoid observation.

He hopped into the elevator and pushed "Five." The doors squeaked closed, and the elevator began to rumble upward. Then his cell phone rang. *Damn.* Yarik pressed the answer button immediately to stop the ringer and then looked at the display: Sergey Shipilov.

Sergey was the young agent Yarik had posted at Moscow's Sheremetyevo airport to watch for Ferris, the former Green Beret Yarik had been hoping to get his hands on, until Victor took him out in a blaze of glory.

"I'm listening."

"Sir, it's Sergey Shipilov. I'm calling to report that Alex Ferris is alive. He's alive and in Russia and staying in room 212 of the Hotel Irkutsk."

"What!" Yarik hit the stop button on the elevator. It was early; traffic would be light.

"It's true, sir. I know you called off the watch, but as I had no other pressing business, I decided to go the extra mile for you. There's nothing I wouldn't do for—"

"Where are you now?"

"I'm in the hotel lobby. I've questioned the receptionist and the taxi driver and learned that Alex plans to sleep all day before going out at nine o'clock this evening. The driver didn't know for sure where he would be going, but he has reason to believe it's Max's Place."

"The strip club?"

"Yes, sir. He said Alex asked him where he could go to have a good time with a beautiful lady, or six."

"And you're absolutely sure it's him?"

"He looks just like the photos you gave me. He has the six-foot athletic build and bright blue eyes described in the memo, and he arrived from San Francisco. He's got a Soviet passport with the name Alexander Grekov, but unless you're a believer in huge coincidences, it's got to be Alex Ferris."

"I don't believe in coincidences. When is Alex scheduled to check out?"

"Not until the middle of next week."

"Good. Now, listen carefully, Sergey. You are to stay on him like glue, invisible glue. Is that clear?"

"Yes, sir."

"Did he do anything to indicate that he knows he's being followed?"

"No, sir. I was very careful."

"Then you should be able to handle him on your own until morning. I happen to be flying to Irkutsk in an hour, but I'm going to be in a meeting until noon, and then I have other business that will keep me occupied until around midnight. I doubt Alex will last that long at Max's—I've seen the girls—so I'll plan to catch up with you at the hotel around this time tomorrow morning. Meanwhile, you are not to arrest Alex, just observe him. Take detailed notes on everything he does and especially everyone he sees and call me on this number if anything extraordinary happens."

"Yes sir, general."

"Are you sure you can handle Alex alone, Sergey?"

"Yes, sir."

"That's good. I'd just as soon not involve the Irkutsk office. I will make the decision on what to do with him when I see you tomorrow morning, based on what Alex does between now and then. Understood?"

"Yes, sir. I'm your man, sir."

"We're about to find out. If you start getting tired, Sergey, just remember that in twenty-four hours you'll be a hero. Don't make a fatal mistake before then." Yarik hung up without waiting for acknowledgment.

This was bittersweet news. Yesterday Yarik had made a point of lavishing praise on Victor to Karpov, and now he looked like a fool. On the other hand, now he could have his way with an American spy. Overall, it was probably a net gain. How big a gain would depend on Alex's stamina. Instinct told him it was going to be good.

Then there was Sergey. Yarik didn't buy the young agent's tale of going the extra mile. He found if far more likely that Sergey had temporarily misplaced his pager, or had forgotten to check it until he had already picked Alex up. That was all right. Yarik could appreciate a man taking an advantage when presented. Just so long as there were no other anomalies. On second thought . . .

Yarik called the office and had them transfer his call to the Hotel Irkutsk. He identified himself, reconfirmed what Sergey had told him, and left a message with his mobile number for whomever was at reception: He was to be discreetly informed *immediately* if Mr. Grekov had any change of plans. Then he hung up and pressed "one" on his speed dial.

"Karpov."

"It's Yarik. I have some bad news. Apparently the American private eye escaped Victor's explosion and hopped on a plane. He arrived in Irkutsk ninety minutes ago using a Soviet passport. Fortunately, my redundant security measures at Sheremetyevo compensated for this shortcoming."

"Why didn't the bomb work?"

"I don't know. I haven't talked to Victor yet."

"I see. Don't mention this to him. I'd like to bring it up myself."

"As you wish."

"Why were you employing redundant security? Is there something else I should know?"

"Just instinct. Alex's bio raised my defenses."

"I love those instincts of yours. We'll come back to the bio later. It gave me an idea. Where is Alex now?"

"He's staying at the Hotel Irkutsk under the name of Alexander Grekov. My man is going to watch him for the next twenty-four hours. We will probably pick him up together early tomorrow morning after he leads us to whatever fountain of information brought him here. That way we will be able to cut off the source as well. I'm planning to interrogate Alex personally, and should have everything there is to know by noon tomorrow."

"Excellent. I want to talk to you about that as well. See you at nine."

Yarik closed his phone. Victor was not going to be happy.

When the elevator doors opened on the fifth floor, Yarik found himself face-to-face with an early riser. Having been spotted on the scene, he began to curse his luck but then recognized the face between the fur hat and collar: Luda Orlova, SibOil's diligent and dedicated senior accountant. His victim had literally walked straight into his arms.

CHAPTER 17

Irkutsk, Siberia

The boardroom at Irkutsk Motorworks was as dilapidated as its product line. Chairs once grand were now wobbly and frayed, the laminated table had long since given up its shine, and even the walls seemed somehow sad. To Karpov, this room represented Russia's state of affairs, and the very sight of it steeled his will. It was a disgrace, it was a shame, and it was about to change. The people of Russia deserved better.

Stepashin and Yarik sat to Karpov's left and right. The Knyaz were about to meet. As the wall clock ticked nine, Karpov's watch beeped twice, and the telephone rang. He pressed the speaker button and began. "Victor?"

"Good morning, gentlemen."

"Good afternoon, Victor. How are you?"

"I'm just fine, sir."

"Well then, I'll get right to it. This afternoon I'll be sitting down with the management of Irkutsk Motorworks to discuss the launch plan for the *Acula Engine*. They've already cranked out a dozen of the

UE-2000 copycats, and I expect to learn that they will be ready to tool up for full-scale production within the month. Can you confirm that we'll have no competition from United Electronics?"

"The UE-2000 project is virtually dead."

"Virtually?"

"Well as you know, the brain behind the project, Frank Ferris, is now dead. I had arranged to destroy their prototype as well, to have it explode at the weekly test run. That would have taken out additional project personnel and almost certainly led to the project being shelved, if not canceled. But a software glitch shut the engine down before my sabotage had a chance to kick in. Still, the project is severely crippled.

"I was, however, successful with another related explosion. This one took out Alex Ferris, the PI who had been snooping around after I eliminated his brother."

"That explosion didn't work, either," Karpov said, sounding every bit the disappointed general that he was. "Alex Ferris arrived here, in Irkutsk, early this morning using a Soviet passport. He's at the Hotel Irkutsk now, under the name of Alexander Grekov."

There was a painful silence before Victor responded, his voice calm and cool but uncharacteristically strained. "I don't know what to say. I put a bomb on the ignition of the car that Ferris drives. It blew up. Those facts are certain. The press identified the victim as Alexander Ferris of San Diego. That is also certain. For reasons I'm sure you can appreciate, I did not hang around to witness the explosion personally, so I cannot give you a firsthand account of Ferris's fate, other than to say that I have not seen him since then."

"It would appear that you haven't seen him because he was on a plane. But believe it or not, according to what Yarik has told me, that may actually be a good thing."

"How so?" Victor asked, his tone cautiously optimistic.

"Tell me what you know about Alex Ferris. I understand you were at Stanford together as undergraduates, and that you knew each other socially?"

"That's right. I knew Alex fairly well. He grew up in Geneva, Switzerland, which is where his American father met his Russian mother. So he's a polyglot, got the Swiss German, French, and Italian trio plus native English and Russian."

That was news to Karpov. Good news. "What were they doing in Switzerland?"

"His father was a banker, and his mother worked at our consulate."

"Really? I wonder if we ever met."

"In any case she's dead now. Both Alex's parents were killed in the terrorist attack at Rome's airport in seventy-three. I'm sure thoughts of revenge drew him to the military and eventually the Special Forces. The CIA scooped him up after a few years in the Green Berets and put him in the field, in covert ops. I'm sure they made good use of both his language skills and military training."

"Where did he serve?"

"I don't know. He never talked about it, but I got the impression he was all over the Eastern Bloc and Middle East. But he's done with that now. Opened 'International Private Investigations' about six months ago down in San Diego."

"Is he married?"

"No. No girlfriend either. If he had one, I would have Peithoed her as insurance. As far as I know he's never had a serious relationship, although the women line up."

"Is he gay?"

"No. He enjoyed himself in college as much as any guy and more than most. I think he just prioritized his career, and it wasn't compatible with marriage, something I know we all can appreciate."

"Close friends?"

"Not since college. His career kept him moving around and wasn't conducive to relationships, plus like most good spooks he's naturally independent. He didn't even talk to Frank very often, and they were twins."

Karpov put both palms flat on the table and said, "He's perfect," more to himself than anyone else. "Yarik, I want you to go ahead with your plan to follow Ferris for the day to learn what he's up to. Then bring him back to Academic City for interrogation as discussed. I also want you to ensure that Ferris is . . . undamaged. I intend to put him to good use."

CHAPTER 18

Irkutsk, Siberia

There were five metro stops between the Hotel Irkutsk and Irkutsk Motorworks. Alex stopped at every one of them, exchanging five twenty-dollar bills with five different black-market traders. Now, in addition to ninety-eight hundred dollars he had smuggled into Russia in his boots, he had ten thousand rubles in his wallet. It was enough to live for a month like a czar. He could have gotten twelve thousand, but he wanted the rarer hundred-ruble notes to keep the volume down, so he had accepted a lower exchange rate with an internal chuckle; a hundred dollars and he was rich.

On the bad-news side of the coin, he had picked up a tail while clearing customs in Moscow, a green agent with distinctive gold-framed glasses. Alex had masked his discovery and extreme disappointment and had strung "Gold Frame" along in order to ditch him at the most opportune time. That time had come a half hour ago, when he left the Hotel Irkutsk by window after priming both the sexy hotel receptionist and a shifty taxi driver with disinformation. If the next couple hours went according to plan, it would be midnight before Gold Frame realized that he'd been outmaneuvered.

At the last metro stop, Alex used fifty rubles to buy himself a change of wardrobe at a flea market. It was unattractive but warm. The only things he did not change were his boots, socks, and gloves. Every soldier knows you don't compromise on footwear or jeopardize your trigger finger. Alex had come into Russia wearing a pair of high-end winter trekking boots, and he would go out wearing them, hopefully not feet first. To blend in he had cut off the logos and used a marker to blacken over the accent marks. Now they were a secret weapon.

Although Alex had no prior knowledge of a specific bar near Irkutsk Motorworks, he knew that every factory in the civilized world had a watering hole within a few steps of its doors. The Engine Room turned out to be one of two establishments that catered to Irkutsk Motorworkers.

Whereas the day shift would always wait until after work to hit the bar, Alex knew that night-shift workers might well go in for an aperitif. It wasn't that the day shifters were more virtuous; it was just that the night shifters could drink inconspicuously before work. At least that was the case in the US, and Alex figured that when it came to drinking, anything Americans could do, Russians could do better.

Before heading inside, he took an inconspicuous look through the fence at the factory complex, lest he be caught without even the most basic knowledge. Then he paused for a moment to gather his thoughts.

The bar did not look particularly cheery given the dim lighting, but Alex had a feeling it would look even worse with the lights turned up. The floors were either grungy-blue linoleum or blue linoleum that was grungy. Alex decided not to dwell on that; vodka was a sterilizer. The plaster walls were painted different shades of green, but not according to any pattern or style that he could discern. The flat paints were most likely acquired one bucket at a time on a take-it-or-leave-it basis. The crowning jewel of the decorum was the bar itself. It had machine parts nailed, bolted, or welded to every square inch of its surface, and the countertop was the wing from an old airplane. It reminded Alex of something he had seen at the Museum of Contemporary Art in Chicago, but he decided that it would be unwise to inform the proprietor of the fact.

He sat at the bar and simply asked for two hundred grams, knowing that he would immediately be marked as an outsider if he used the superfluous word "vodka." Although The Engine Room wasn't busy yet, he still didn't have his order five minutes later. Alex couldn't figure out why the man was so slow to move, but as long as it wasn't personal, he didn't mind. With sixteen hours of jetlag, this evening was going to be one rough ride. Russians don't sip their vodka with olives and vermouth. They slam shots. So it's hard to fake drinking unless you have water in your glass, and Alex couldn't afford to get caught in that old trick.

He was getting nervous about the implications of the bartender's rebuff when a chesty waitress walked in the front door, wearing a big white fur hat and stomping the cold from her feet. Alex got his two hundred grams and a hello-lover look less than a minute later. As Olga walked away with her first tip of the night, she undid the top button on her strained blouse, giving Alex something to look at while he waited to get lucky. He had decided to give The Engine Room thirty minutes to produce what he was looking for. Then he would move down the street to the competing establishment.

Alex was hoping to find an Irkutsk Motorworker that looked like him. Thanks to his mother, he knew he was fishing in the right gene pool. Of course, even with a perfect facial match, there would still be issues. He looked happier and healthier than anyone in Siberia, and he had a light California tan. There was little he could do about that but hope that his jet lag, five o'clock shadow, and the dim lighting would help compensate. He prepared a story just in case.

The first half dozen patrons to enter were no good for one reason or another, too old or fat or dark or disfigured or all of the above. Then at four fifteen a large man in well-worn, navy-blue coveralls entered the bar and took a seat at a small table in the corner. Alex tried to picture him as he would look in a black-and-white passport photo. He was a good match overall, but there was one glaring exception. The man was bald. Alex cursed his bad luck. If worse came to worst, he could shave his head, but given the temperature outside—*the temperature outside, that was it.* With a sigh of relief Alex remembered that he would still be dressed in outdoor clothing when passing through security, and that included his fur hat. The man, for his part, might also be convinced to leave his *shapka* on. Yes, this would work. Alex had found his fish. Now he just had to plant a hook and reel him in.

Coveralls looked up at Olga, who in turn nodded to the bartender, who poured a flask like Alex's without further prompting. Alex intercepted Olga with a wink and a ten-ruble note and asked for a bottle of Stolichnaya with three glasses, which, thank you very much, he would personally deliver to the man's table. In Russia it was customary to drink in groups of three. No further explanation was required.

Alex sat down across from Coveralls and poured two shot glasses to the rim. Then, without saying a word, he lifted his glass and held it at eye level, looking across the small table at his new best friend. The man looked puzzled at first, like a guy who sees a hundred-dollar bill on the sidewalk and can't believe that what he sees is real, then, afraid it will vanish, pounces before it can disappear. *Za zdarovye.*

They drained their glasses.

Alex poured another couple of shots, and the two drank again, still in silence. The man seemed afraid to speak, apparently fearing he would break the spell. Alex, now satisfied that he had the hook in the man's mouth, opened with the universal male icebreaker, "You see the tits on that chick?" tilting his head toward Olga.

The man seemed relieved. Alex's remark had indicated two things: one, that he was just a guy drinking in a bar, and two, that he wasn't gay.

"Tastiest pair in town."

"You been there?"

"Oh yeah. Nice," he said, drawing the word out with a smile and a nod. Then added, "You want an introduction?" He reached out to hold the bottle of Stolichnaya as he offered. Alex wasn't sure if the gesture was subconscious or not.

"Nah, thanks. I've got enough woman problems."

Noticing with seemingly genuine surprise that the bottle was now in his hand, Coveralls took the initiative of filling the glasses the third time. Alex started getting nervous. He was planning on finesse, but at this consumption rate he wouldn't be able to beat a chicken at tic-tac-toe in half an hour. He needed to buy time. Alex made a point of directing his gaze at Ms. Titties for a while, and sure enough, his new friend went ahead and drained his glass alone.

"Speaking of introduction, I'm Alex."

"Boris. You new to town?"

"Just this part. I'm avoiding my wife's friends."

Boris nodded with understanding. "That where your woman problems come from?"

Alex faked a surprised look, then nodded as though suddenly remembering his earlier comment. "Her friend saw me with my girlfriend. Of course I said it wasn't me, but she didn't buy it."

"Tell her to mind her own business."

"I wish it were that easy. She's the one with the money. And the connections."

"So dump the girlfriend. A guy like you can always find another once things cool down."

"I've tried. Can't do it. She looks like an Italian film star and fucks like a Swedish one. I'd almost rather die than walk away from that bed."

"Guess you gotta be more careful."

"Exactly, and that's my problem. She's hired a private eye to spy on me."

"No shit?" Boris downed another shot.

Based on Boris' coveralls, Alex was sure he worked at Irkutsk Motorworks, but he did not know in what capacity. If he learned that it was quality control, he would never be able to fly Aeroflot again.

Putting that thought out of his mind, he continued to bait Boris. "Meanwhile Sophia has said that if I leave her sitting at home alone one more Friday night, she'll dump me like yesterday's garbage." While he spoke Alex fidgeted in his seat uncomfortably, eventually withdrawing his very thick wallet and setting it on the table.

Boris's eyes bulged, but he didn't comment. Instead he said, "When's your next date?"

"Ten o'clock tonight."

Boris shook his head. "What you gonna do?"

"I was hoping you might help."

Boris looked startled. Then he grinned. "You want me to fuck Sophia for you, keep her satisfied till you work things out with the missus?"

"Don't you have to work?" Alex asked, nodding at Boris's coveralls.

Boris's eyes bulged, and he paused, clearly unsure if the vodka was interfering with his hearing. Then he said the magic words. "Shit man, I can always call in sick."

If this guy was stupid enough to think a stranger was going to buy his drinks and then give him his girlfriend for the night, Alex knew he would have no problem selling his real plan. "Nice idea, but actually I was thinking we could trick the private investigator into following you, and then *I* could go see Sophia."

Boris gave him a doubtful, crestfallen look. It was time for Alex to reel him in.

"Of course, I would compensate you for your lost wages. And for the inconvenience of replacing a lost ID. You could go spend the evening at Max's Place, on me, as long as you make sure the PI follows you there."

Boris's face lit up like a young Hugh Hefner's. Then, realizing his mistake, he did his best to look concerned. "I dunno, man, I had to miss a few days already this month, and this might be too much. Could cause me to lose my vacation voucher."

Alex thought, *yeah, right*, but said, "I understand," and opened his wallet. "How about I give you a hundred for the inconvenience," he laid a crisp ruble bill on the table, "a hundred to keep things cool with your boss," another bill, "and one, two, three hundred for Max's ladies?"

Alex could tell Boris was trying to control his excitement. It was too good to be true, and in a minute he would figure that out, so Alex said, "I love spending the wife's money this way."

Boris raised his glass.

CHAPTER 19

Moscow, Russia

> "In the short term the question for the Soviet leadership now is not whether reforms will succeed, but how to prevent anarchy and chaos."
>
> —*US Secretary of State James A. Baker III*

Ri-ri-ring . . . swish. The sound of the encrypted call was music to Sugurov's ears. Andrey's critical report was overdue.

"I'm listening."

"Alex is in Irkutsk. So am I. After his stunt with the car bomb, I'm surprised to be reporting that he picke d up a tail in Sheremetyevo. A young KGB agent followed him onto the connecting flight.

"I was able to get close enough to the tail to use my sound surveillance equipment. He placed a call to none other than Yarik."

"Yarik—the KGB's chief executioner—heaven help us."

"Between Victor and Yarik we now know that both the KGB's Illegals and Executive Action Departments are involved. We're uncovering a monster, sir, a hydra, only I don't know how many heads it has."

"There's only one head, Andrey, you may be certain of that. Multiple heads exist only in mythology. And I fear you have not encountered him yet."

"What makes you so sure, sir?"

"Victor's relative age and permanent presence in the US rules him out. Yarik, cunning though he may be, is no grand strategist. With those two names, however, we can begin sketching a portrait of the mastermind we're up against. I daresay he appears to be somebody in the top echelons of the KGB. Let us hope so anyway. If the Knyaz are bigger than the KGB, then there may be nothing we can do to stop them. As it is, my friend, I'm more than a little concerned."

"Why not just expose them now, the members we do know?"

"Suppose we did that, and then they exposed their whole operation on the evening news. What would the average Russian think about a group that was using Russia's intelligence capabilities to create manufacturing jobs, restore pride, and strengthen the economy? Given the current economic situation, I think they might be inclined to overlook the bothersome details, and the devastating long-term consequences. I think they'd take the money and call these guys heroes. Those are the two things everybody loves: money and heroes. And Russia is desperate for both right now."

"You're right, sir. Sorry. I'm just frustrated."

"I understand. Tell me, how is Ferris doing?"

"Brilliantly, sir. He slipped his tail at the hotel, but they don't know it yet. Alex is a very resourceful man. I almost felt sorry for the agent, though. I wouldn't want to be the guy who has to tell Yarik he lost his quarry."

"You just make sure you don't lose yours, Andrey. There is far too much at stake."

CHAPTER 20

Irkutsk, Siberia

Alex watched with a mischievous smile as Gold Frame left the hotel in hot pursuit of the wrong man. He allowed five minutes to be sure they were well on their way and then went to the lobby to check out. The receptionist did a double take when she saw his smiling face. She seemed a bit nervous that he was leaving—fancy that—but brightened up when he asked her for a taxi to take him to the airport.

"Flying home?"

"Back to Moscow."

"Midnight flight?"

"That's the one."

"Bon voyage."

She picked the phone up before he was out the door. *So predictable.*

The air was frigid outside, but no snow was falling, yet. The Channel One News had warned that a major snowstorm was in the forecast, so it was a good thing that he was not really flying. He took the taxi to the airport and then walked around a bit to satisfy himself that he was not being followed. Once convinced, he ducked into a kiosk, where he bought some mascara, a card, a fancy box of chocolates, and a red wool scarf.

Alex addressed the card and tucked it under the ribbon on the box. Then he put the scarf around his neck, tied the ears from his fur hat snugly under his chin, and went back out into the freezing night with an altered stride. To all but the most careful of observers, he was a different man.

He caught a different taxi back to town, this time directing the driver to The Engine Room's competitor, Propeller, which was located a half block to the other side of Irkutsk Motorworks' entrance. When they arrived, Alex held up the card and chocolates and said, "I need these delivered to Isabella Belochkova at 146 Potemkin Boulevard, building twelve, apartment 166. How much will that cost me?"

The driver sucked air in through bad teeth for a long second and then said, "That's clear on the far side of town. Will take me an hour, and that's if traffic is good and the snow doesn't start. Say eighty rubles. Plus of course the ten for this ride."

"You sure you can find it?"

"Sure I'm sure. My sister lives off Potemkin."

"Good. It's worth two hundred to me, or four hundred with a guarantee."

"Guarantee?"

"For four hundred you guarantee you deliver, or I guarantee to . . . make you regret your lack of commitment."

The driver's face blanched, but then his eyes shifted from left to right to left again. "I'll take the four hundred."

Alex handed him the box, the card, and the four hundred rubles. Then he made a point of writing down the car's plate number after exiting.

As soon as his back was turned, Alex chuckled to himself, picturing the driver's desperate attempt to deliver chocolate to a non-existent person at a phony address, while any followers looked on in confusion. Perhaps all these precautionary countermeasures were unwarranted, but after Gold Frame's appearance, Alex worried that he wasn't being cautious enough.

He entered Propeller and made his way through a boisterous crowd to the men's room, where he locked himself in a stall and waited for the other occupants to leave. Once alone, Alex moved to the mirror and began blackening around his left eye with his newly acquired mascara. This would make the guard less comfortable about staring, would give him an excuse for acting coy, and would make it that much more difficult to distinguish him from the photo in Boris's ID.

Alex left Propeller in much better shape than he had left The Engine Room. There was probably still some vodka on his breath from the latter, but that would only serve to augment his disguise.

It was time to get serious. The next two hours were what he had traveled halfway around the world for. If he got this right, he could be home by this time tomorrow.

Irkutsk Motorworks was a complex of three buildings surrounded by a tall chain-link fence with a guard shack on its only entrance. A coil of concertina wire around the top looked much newer than the fence itself. Security had recently been upgraded.

Boris, once loosened with liquor and intoxicated with cash, had vented that management was making major changes. He really was concerned about losing his job. He had tugged at a loose thread on his blue coveralls and explained that he worked on the "blue side" of the complex, whereas all the action was over on the "black side."

"Why not switch to the black side?" Alex had asked.

"I tried. Didn't pass the test. Fucking Perestroika."

"They working a double shift over in black?"

"Still a single, though rumor is that's about to change. Won't help me none."

"And I suppose black services the administration building as well?"

"You got that right."

"Bastards."

Alex spent the next few vodka shots pumping the disgruntled worker for details about the factory's layout and procedures. It became abundantly clear that everything of interest to Alex would be in the black zone. But Boris's identity card and coveralls were blue, and it was too late to try to find a black-zone look-alike now. He would have to improvise once he got inside.

Alex's first hurdle was the entry gate guard. Boris's shift ran from five p.m. until one a.m., but he had called in sick. It was now eleven o'clock. If questioned at the gate, Alex would say he started feeling better and decided to get a couple of hours in. This was thin, but his blackened eye helped fill in the blanks. The social awkwardness accompanying the bruise would also avoid a lengthy comparison of his face to Boris's ID. At least, that was Alex's theory.

One bonus nugget of news from Boris gave him hope. The Irkutsk Motorworkers had just spent three days working hard to get the place shipshape for a big meeting that morning. Human nature dictated that most of the staff would spend the next three days slacking off to compensate.

Alex held up his ID without enthusiasm or a break in his shuffle as he passed the guard's window and clicked through the turnstile. The guard did not even bother to raise his head from his paperback. He just blinked his eyes up at Alex, said "ouch" and then returned his gaze to the book. By reading a detective story, he had just overlooked the real thing.

Following Boris's directions, Alex headed straight for the maintenance room and its lockers. He needed a black uniform. A cross-shaped covered walkway connected the two enormous industrial buildings with the central administration building and the guardhouse through which he'd just passed. Whereas the brick behemoths were trimmed with icicles the size of fence posts and stacked with enough snow to indicate that someone was watching the heating bill, the wind kept the walkway clear of both.

Alex listened briefly at the maintenance room door but couldn't hear anything over the wind. He checked the handle, found it unlocked as promised, and walked in on a legitimate janitor.

"What are you doing here?"

CHAPTER 21

Suhbaatar, Mongolia

As a general in the KGB, Yarik was entitled to the use of a Chaika limousine with a flag on the hood, a siren on the top, and a major in the driver's seat. He rarely took advantage of the perk, however, preferring, instead, to feel the road through the steering wheel of his Ford Explorer. It offered a much smoother ride than the Chaika, and, on days like today, Yarik needed more discretion than he could get with an aide in the car. Today's mission was Knyaz business.

A typical head of the KGB's Executive Action Department would spend his time dealing with administration, leaving the operations end of the business to the young guys. But Yarik was not typical. He detested administration. This was normal enough, but he also cared little for the money, perks, or privileges that came with his rank. This combination made an eloquent solution easy to devise. Yarik delegated the administration and the chauffeur to a colonel in his confidence, and freed himself up for the good stuff. It was almost too good to be true. He got power, respect, and fear, all from doing what he liked best.

Executive Action, they sure found a way to give the group responsible for murders, kidnappings, and sabotage a respectable face. Were they fooling anybody? Did he care? In his opinion, it was the best job in the world.

With two hours of lonely, winding mountain roads behind him, Yarik caught sight of the border-patrol station. Aside from a crinkly old goat herder and his gnarled dog, the desolate shack was the first sign of civilization he'd seen for fifty kilometers.

A soldier emerged, his weapon ready. Yarik readied his passport and pulled to a stop. Crossing into Mongolia would not present him with a problem. In fact, this particular middle-of-nowhere crossing probably didn't present a problem to anyone who had ten rubles to spare.

As the private accepted Yarik's identification, his jaw dropped a bit. Yarik's reputation had preceded him. Due to the combination of his size, title, and the bloody trail he left behind, Yarik encountered slack jaws several times a day. He found it very satisfying and always kept it in mind when planning his kills. After all, when you've got the best job in the world, you have to defend your title.

Just past the border was an open-air bazaar, duty-free shopping, so to speak. Yarik stopped to make a quick purchase, garnering an odd look from the vendor when he asked to have it wrapped in newspaper and tied with twine. The Mongol complied without comment, and five minutes later Yarik reached his destination.

"Good afternoon, general, and welcome to the Lone Spruce Hotel." The manager gave a slight bow.

Yarik recognized the voice of the man he had spoken with by phone earlier in the week. "Are they here yet?"

"Not yet, sir, but I expect the Ivanovs within the hour, assuming this Friday is no different from most." He handed Yarik a duplicate key for the Ivanov room and looked inquisitively at the oddly shaped package Yarik was carrying.

Yarik did not comment on it. He just handed the manager fifty rubles, enough to rent half the Mongolian hotel. As the man took the money from his right hand, Yarik grabbed the manager's genitals in his left and looked down into his eyes. "Keep your mouth shut and you will never see me again." When he released, the manager wet himself but said nothing. Yarik began to whistle as he walked up the stairs.

He made his way to the room the couple had reserved and concealed himself in a convenient closet. The latticework afforded him a full view of the bed, and there was room to shift about.

As he set about unwrapping his package, he felt a familiar hunger building within. His rage was like a beast that rarely ate its fill. The Orlova execution had not satisfied him for breakfast. There was no sport in snapping a woman's neck. Dinner, however, would likely compensate. He would be procuring it with a Mongolian hand scythe. He tossed the instrument back and forth between his enormous hands, getting a feel for its weight and balance. It had a curved, steel blade half a meter long attached to an equally sized wooden handle: beautiful, simple, deadly.

Yarik had decided to make the killing look like a jealous husband or another boyfriend was the perpetrator. He did not know if the woman had either, but it did not really matter. The hand scythe would mislead any official investigation, but bar talk would still stoke his legend. The hotel manager and border guard would see to that.

He did not have long to wait before the happy couple arrived. They burst into the room in a torrent of kisses and giggles and dove hungrily onto the bed.

The woman was attractive, even striking, and she had a warm, smoky voice. She was a good fifteen years younger than the forty-four-year-old engineer, and well proportioned. She had honey-toned skin; long, thick black hair; and voilà, shaved genitalia. Now Yarik understood why the engineer made the expensive and illegal trip each week.

He also had to wonder what she got out of it, and hoped it was not related to the Knyaz project. Yarik was not overly concerned about that possibility. If Miss Mongolia had gotten what she was looking for, she would not be wasting any more time boffing this guy.

Having watched with voracious eyes while his lover stripped, the engineer stood and shed his own clothes like they were on fire. Then Yarik understood. The engineer was half man, half beast. As the woman coaxed the beast out of him, Yarik thought the man might pass out from lack of blood to the brain, but he remained standing. This new evidence did not commute their sentence; in fact it didn't rule out the espionage theory at all. But when she was gone, Yarik would consider the case closed. It would probably be a waste of time to scour Mongolia for those behind her.

Meanwhile, there in the bedroom, the woman used both hands to push the naked engineer backward onto the bed where he lay with his prick raised in salute to her beauty. Then she dove on it like a seal on salmon. Yes, Yarik thought, the best job in the world.

From where he stood, Yarik could see the Mongolian woman's breasts knocking together rhythmically as she performed her service. He was finding it difficult not to moan along with the engineer. Yarik considered doing just that for the thrill of her reaction, but he didn't want the show to end. There was something of a tigress in this woman, and that made her just his type. If he lasted to retirement, Yarik thought, he would want a woman like that by his side. But not until then.

He considered killing the man first and taking the woman before dispatching her, but decided to resist the urge. It would be a sloppy, amateurish thing to do, and probably unnecessary.

Act one of the show ended, and Miss Mongolia moved up on the bed. Her sailor was at half-mast, so she dangled her heavy breasts in his face for a moment to put some wind in his spinnaker before commencing with the second act. She took the leading role in this scene as well. *Where did she get so much energy?* Judging by the stamina in her legs, she must be an equestrienne . . . or a circus performer. Like the fated scientist beneath her, Yarik was finding it hard to control his enthusiasm.

Halfway through the second act, Yarik's phone began to vibrate. *Damn!* That was twice today. He looked at the display: Hotel Irkutsk—*the receptionist; Alex must be moving*. Yarik pressed the answer key and said, "Hold on." The bed stopped squeaking at the sound of his voice. He dropped the phone and crashed open the closet doors, bringing the scythe to bear with a roar as he leapt toward the bed. The two lovers, caught up in the delirium of their lovemaking and startled by the incomprehensible sight of a screaming giant wielding a scythe, froze for an unbelieving moment to stare in shock. A moment was all the time Yarik needed. With two quick flips of his wrist, he slit both their throats. Screams turned to gurgles, gurgles to silence. Then he speared them to the bed like ketchup-splattered french fries on a toothpick. *Love gone astray.*

The scene would look horrendous to the poor chambermaid that found them, but two seconds of shock aside, they had died happy. Objectively speaking, Yarik had quickly and painlessly executed a traitor and a spy. The rest was just theatrics.

Yarik was certain that he, too, would someday die a soldier's death. It would likely not be as painlessly quick or as blissfully unexpected as it was for these two, but it would almost certainly be as bloody. That was okay with him.

Yarik remembered the phone and returned to the closet. "What is it?"

The phone was dead.

CHAPTER 22

Palo Alto, California

Victor was steaming when he disconnected the conference call. *Alex was alive!*

He went straight from the telephone to the gym, where he spent an hour working those three words into a heavy bag. There was nothing that got under his skin more than being played for a fool. And this time, this time it had happened in front of his father. He was apoplectic.

It wasn't until he stepped out of the shower that he found the wherewithal to focus on anything but his own humiliation. That was when it struck him. All Alex had accomplished with his deception was to exchange a sudden, painless death for a lengthy, excruciating one. A warm feeling enveloped him, and it was not just the towel. The more Victor thought about it, the clearer it became that there was nothing he would rather have happen to his rival than an encounter with Yarik. The largest member of the Knyaz made Torquemada look like the tooth fairy. At any moment now, Yarik would pick up Ferris for interrogation, and the fun would begin.

Victor would give anything to participate in that soirée. Perhaps he should fly to Russia to watch. *Now there was a thought.* A quick in-and-out would also give him a chance to pick up his shares of Knyaz AG stock. But no, there was still too much going on. And besides, Karpov had wanted Ferris brought to him unharmed, so there would be nothing quick about it. *What was all that about, anyway?* He would have to ask Yarik the next time they spoke.

With those intriguing thoughts running through his mind, Victor returned to the Shell station. He found a pile of *Lucy's Ladies* business cards stacked in his phone booth. He hoped it wasn't a sign that he would soon be sharing his office with call girls. *Then again, perhaps that wouldn't be so bad . . .*

He flipped through the cards. Each had a different picture. He pocketed a few. Then he took a special black box out of his pocket and set it lovingly on the metal shelf. Reading from a little address book, he keyed fourteen characters into the box but did not push the transmit button. Instead, he picked up the telephone receiver, inserted twenty quarters, covered the microphone with his voice-distortion disk, and dialed Seattle. He expected to find Dr. Davis home alone, as Clara had dance class Friday evenings.

"Hello?"

"Good evening, Mark, how are you?"

"I'm sorry, who's asking?"

"Okay, right to business then. I need you to mosey on upstairs to Clara's room, please."

"What? Who is this?"

"Look, Mark, don't wear out my patience. Now get your ass up the beige staircase, past the pink bathroom, the linen closet, and the circus poster, to Clara's room, pronto."

"Oh, okay."

Victor liked this part. It was like stepping into a Hollywood studio and acting out a role. That was why he used words like *mosey* and *pronto*, and said the cruelest things with the kindest voice.

"Now, on the wall over the head of Clara's bed, there's a picture of Winnie-the-Pooh holding a red balloon. I want you to take it off the wall and tell me what you see."

"Jesus!"

"Tell me what you see."

"It's a page from a magazine."

"And what's on the page, Mark?"

"It's a picture of a girl. A . . . a dead girl."

"And what does she look like?"

"She's been murdered. Cut up."

"And who does she look like?"

"Clara. She looks like Clara."

"I thought so, too. So, Mark, do I have your attention now?"

"Yes."

"Good. Now, call Taffy. Let me know when you've got her in your arms." It was hard for Victor to keep from laughing as he pictured the scene: panic mixed with confusion, rage with supplication. Victor had half a mind to have Davis jump on one leg and cluck like a chicken.

"I've got her."

"Good. Now look into her eyes, please."

"Okay."

"Are you looking, Mark? Don't bullshit me now."

"Yes, yes I'm looking."

"Good. Now I want to hear you tell her 'good-bye.'"

After a long pause Victor heard the word, soft and slow, and he pushed the transmit button on the black box. A moment later, eight hundred miles away, there was a yelp, and then Victor heard a lot of rustling. Eventually Mark got back on the line.

"What kind of a sick bastard . . ."

"Focus, Mark. Focus. What kind of a bastard I am is not what you should be concerned with at a time like this." Victor spoke with a voice as kind as a granny on her wedding day. "Would you like to take three guesses as to what you should be concerned about?"

Victor heard the programmer crying, and smiled.

"Clara?" Mark's voice was a whisper.

"Very good, Mark, Clara. You are exactly right. I knew you had potential. Now, first of all I have some rules for you, and then I'm going to tell you what you are going to do for me."

CHAPTER 23

Irkutsk, Siberia

"I said, 'What are you doing here?'" The bleary-eyed janitor in black coveralls repeated his question.

No doubt Alex's contrasting blue garb was the reason for the immediate challenge. Alex kept his cool. You didn't position your best men in the maintenance room, and besides, Mr. Black's tone was more startled than hostile. Alex suspected he had caught the man sleeping.

Mindful of his expression, Alex looked around, as though he, too, were confused.

"Shit. I got myself turned around." He started to leave then stopped.

"Say, you got a cigarette?" Alex walked forward a few steps before the man could collect his wits, then sprang like a mousetrap. Alex drove his fist up under Black's chin just as he was opening his mouth to respond. It was a perfect punch, timed to catch the jaw as it dropped open in preparation for speech. Alex used just enough power to get the job done without causing permanent damage. No need to cripple the guy; this wasn't personal. Black's jaw slammed shut with a satisfying crack and bloody spittle sprayed forth onto Boris's blues. Alex whipped around and caught Black in a headlock before he could react.

Alex used his right arm to help crimp his left tightly around the janitor's neck, going for carotid closure and blackout. The janitor seemed to comprehend the strategy. He began bucking and spinning like he'd swallowed bees. He had a good eighty pounds on Alex, and in this situation, weight made a difference. Alex ran the calculations and switched to plan B. As they careened into the janitor's cart, he released his right hand and used it to grab the hickory handle of a long scrub brush then, on Black's next downward buck, Alex released his left arm as well. As Black stumbled forward, Alex clubbed the base of his crew-cut skull with the brush's backside.

Black dropped like a stone.

Alex looked around while catching his breath, thinking ahead. The wind had surely drowned out the scream, but nonetheless it was time to slip into high gear. He stripped the slacking janitor, noting by his ID that his real name was Yuri Petrovkin. He dragged Yuri over to a large storage cupboard, where he used a spool of wire to bind Yuri's hands, and dirty rags to gag his mouth. Then he rearranged the cupboard's contents, and locked Yuri inside.

Still moving quickly, Alex donned Yuri's black coveralls. He'd expected to find a modern electronic keycard in the pocket, but found a big ring of metal keys instead. Upon inspection, however, he noted that they were considerably more sophisticated than traditional keys. It was as though the black zone was set up to appear just like the blue one, when in fact it was much more. The puzzle pieces were locking into place.

His plan was to take a quick, confirmatory look at the black production facility. Then he would head for the administration building and whatever documentation he could find in the executive suite. Before leaving, he routed through the janitor's toolbox looking for weapons. He selected a long awl and a sharp steel chisel, and threw both onto the janitor's cart. Then he unscrewed the long wooden handle from the industrial mop head. It was thick and heavy and had a weighty iron screw head. He left it propped up in the bucket at the front of the cart. These wouldn't be much good against an AK-47, but they'd be deadly enough in close-quarters combat.

Alex found himself shivering by the time he'd pushed Yuri's cart to the main entrance of the black production facility. His quivering hands made it difficult for him to work the keys. To take his mind off the imminent danger while he worked, he let his thoughts wander to the scene that would be transpiring about this time at Max's Place. He could picture Boris drinking vodka from the navels of half a dozen Siberian hotties. Eventually his hat would slip off, exposing the deception along with his bald head. He hoped that wouldn't be too soon.

With that wishful thought, the lock responded to one of the keys, and a moment later Alexander Temogen Ferris, International Private Investigator, stepped into the hot zone. It had been a long trip.

Alex found himself looking into the electronic eye of a security camera. He spun around to grab the janitorial cart, and backed in until he'd passed beneath its gaze. Then he turned back around to survey the scene before him. The sight made him feel as though he'd moved forward fifty years in time. The factory floor was spotless and covered with row upon row of modern manufacturing equipment. It wasn't the equipment that riveted Alex's attention, however, so much as the product of their labor.

Lined up on both sides of the mammoth room like eggs in a carton were a dozen enormous aircraft engines. Alex pushed the squeaky cart toward the closest engine to confirm his expectation. There was no doubt as to what he was seeing. This was his brother's design. The engines had the same unusual sharklike "gills" he had seen on the prototype at United Electronics.

Alex had expected to uncover something like this, but nothing so grand or advanced. To his eye, Irkutsk Motorworks was better equipped than United Electronics. Its production was certainly more advanced. The student had surpassed the teacher. Where did they get the money? Surely the State had not sanctioned this? If so, then Perestroika would take on a whole new meaning, Gorbachev's halo would rust, and the Cold War would heat up.

Alex would have liked to ponder the implications of his discovery further, but this was neither the time nor the place. He had gotten what he needed from the production facility, but he still had a lot to accomplish before escaping during the shift change. The whistle was just ninety minutes away.

He pushed the cart back out into the wind and cold, careful to keep his back to the security camera. Thirty seconds later, he reached the entrance to the administration building. It was locked, but he found the right key on his second attempt. He headed straight for the elevator, assuming the executive suite would be on the top floor.

It was a U-shaped building, with offices running along the outside wall, and the hallway running along the inside, overlooking the courtyard. The bottom section of the U, where the elevator was located, was built twice as wide as the wings. This accommodated conference rooms overlooking the courtyard and secretarial stations outside the executive offices.

The decor that met his eyes when the elevator doors pinged open was typical of the Soviet era. Sad laminate furniture with chipped edges, and shabby seat cushions that gave the air a sour smell. Clearly the black modernization had been limited to the factory floor. None of that mattered to Alex. He was there for information, not accommodation.

His first choice of places to pilfer was the central office. It was twice as wide as the others before him, and no doubt held the juiciest files. It also looked directly over the guardhouse, and thus was the most exposed. Alex didn't know if janitors were allowed to clean it or not. He would have to risk it.

Reaching for the key ring, he thought back to Boris's words and had a change of heart. He crossed back through the secretarial section and tried the boardroom door on a hunch. It was unlocked. Stepping in, he closed the door, flipped the light switch, and felt another drop of adrenaline hit his bloodstream.

It was obvious that the room had just been used for a long meeting, undoubtedly the one about which Boris had spoken. There were empty coffee cups and bits of leftover sandwiches on the table. More confirmation that Yuri had been slacking off. The chairs were all over the place as though the meeting had dragged on far too long and people had gotten restless.

Alex scanned the table for papers. He checked underneath it and around the chairs. He found nothing. He walked over to the whiteboard and tried to read its post-erasure markings. That was hopeless. Then his eyes came to rest on something else, something that appeared out of place. He walked to the end of the room and lifted the overhead projector off its cart. A single lost acetate was hiding there atop a film of dust and a bent paper clip.

Alex took a quick survey of the courtyard below, confirming his solitude, and then brought the projector to life. The acetate displayed a map on the wall. It was Siberia, and it had several locations marked by flags. Irkutsk had a flag labeled "Irkutsk Motorworks," Krasnoyarsk had one labeled "RuTek," and Novosibirsk had two: one in the center labeled "SovStroy," and the second in the famous scientific suburb of Academic City. It made Alex smile. Positioned beside a crescent-shaped lake, it read "HQ."

Alex burned the map into his mind. It completed two-thirds of the puzzle, the *what* and the *where*. The missing piece of the puzzle remained the all-important *who*. None of the pages contained names, and he could not fly home without them. That would be like predicting the end of the world without forecasting the date.

He would have to risk searching the chief executive's office.

Alex folded the acetate and stuffed it into a pocket. He'd just grabbed the cart's handle when the boardroom door opened, and an enormous figure darkened the doorway.

“Not quite done cleaning yet,” Alex mumbled, stooping down to pick up some trash.

“Oh, I think you’re done.” The voice was gruff, but its tone seemed satisfied.

Alex surreptitiously slid his hands toward the chisel and awl while looking slowly up at the man who had discovered him. He was a bald-headed giant with a face like a clenched fist and a neck that would moor a ship. Alex knew the fight was over before it began. Hand tools were no match for Mr. Clean, or the hand-cannon leveled before him.

“Sandwich?”

CHAPTER 24

Irkutsk, Russia

Ri-ri-ring . . . swish.

"I'm listening, Andrey," Sugurov said, anticipation in his voice.

"Sorry for the early call. Alex has been captured. He was caught inside Irkutsk Motorworks, one of the factories that supplies the Tupolev aerospace company with their engines."

"There's our first solid connection."

"Exactly."

"Do you know if he found anything other than copycat engines? An organizational chart? A strategic plan?"

"No, sir."

"So if we lose him now . . ."

"We won't be back to square one, but we'll still be a long way from home."

"What else do you know?"

"Yarik caught him, personally."

"And he's still alive?"

"Yes, surprisingly. Seems Yarik wants to take him elsewhere, for interrogation, I assume. That may give us a shot, both at saving Alex and at identifying the Knyaz."

"Where are you calling from?"

"I'm outside Chulin Air Base, where they're holding Alex. It's just east of Irkutsk. The snow is coming down pretty heavy now, and there's a nasty wind, so obviously they're waiting until the weather improves to take off."

"Do you think you stand a chance of getting him out of there first?"

"I don't know, sir, but I am going to try. It will be very risky. That's why I wanted to check in with you now, to let you know what was happening in case things don't turn out."

Sugurov stopped pacing and dropped into a chair as he exhaled. "Listen, Andrey, I know I don't need to tell you how important this mission is to Russia. You understand that better than anyone. But don't go throwing your life away either. If it can't be done, it can't be done. We will find another way."

"Do we have time for that?"

Sugurov was not one for candy coatings or wishful thinking. As foreign minister he could not permit himself such indulgences. Still, knowing and loving the man he was speaking with, he dreaded the consequences of the only answer he could give. "We don't have time."

"Then I will do everything in my power to ensure that Alex does succeed."

"Can I send you some help?"

"No, sir. I doubt there's time, and in any case it's too risky. Any overt help would expose our connection to Alex and alert the Knyaz."

"What about tracking the plane to see where they take him?"

"Won't work, sir. You'd need to work with the air base here, and we have to assume it's been compromised. In any case I doubt they could help. Yarik knows his business and will surely dip below radar long enough for us to lose him."

"Godspeed then."

Sugurov put down the receiver and noticed that his hand was shaking. He had not experienced that before. Was it age, or nerves?

He slid aside one panel of the oak headboard on his bed, revealing the door to a safe. Sugurov keyed in the long combination and was rewarded with the familiar whir and click before thick steel door swung open. He removed a metallic briefcase, set it down on the bed, and pressed his thumbs down squarely on the two large clasps. A microchip verified the thumbprints of the foreign minister, and the case popped open.

The briefcase contained the single red file that had started it all. The file that had survived a helicopter crash and exposed the existence of a powerful, clandestine organization within the Russian government. The file that had proved that organization's ability to infiltrate the elite and coerce cooperation from the trusted. The file that had led Sugurov to Victor Titov, and then Elaine Evans, and then Frank Ferris, and then Alex. It read:

> I am pleased to report that I shall deliver US projects two and three and complete my assignment as scheduled. I would like to add that the latest figures from the parent companies estimate sales of between one and two billion dollars for each project in the first year alone. We have chosen wisely. With the war coffers secured, I trust this means we will keep to the master schedule and launch in full force by New Year's, assuming Gorbachev continues to be ripe for the plucking.
>
> Here's to the New Russia. Long live the Knyaz—
> BUKTOP

CHAPTER 25

Irkutsk, Siberia

There's a thick black bag over your head, and your hands are bound tightly behind your back, securing you to a thick D ring riveted to a metal floor. Your hands are numb, your legs are freezing, and your jailer looks like the Hulk's bigger brother. You've got information that could alter the global geopolitical landscape, but you're thousands of miles from anyone who cares. What do you do?

It was not an easy question, but one that Alex was determined to solve. He began by asking himself what he knew. To manipulate a situation, he first had to understand it.

Alex knew that his captors were KGB and that the giant in charge was named Yarik. The first bit of intel came from the uniforms, the second from a slip of the tongue. Yarik had rewarded the loose-lipped soldier with a punch to the face so brutal that he had lost consciousness to the sight of spurting blood and the sound of snapping cartilage. Alex appreciated the sacrifice, and added *Yarik* to *Victor* on his list of names.

Alex also had a list of locations. The map left beneath the boardroom projector indicted that in addition to Irkutsk Motorworks they controlled factories in Krasnoyarsk and Novosibirsk. Best of all he knew that their headquarters was also in Novosibirsk, next to a crescent-shaped lake just east of Academic City.

Perhaps that was where they'd be taking him.

Regarding his present location, Alex's best guess was that he was in the belly of a stationary cargo plane somewhere near Irkutsk. He had no way of telling how long he had been there—each minute beneath that hood seemed like an hour—but he guessed that it really had been hours. Surprisingly, they hadn't removed his watch, although of course he couldn't see it.

Oddly enough, they hadn't tried to interrogate him either. They hadn't spoken to him at all, other than a few barked commands, with one notable exception: "Now I've got your number."

Yarik had uttered those words just after stabbing Alex in the ass with a syringe that looked more suited for a horse than a human. That had put the fear of God in him. Alex had seen what interrogation agents could do to a man's brain.

Sitting in the dark, trying to mentally overpower whatever chemical cocktail was coursing through his veins by playing out his what-do-you-do game, the significance of Yarik's five words finally came to him in a flash of understanding. A cold hand clamped his heart. The giant had not injected him with an interrogation agent. He had implanted him with the same device they had used on Elaine's mother and daughter, the Peitho Pill.

Escape was now impossible.

Alex was bound by an electronic leash he could not outrun.

Those five words, spoken in that gruff voice, began to echo over and over in his mind like a catchy advertising jingle. *Now I've got your number*. He found it hard to think of anything else. He began to truly appreciate the tortured life Elaine had been living, and the awesome power held by the people he was up against.

Rather than continuing to churn desperate thoughts, Alex focused on funneling the nervous energy into formulating a solution. He forced his mind to return to unraveling the conspiracy that had killed his brother, enslaved Elaine, and imprisoned him in Siberia.

His visit to Irkutsk Motorworks made the grand plan clear. The KGB was using a diabolic device to commit industrial espionage. They were simultaneously sabotaging product development at US corporations while establishing parallel operations in Russia. Alex supposed it was a sound business tactic, if laws and ethics weren't of concern, but it hardly fell under the purview of the KGB. This didn't concern state security. Or did it?

Russia was in desperate need of a solid industrial base, one that would be competitive in a modern capitalist marketplace, one that could replace their military-industrial complex as the foundation of a restructured economy. Soviet factories were elephants—too big to maneuver, too slow to respond, and too expensive to maintain. But with the Iron Curtain now down, they were being forced to compete in a world of tigers. Crisis and bloodshed were imminent.

Still, it seemed to Alex an odd undertaking for the KGB. They were essentially a group of spies and thugs. What did they know about industry and economics? It was with that thought that Alex understood his mistake, his bad assumption. The KGB was no more a single organism than was the CIA. While the rank and file would be relatively homogenous, at the top they too undoubtedly had a series of interlocking power structures, each vying with the other for ultimate control. Politics surely drove the KGB just like any other large organization.

Alex probably wasn't dealing with the KGB. He was likely dealing with a faction of the KGB, a politically ambitious faction.

If he was right and this group was doing what it looked like it was doing, his adversaries were attempting to fill an economic and political vacuum that would suck them right to the top of their transforming nation. This was Perestroika, but a very different flavor from Gorbachev's.

Alex felt the scope of his mission growing a hundredfold, and with it the weight on his shoulders.

But he was still stuck there, bound, blind, and helpless. But not deaf . . . Someone had just entered the cargo hold.

The intruder walked toward him and paused. Then Alex heard something thump to the ground beside him, something heavy enough to cause the floor to vibrate. Another body? A cauldron of boiling oil? Alex braced himself for a kick in the chest, but instead he got a very different kind of wallop.

"Alex . . . Alex, can you hear me?"

It was the voice, *the* voice. He had only heard it once before, but he knew it like his mother's. That same voice had said the words: "They're about to kill your brother."

CHAPTER 26

Novosibirsk, Siberia

The Chaika limousine bounced along with Karpov's emotions as he considered his oldest friend's request.

Beside him in the back seat, Stepashin continued to make his case. "You're far more charismatic than any of the other presidential contenders, but you are a KGB general. While Russians like, need, and respect strong leaders, the wounds inflicted by life under Stalin remain fresh. Voters are very wary of militant personalities."

"Nothing I can do about that," Karpov said.

"Actually, you can. We can put you in a whole different category, by splitting your personality."

Karpov gave Stepashin an incredulous stare.

Stepashin ignored it. "With the right wife by your side, you'll convey the proper balance of strong and visionary with charismatic and trustworthy."

Karpov grunted noncommittally. He agreed but wouldn't concede immediately. He wanted something in return. Something big.

"You've already fallen for the perfect candidate," Stepashin added. "Anna Zaitseva is another Raisa Gorbachova in the making. A beautiful doctor from a common but respectable family, she'll complete both your public persona and your private life."

Karpov turned to look out the window at the snow-covered country landscape rushing by. "She's not interested. I've asked her out. More than once."

"People change. She's older now, twenty-eight, and surely becoming aware that her biological clock is ticking. I could easily find other candidates, eager candidates who look the part . . . but I've never seen anybody but Anna get under your skin. I want you to be happy. The country needs you to be happy. And you deserve to be happy. Tell me you'll try and I know you'll succeed."

Karpov turned back to face his friend. "You really like her?"

"I don't know her, but she appears perfect on paper, and I like what she does to you. She adds sparkle to your eyes, and a surge to your stride. You should see your face when you mention her name."

That was news to Karpov. He wasn't sure he liked it. It gave her too much power. But that was beside the point of this discussion. "Okay. I'll try. And I'll succeed. But . . ."

"But what?"

"I need a similar effort from you on a project no less crucial to our cause."

"Name it."

"Even with the people behind us, the KGB in our corner, and the economic power that will soon be at our disposal, there remains one unpredictable force that could still cost us the presidency." He paused to let Stepashin think. "A force of which our opponents are sure to avail themselves."

"The courts."

"The courts. The Supreme Court in particular. We need to own it."

“It can be bought.”

“We’re not the only ones with oil money. And the power of money is unpredictable. We need the kind of certainty only Peitho can provide. I need you to implant the chief justice.”

CHAPTER 27

Irkutsk, Siberia

Alex's hood lifted, and he found himself looking into the eyes of the man whose call had sent him to Frank's house minutes after his death, the man who topped his list of murder suspects.

"I'm here to help," the Russian said, producing a pocketknife and locking the blade into place.

Alex leaned forward to expose the ropes that bound his wrists.

"Name's Andrey. I'm sure you have a hundred questions, but we've only got seconds. Here's our situation. We're in the KGB's airplane hangar at Chulin Air Base. There is little to no chance of your walking out of here unobserved. The KGB's lead enforcer, whom I believe you've met, is in the building, preparing to fly you out of here. His presence has everybody fearful, alert, and eager to impress. Can you handle a jump?" He nodded toward the parachutes on the floor beside Alex.

So that was the thump. "Yes, I can handle it. Now please cut the ropes."

"I'm not going to cut them. Too risky. But I'll loosen them to restore your circulation and leave you the knife so you'll be ready when the time is right. Sit on the knife for now. Just make sure you can get to it when the time is right." Andrey bent down and got to work.

"Who are you and why are you helping me?"

"It's complicated. Suffice it to say that the people who murdered Frank also killed a dear friend of mine."

While Andrey worked his bonds, Alex wrestled with the disconnect between what he was seeing and hearing, and what he had concluded upon hearing the familiar voice. Andrey struck him as stressed but sincere, not slick or subversive. Then again, Frank had clearly been fooled by his killer.

"I'm going to hide in that container over there," Andrey said, pointing to a long cargo bench running along the opposite wall. "Once we're in the air, I'll come out blasting." He tapped his sidearms. "You be ready to cut yourself free and lend a hand with the knife. I don't know how much company we'll have."

Andrey then dropped the hood back into place, and Alex's world became dark again. A moment later Alex heard the parachutes thunk into the cargo bench. Then Andrey cursed softly as he jammed himself in after them.

"I'll keep an eye out; meanwhile we can speak softly," Andrey said. "Tell me what you've learned."

Whether he was a true friend or a subversive foe, Andrey's question was right on cue.

"You still haven't told me who you are."

"This is not the place for that discussion; it's . . . complicated. The knife in your hand should convince you that I'm your friend."

"Given that you've got a gun, I'm more inclined to trust my ears. They recognize your voice."

After a pause Andrey said, "From the phone call?"

"That's right."

"I appreciate that looks bad. There's a lot that's not as it seems. The fact of the matter is that it's about to get messy, and you might not survive. I need to know what you've learned but don't have time to convince you to trust me or to prove that this isn't some elaborate ploy. So let me ask you this: Do you think Yarik is someone who would need my help with an interrogation?"

Alex had to concede the point. He was processing other angles when Andrey continued.

"Look, Alex, I know you're a pro. So am I. But there's no time for the two-step. Bullets will be flying soon. Just tell me things they already know you know. That might suffice."

"Fair enough. I have learned that a group within the KGB is stealing the blueprints of highly lucrative American products and then manufacturing them here in Russia. They are doing this at factories in Irkutsk, Novosibirsk, and Krasnoyarsk. Their headquarters is in Novosibirsk, near Academic City. Simultaneously, they're sabotaging the American companies that invented those products, presumably so the Russian versions will have a monopoly on the world market. I do not know how they expect to get around patents. I do not know who they are or how long this has been going on. I do know that they are high-tech, and ruthless."

"What members of this group do you know? What names have you come across?"

"I only know two names: Yarik and Victor."

"If you learned Victor's name, why are you suspicious of me?" Andrey asked.

"I already told you, I recognize your voice from the phone. And I don't follow your logic."

"It was me on the phone. But it was Victor who killed your brother. Victor Titov."

"I didn't know his last name. Or that he had killed my brother."

"Actually, you do know his last name. His other last name. His American last name. Victor Titov's cover name is Jason Stormer."

Alex felt a surge of adrenaline. He had sensed it, even investigated it, but then had ruled Jason out. "I verified that Jason was on a plane when Frank was killed."

"No, Alex, another KGB agent was on a plane disguised as Jason Stormer."

Of course! Alex felt like a fool. That snapped one piece of the puzzle into place, but Andrey's appearance had opened another, bigger hole. "Tell me why you're helping me."

"Because I need you to succeed."

"From where I'm sitting, it looks like you do okay by yourself."

"I'm just back-office support. Look, Alex, as a foreigner you can do things in Russia that I cannot do. My actions could have severe political ramifications."

"What does that mean?"

"I hold a prominent position working for a very powerful man. One of Gorbachev's cabinet ministers."

"So find a Russian with a lower profile."

"I wish it were that easy. I need somebody with two specific features: one, he has to be clever and resourceful enough to unravel and penetrate a very sophisticated operation. Two, he has to be someone I can be one hundred percent certain has no connections whatsoever with the group we're going after."

"Why are you so concerned about that?"

"They recruited someone very close to me. Someone whose loyalty and integrity the minister and I would never have questioned."

Suddenly Alex understood. "Does the word *Peitho* mean anything to you? Peitho Pill?"

"No . . ."

"These people have a device that they implant in people. Apparently, once this Peitho Pill is in place they can kill a person with the flip of a switch. They use that threat to coerce people. With Peitho implanted in someone's child, they can make him do anything. It is truly diabolical."

"Oh my God. That must be how they got to Leo. This makes things even worse than we thought." Andrey's voice sounded strained. "They—"

Alex heard footsteps, and then his new friend said, "They're coming."

CHAPTER 28

Palo Alto, California

Piloting his Beamer toward the Sunset Palms Hotel and his rendezvous with one of Lucy's Ladies, Victor found himself rehashing the stressful question that drove him to seek that kind of release. Could coincidence account for all his recent problems? It seemed unlikely, yet the alternative—that someone was finally on to him after all these years—seemed impossible.

For seventeen years, half of his life, Victor had been living a lie so skillfully conceived and flawlessly implemented that he had sailed through the background checks required for a government security clearance. In fact, his placement had been so flawless that it had become the standard by which he judged all his future endeavors.

Victor was one of a dozen deep-cover Soviet moles the KGB planted in the US that year in an operation codenamed *Immaculate Conception.* None had been rooted out. He vowed he would not be the first.

Immaculate Conception began with the KGB placing an agent named Sparrow at U-Haul's headquarters. Sparrow's first job was to go through the reservations database, looking for families making one-way, long-distance moves. Then he called everyone that fit the general profile, and began narrowing down the list. The first criterion was children. He was looking for families with teenage children.

"Hello Mrs. Murphy, this is U-Haul Customer Service calling. I just wanted to check if any children would be accompanying you and Mr. Murphy on your move this summer?"

"Why yes, our son, Michael, will be with us."

"I see. And how old is he?"

"He's twelve. Why do you ask?"

"We just want to be sure your truck is equipped with the proper safety equipment. It's just one more way U-Haul works to serve you better."

"It's kind of you to ask, but we won't be needing any of that."

"Thank you, Mrs. Murphy, and have a good day."

Once Sparrow had prepared his list of finalists, he quit U-Haul, donned a suit, and set off to visit each family. His tack was to pretend to be with the Census Bureau; his job was to determine if the family had any close friends or family. Most did, and Sparrow ended up visiting over two hundred finalists before producing the dozen target families Immaculate Conception required.

The Stormer family was moving from Detroit to Sacramento, where they planned to start a fresh life and a new business. Sixteen-year-old Victor and his "parents" intercepted the Stormers one night at a motel in Wyoming, killed them, and continued the drive the next day in their place.

They buried Jason in a deep grave with enough lime to dissolve him in no time. He was never found. Nobody was looking. Mr. and Mrs. Stormer, on the other hand, made the journey to Sacramento in an ice cream truck before the KGB transferred them to a deep freezer plugged in at a U-Store facility.

Six months later, the new Jason Stormer graduated from high school and applied to Stanford. Shortly thereafter, his KGB parents thawed

Jason's real parents, put them in a car, and "killed" them in an accident that burned them beyond the reach of an autopsy.

Victor's KGB parents flew on to another assignment while Victor himself went off to college fully armed. He had friends and a history in Sacramento, a high school diploma, a fat insurance payment from his dear parents' death, and a bulletproof cover. With seventeen years of citizenship now layered on, he was confident that nobody in America could possibly guess, much less find a way to prove, that Jason Stormer was born Victor Titov.

The string of problems he had been facing had to be a coincidence.

Victor entered the hotel room to find that the evening's entertainment had already arrived. She was waiting for him on the bed in one of the suite's white terrycloth robes. "My name's Nikki," she said, setting down a jar of minibar pistachios and standing. She dropped the robe around her ankles without another word.

Nikki was exactly what he had ordered. That was, of course, what one expected when putting a thousand dollars on his AmEx, but in this business, you never knew. She had slender arms rising to supple shoulders, which she pulled back gracefully to parade two golden apples, ripe for the plucking. They were teased from atop by her thick brown hair. Nikki had it coiffed in a wild, unkempt look, akin to the one in her eyes.

Victor felt his mouth go dry.

Still mute, Nikki walked over, crouched to her knees, and unbuckled his belt. She might have been nineteen when she walked in the door, Victor thought, but she'll feel twenty-five by the time she leaves. Victor's mind began to bathe within the carnal pleasures of the moment. Tensions released. Concerns assuaged. Then his pager leapt to life.

Some people react to spiders, others to blood. Some fear heights, others enclosed spaces. Nothing knocked the joy out of Victor like the vibration from his pager. The heavens might as well have opened up to drop a rattlesnake into his shorts; his reaction would have been the same. He had no illusions about what that hum signified. To Nikki, however, it was just another toy. She picked the vibrating box off his belt with a giggle and began pleasuring herself with it, staring dreamily into his eyes as she moved it in slow circles. Victor found himself paralyzed with shock. It was like watching a baby teethe on a hand grenade—hard to process. But the spell didn't last. He snatched the pager away and went to the bathroom to read the message in private.

Sight unseen, a vibrating pager meant two things to Victor. It meant something was wrong, and it meant that his father was upset about it. Then there was the message format. Like an EAM sent to a submarine, Karpov's messages did not allow for discussion or debate. They just demanded emergency action without providing explanation. It was a father's way of getting the last word without even having to speak to his son. The pager was the voice that commanded him, the collar that enslaved him, and the whip that lashed him. Victor hated the pager.

He punched in his nine-digit security code and looked at the screen. *Ferris slipped his tail in Irkutsk.* Victor's blood pressure surged such that he thought his eyes might pop like champagne corks. "No!" He punched the bathroom door hard enough to put his fist through both sides of the flimsy wood.

Nikki yelped.

Still fuming, he yanked his hand back through, driving splinters and drawing blood.

The pager went off again.

"*Damn it!*" he yelled, tossing the pager skyward in a mixture of shock and rage. He snatched it from the air with a slippery hand, and read the second half of the message: *but Yarik has him now.*

A calm settled over him like a warm blanket. He read it again, then wiped the blood from the pager and tended to his hand.

Victor liked Yarik. The giant was strong, sincere, and straightforward. He was also, without a doubt, the most instinctively sadistic person Victor had ever met. He wondered how that pursuit had unfolded and made a mental note to ask Yarik for the details the next time they spoke. Victor recalled the story of a fur trapper who had stolen supplies from a remote base while Yarik was visiting. Yarik chased him over the Siberian countryside, in the dead of winter, for four days, just for sport. What mortal could enjoy spending nights outdoors when the temperature was forty below zero? And over what, a rifle and a couple boxes of ammunition? Not this California boy.

The soldier sent to accompany Yarik reported what happened when they finally caught the trapper. Yarik zipped him up in a sleeping bag with his arms sticking out the top. Then he bound his wrists together around the trunk of a tree, and then left him there overnight. In the morning, while Yarik sipped his tea, he began interrogating the thief. What else had he stolen? To whom did he sell things? Did he have help on the inside? Questions like that. For each answer that Yarik didn't like, he ceremoniously snapped off one of the trapper's frozen fingers. When the interrogation was over, he just left him there. Victor superimposed Alex's face on that mental image and grew a grin. Enjoy yourself, Alex.

With that thought, the blood returned to Victor's loins, and he walked back into the bedroom intent on giving Nikki the good news. She was gone. He punched his palm in frustration and recoiled in pain. His grimace turned to a smile as he pictured the look that must have crossed the call girl's face as his fist crashed through the door. He was too much of a man, even for the pros.

CHAPTER 29

Siberian Outback, Russia

Without warning, four of the seven KGB soldiers began convulsing wildly as bullets tunneled through their bodies from below. The three remaining soldiers jumped to their feet from the opposite bench and stared in uncomprehending horror as their team members disintegrated before their eyes, the victims of an unseen power.

With the roar of the aircraft's engines drowning out all sound in the cargo hold, it was unclear if gunfire or lightning or Satan himself were powering the bloody boogie. That doubt vanished a moment later when the Devil incarnate, all glistening red and bristling with rage, burst forth from beneath the four lost souls and turned his fiery gaze toward them.

♦ ♦ ♦

Blood from the soldiers' bodies poured down onto Andrey as the savage smells of cordite and copper filled the bench. The vile combination sparked an adrenal blast that primed him for the fight ahead. He swallowed an acrid cloud, summoned a barbaric cry from deep within, and sprang from the cargo bench like a demonic jack-in-the-box.

Andrey had the steady nerves of a twenty-year combat veteran, so he remained calm even though the sight that met his eyes sucked the wind from his lungs. Three soldiers were still standing, and he was out of ammunition.

The survivors stood before the opposite bench, a meter to the right of where Alex sat bound. Each wore the same wide-eyed expression of horror—despite having youth, numbers, and arms on their side. Andrey had burst forth prepared to neutralize a surviving soldier or two during their moment of shock, but he was facing a couple assault rifles and a large, menacing knife.

He spun around, whipping a packed parachute by the end of its harness straps through a 270-degree arc, channeling all the power of his arms, legs, and back into building momentum before slamming it into the soldiers' weapons and sending them sailing. The overextended swing also sent Andrey tumbling right into the trio, and the four of them landed violently in a heap on the floor.

From the writhing muddle, Andrey caught a glimpse of his comrade in arms. Alex was unmasked now and on his feet. Judging by the fire in his eyes, he was ready for redemption.

Andrey disabled the soldier above him with a double-armed bear hug from behind, while the dazed man on the bottom worked to wriggle himself free. Andrey used his left leg to pin the third soldier's neck against the bench. With his right he kicked the man's skull against its base with the heel of his heavy boot until it gave way with a crack loud enough to hear over the engine roar. Meanwhile, the soldier in Andrey's arms kept flailing his head back in an attempt to break Andrey's nose.

Then Alex arrived. He swooped in and slashed the bear-hugged soldier's throat with a quick, fluid move of his knife.

Andrey turned his head to avoid swallowing arterial spray and yelled, "Go block the cockpit door!" Then he rolled free of the corpse and stood to face the remaining man, the Armenian brute who had favored a blade. No longer dazed, he rose to his feet wearing an air of confidence the surrounding scene did not support. As Andrey met his eye the Armenian flared his upper lip, flashing canine teeth while assuming the cool, forceful stance of a skilled martial artist.

Andrey had always been more of a wrestler than a fighter, his large frame better suited to developing a gorilla's strength than a gazelle's speed. But if he followed his natural inclinations and dropped into a wrestling pose, his opponent would understand the score and adapt his attack accordingly. So, instead, Andrey squared off with fists and forearms before him, announcing himself as a student of the sweet science.

The soldier feigned a punch then leapt and twisted with a spinning kick to the side of Andrey's head. His practiced move was lightning quick and nearly impossible to block, but it was not Andrey's intent to try. He accepted the blinding blow in order to catch the recoiling leg, trapping it high above the ground. Clamping down with viselike hands, Andrey somersaulted forward in a diving roll, snapping the soldier's leg at the knee.

Were it not for the earsplitting screams, Andrey might have let the Armenian live. Instead, he planted his boot deep in the soldier's solar plexus, momentarily extinguishing his anguished cry. Then Andrey smacked the switch for the tail landing gate with the side of his fist. As the rear of the craft began to open, he stooped and grabbed the back of the soldier's uniform with both hands. Then he lifted and twisted like a hammer thrower, sending the silenced soldier soaring through the burgeoning crack and out into space.

CHAPTER 30

Siberian Outback, Russia

Andrey bent forward to rest his palms on his knees while he chased his breath. When he looked back up Alex was there, buoyed with newfound freedom and percolating the energy of youth. Facing each other eye to eye for the first time, the two panting predators spent a silent moment sizing each other up.

"Is the door secure?" Andrey asked, breaking the verbal silence as he repocketed his knife. He leaned inward toward Alex so he could hear his response over the sixteen close-quarter pistol blasts that still rang in his ears.

"I blocked it as best I could," Alex shouted, "but I don't know how long it will hold. Let's hope we can get out of here before they learn what happened."

A murderous clamor erupted from the direction of the cockpit before Andrey could concur. He looked over at the vibrating door and pictured a red-faced Yarik fuming on the other side.

It was not the best time for such a ceremony, but something about the warrior's code made Andrey pause and extend his hand. "Andrey Demerko."

Alex looked at him for a moment before reciprocating, "Alex Ferris." Then he added, "Thank you," indicating the pile of bodies with a sweep of his head.

Andrey brushed off the latter remark and said, "Suit up" as he turned to appraise the landscape now visible far below. It looked as cold as a glacier, and no less desolate.

"Not yet. I have to kill Yarik before we leave."

"We can't risk a cabin assault. It's too risky."

"You don't understand. He put that device in me, the Peitho Pill. Even if I get away, I can't escape."

In the background Yarik's pounding intensified and then ceased altogether. He was up to something.

"Don't worry," Andrey said. "This plane is going down." He withdrew two hand grenades from his belt, wedged them in the tailgate's hydraulics, and pulled the pins. "Compliments of the Chulin Air Base arsenal."

Alex gave him an understanding nod. When the pilot closed the gate, the grenades would release, and it would be bye-bye, birdie.

"Now shut up, suit up, and grab an AK. I don't have any more ammunition for my Makarovs."

Alex complied, nodded, and then leapt out into space. He had obviously endured all the Yarik he cared to take.

With a somber smile and a silent prayer, Andrey dove after his charge. It was his first flight as a guardian angel. He hoped it would also be his last.

Their altitude was somewhere in the range of six to seven thousand meters, so once they established eye contact, each assumed a diving pose. The increased speed made it harder for them to stick together, but the thin air demanded the quickest possible descent. This was no place to pass out.

As they rocketed toward the white expanse below, Andrey caught sight of the airplane above. It was circling back. They were not yet out of the woods. A long sixty seconds later, they leveled out, preparing to deploy. The two unlikely comrades looked each other in the eye for a moment, then nodded.

Andrey had to shift his AK from his right hand to his left in order to pull his rip cord. As he did so, he saw Alex's canopy fail to inflate. His parachute had deployed, but the harness that connected the risers on the right side was severed, and the silk just streamed out uselessly above him like the luminous trail of a plummeting meteorite. The Armenian had probably slashed it with his hunting knife during Andrey's swing for the bleachers. Would he get the last laugh?

Andrey discarded his AK and assumed the soaring-eagle position to slow his descent, grateful that he had not yet deployed. Then he looked over at the man he had chosen to save his country. Alex seemed to have his wits about him. The two men locked eyes as Alex released his useless chute.

Paratroopers were not skydivers, and thus unaccustomed to free-fall acrobatics. They made one unsuccessful pass, and then another, attempting with increasing desperation to converge in three dimensions as they fell to Earth. How many more tries did they have?

On the third pass, Alex caught Andrey by the ankle. Then the two veterans began to work the drill they had studied decades apart with different forces on separate continents. Working face-to-face, they attached the clips on the front of Alex's harness to the D rings on the front of Andrey's. Andrey gave them a quick test and then pulled his own rip cord. A second later his parachute bellowed open, and both men began to breathe again.

Their descent slowed, but it soon became clear that it had not slowed nearly enough. Looking up, Andrey saw the problem; it was an extra-light chute. All military parachutes were lightweight compared to sport parachutes, and this one was at the small end of that spectrum. It was designed for lightly equipped troops descending under fire. How one of those had gotten packed into a regular harness, Andrey did not know, but whatever the reason, the outcome was indisputable. They were both going to break their legs and probably their backs unless one of them found a way to substantially lighten the load. There were not many options available, and the rocketing ground left little time to experiment.

Alex dropped his AK, but that was like bailing a boat with a thimble. Then Alex lifted a leg to undo a boot, but Andrey stopped him. He knew what he had to do. These past months had just been borrowed time. He had used them well.

He grabbed Alex on both sides of his head, looked him in the eye, and shouted, "Don't you fail me, Alex! Don't you let my children down!" Then, before his charge could respond, Andrey Demerko, veteran of Afghanistan, Chief of Staff for the Russian Minister of Foreign Affairs, and architect of the plan that would save his beloved nation from the clutches of criminals, cut himself free.

At one time or another, everyone wonders what he would think about if he knew he only had a moment to live. This was the second time Andrey learned the answer. He saw the smiles of his wife and children and those of the grandchildren to come, and he knew that he had done the right thing.

CHAPTER 31

Novosibirsk, Siberia

Doctor Anna Zaitseva's lower lip was quivering as she looked up after finishing the day's first operation.

The assisting nurse caught her eye. "It's okay, Anna. You saved him." Vova nodded down at the patient she had just closed.

Vova knew her well enough to guess what she was feeling; industrial accident cases always reminded her of her brother Kostya. "What's next?" she asked.

They were a good team, she and Vova, albeit an unusual one. As a female doctor with a towering male nurse, patients almost always addressed him first. Then Vova would open his mouth and suggest in his effeminate lilt that they ask the doctor.

She gave Vova a grateful smile before repeating her question. "What's next, Vov'?"

"Frostbite in theater three."

As they went through the perfunctory interoperational routine of changing from soiled gowns to fresh, scrubbing, and regloving, Anna found that she couldn't get her mind off Kostya. Her brother had died along with twenty-four fellow villagers from the vilest type of industrial accident: a radiation leak. She suspected it was also the worst possible kind: avoidable. But she didn't know for sure. Not yet.

"You went to the memorial service last night, didn't you?" Vova didn't wait for her reply. "I wish you'd stop going, Anna. It gets you too worked up. And besides, it's been five years now."

"It's become more of a social event than a memorial service."

"But it still upsets you."

"Of course it still upsets me. We still don't have closure. They still haven't explained how it happened."

"And they never will. The government is still living down Chernobyl. They're not about to turn an anomaly into a pattern by adding Academic City to the list."

She knew he was right. The legal system had gotten them nowhere. "You're right. That's why I've decided to get the information another way."

Vova pounced on that, as she knew he would. "I don't like the sound of that."

"It's nothing too radical. I just agreed to take General Karpov up on his latest dinner invitation."

Vova squeezed his bar of soap, sending it bouncing around the sink. "You're going to try to finesse classified information out of Vasily Karpov, the slickest politician in Siberia? The most powerful man east of Moscow? A KGB general? And you don't think that's radical?"

"It's just dinner. He's been after me for months. He'll be motivated to please me. To impress me. And his office is right there in the same compound where the accident occurred, so it won't be hard to steer the discussion that way."

"It's still a big risk, Anna."

"You weren't at the hospital back then. You didn't see the endless stream of our best and brightest as they were wheeled in looking like sausages off a grill. You didn't hear the animalistic groans escaping their charred throats. They were burned so badly that their skin sloughed off their hands like gloves while I held them, waiting for the morphine to work. I've never felt so powerless, so ashamed."

"Ashamed?"

"I didn't even recognize Kostya. Didn't know I'd . . . didn't know that one of them was my brother until I opened his documents to fill out the death certificate."

Vova clearly didn't know how to respond to that.

Anna nodded toward the clipboard beside the sink. "Frostbite, you say?"

"It looks like his fingers are going to make it, but his left foot has to go."

Anna nodded. They were seeing a lot of severe frostbite cases this winter, especially on Saturday, Sunday, and Monday mornings. Men would go out on payday weekends, drink themselves to within an inch of their lives, and then try to stumble home, only to pass out in the snow somewhere along the way. In the winter they usually died from exposure, but this patient had been very lucky. Professor Petrov had been warmly dressed and had probably fallen within an hour of being spotted by a snowplow.

Many of Anna's colleagues turned their noses up at men like Petrov. They figured he got what he deserved for behaving the way he did, and saved their compassion for the wives left home alone to worry if their alcoholic husbands would ever return. Anna, however, did not blame these men. She blamed the system that had failed them.

Perestroika had turned Russia on its head, and not everyone could adjust to the new reality. Gorbachev's great restructuring pulled them relentlessly forward toward an unknown future while they clung stubbornly to the past they knew. The tension ripped many apart. For Anna, the plight of the Petrovs was easy to understand. These men had lived in a very proud and stable system for decades. They had purpose. As the signs and posters that still hung everywhere proclaimed, *"They were*

Building Communism!" But not anymore. Now they were limping to their graves on plastic feet.

Anna used a marker to circumscribe three-fourths of Petrov's ankle and then drew the flap she would fold up to stitch over the stump. *This was so sad.* The leg barely bled as she cut through it with her scalpel—lack of blood supply was why it had to go.

She looked up at Vova, got a nod, and began to cut. As she put saw to bone, Petrov suddenly began convulsing. "Defibrillators," she yelled to Vova.

"On it," he said, flicking the switch to power them up and then handing her the paddles.

Anna placed one on either side of Petrov's sternum and pushed the buttons. Nothing happened. She looked up and saw that the status light on the machine was still red. Anna stood there, paddles poised, waiting for the green light to indicate that the defibrillators would fire. Three seconds, ten seconds, thirty seconds, and then the EKG went flat. Petrov was in cardiac arrest. Forty seconds, forty-five, fifty, sixty seconds, and then it was too late. Petrov died with her hands on his heart. He died because the mighty Soviet Union could not afford to replace a battery. How long could this go on?

CHAPTER 32

Siberian Outback, Russia

Yarik came out of his daydream to the sound of a buzzer and the blinking of a dashboard light. The tailgate was open. This could only mean problems, problems caused by the incompetence of others—again. First Sergey had lost Alex and now, now was it possible that seven armed guards had been so incompetent that Alex, bound and blindfolded, had managed to overcome them? No. It was not possible. It had to be a malfunction. Yet his instinct begged to differ . . .

Yarik got up to check. A twist and shove found the door to the cargo hold blocked from the other side. Until that moment, the safe bet was that either an electrical problem or the antics of an undisciplined soldier were behind the blinking light. Now with the door also blocked, Yarik knew there was a serious problem. One or more of his men must be a traitor.

But why? Who was this American? Victor had clearly underestimated Alex. Then Sergey had done the same. Now, Yarik realized with infuriating clarity, he, too, had not given Alex Ferris his due.

Yarik ordered the pilot to circle back and then turned to throw his 120 kilograms against the iron door. After a few tries he could tell that there was a blockage wedged between the overlap at the hinged end of the door and the bulkhead. His blows were flexing the metal, but only slightly. Fortunately a few millimeters of permanent deformation in either the door or the blockage would likely release the tension and allow the blockage to drop free.

To create those millimeters, Yarik dropped to the floor and braced his back against the copilot's chair. He took a deep breath, pictured Ferris's smug face, and pushed his legs into the door with the force of a hydraulic press. He knew from experience in the gym that he could apply over a thousand kilograms of pressure that way. The question was, which would give first, the door, the chair, or his back?

Thirty seconds later, his face red and his thighs sweaty, he relaxed his legs, stood up, and pulled the door fully closed. Then he kicked the spot where the bulkhead had bulged and was rewarded with the sound of the blockage dropping free.

Carnage greeted Yarik's eyes when he opened the door. Normally it would have brought a smile to his face, but this was a victory for the other team. Team? Yes, team. Someone must have helped Alex. He could not have done this alone.

Yarik counted bodies and found only six. He checked their faces and deduced that the missing man was Bagrat. Could the Armenian be in cahoots with Ferris? No way. Bagrat had a large family, three sisters and four brothers. If he turned traitor, it would be a death sentence for them all. But then who? How?

Yarik checked the cargo benches to see if Ferris had stuffed Bagrat's corpse inside, and found the bullet holes that told the tragic tale. Someone had stowed aboard and come blasting out of the bench. Had one of the Peitho victims learned something about the Knyaz and sent a mercenary to dispatch them? Did Alex have a partner that neither Victor nor Sergey had spotted? No matter, he would catch up with this mercenary soon enough. Then Alex's secret partner would cease to exist—but only after Yarik made him talk.

Once again, Yarik would have to see the mission through personally. He knew this should infuriate him, but instead found himself anticipating the hunt. He withdrew a parachute from the untouched cargo bench and walked back into the cabin, donning it as he went.

As soon as he entered the cockpit, the pilot shouted, "There they are," and pointed toward the eastern horizon.

Using aviator's binoculars, Yarik watched with fascination as the two fugitives dealt with the nightmare that haunted every paratrooper at one time or another. Then he gasped in unison with the pilot when one of them cut himself free and broke into a terminal plunge.

"I'm jumping after them," Yarik barked. "You land as close to that corpse as you can and wait for me." Then, without a pause or second glance, Yarik ran and dove out the back of the plane.

The airplane's altitude was less than half of what it had been when Alex and the mercenary had jumped, so Yarik deployed his parachute after the standard three-one-thousand count. Once it snapped open he checked his canopy, twice, and then began a sweeping search of the ground for his prey.

If Yarik could spot him fast enough, and the wind worked in his favor, he would be able to crash down on the survivor like a hammer from heaven. The wind, however, had other ideas. It worked so strongly against him that he couldn't even catch sight of his quarry. It was all he could do to steer toward the martyr's crash zone.

The landscape below was spotted with drifting snow in some places and covered with windswept rocks in others. There was no civilization to be seen. Yarik estimated they were at least a hundred kilometers from even the smallest of villages. It reminded him of the time he had parachuted with a group of hunters into Kamchatka looking for snow leopards. It was perfect.

A powerful explosion rocked Yarik's ears when he was just a hundred meters from the ground. The blast sent a wave of heat billowing forth, slapping his face and sucking the wind from his chute. He dropped like a stone for twenty meters before reinflation, and then looked up to see the airplane plummeting to Earth. *The resourceful bastard booby-trapped the plane.*

With the plane gone, nobody knew he had parachuted after Alex. Even worse, the only member of the Knyaz who knew that Alex had an accomplice was now stuck in the middle of nowhere. Of course, either Alex or that accomplice was already dead, but like cockroaches, where there was one, there were likely to be others.

Was the Knyaz infested? Apparently it was. Yarik cursed Victor, but was just as mad at himself. In all these years, they had only let one slip through, but if the past twenty-four hours were any indication, that one could cost them the game.

A moment later Yarik did a parachute landing fall on the same frozen plane where one fugitive had planted himself at full speed, at "terminal velocity," as they called it. He released his chute as soon as he planted his heels so that the raging wind would not drag him across the ground, plowing a furrow with his bald head as it went. Then he sprang to his feet like a panther released and ran in the direction of the corpse. It was extermination time.

While searching for the body, Yarik found himself hoping that it would not be Alex. Learning the identity of the mercenary could be far more valuable to the Knyaz than just having Alex himself out of the way. Plus, both he and Karpov wanted Alex alive, although for different reasons.

Six anxious minutes after landing, Yarik found it: A blood-soaked corpse staring blindly at the sky. It was not Alex.

Superficial gore and blind stare aside, the victim appeared to be asleep. The illusion would not last. Yarik had seen fall victims before. He knew that the impact liquefied their insides, and that the body would feel like a water bed to the touch. At the first bite from a wolf's mouth, or peck from a vulture's beak, the innards would ooze out through the gash like honey from an overturned pot.

Judging by appearance, the mercenary was both a Russian and a soldier. He wore a combat uniform stripped of rank and insignia like a special operative's, and cut his hair to regulation. Given what he had done in the cargo hold, he was clearly no stranger to combat either. But he was more than just a soldier. This man had released himself from the parachute in order to save Alex. He had a martyr's sense of honor.

Yarik pondered the implications for a moment as a frosty northerly wind howled about him and ice crystals melted on his face. Martyrs did what they did for a cause. Yarik felt a hollow pit open in his stomach. That cause was most likely the downfall of the Knyaz.

He did not have much patience for martyrs. In his eyes, they were fools. He had to acknowledge, however, that their principles did make them dangerous. He could respect the threat imposed by a man who lent fanatical courage and discipline to his convictions. But that was one weapon Yarik did not want in his arsenal. There was no one and no thing for which he would have cut himself free. To the contrary, as a predator and a survivor, he would have seen it as his duty to cut the other man free.

Enough philosophy. It was time to learn the martyr's identity. With that information, he could look forward to hunting down all the fanatical associates inclined to assist Alex in his cause. Yarik searched the body for a wallet or dog tags. Both were absent. He looked for some other type of identification, something that would tell a tale. He found nothing. The man's pockets only contained a couple of wigs and three pairs of glasses. The martyr must have had ID to enter the air base . . . Fucking Ferris must have taken it.

The martyr's lack of identification was frustrating, but a setback of no consequence. He would pry it from the American by the skin of his—Wait a minute. Suppose Alex died before Yarik could reach him? What if he were to fall through the ice of a frozen lake, or twist an ankle and become wolf chow? Yarik had to catch Alex before Siberia did. It was crucial that he learn whom the Knyaz were up against.

Yarik paused to consider his backup options. He did not have a camera—he wasn't the sentimental type—and he knew wolves would devour the body before he could return for it. Furthermore, the ground was too hard to dig a grave, and there were not enough rocks around to build one, not that he had time for either of those. Had Alex anticipated this predicament? Probably. He was a cunning bastard. Well, Yarik mused, he could scheme too.

It took but a moment for him to devise an elegant solution. This time it was Alex who had underestimated his opponent. Alex's move may have been clever, but it was not clever enough.

Yarik's blade was long and heavy, a cross between a hunting knife and a machete. He had acquired it a decade ago on the Ivory Coast from a man who had intended to take Yarik's head but lost his own instead.

Yarik loved the feel of the finely carved cocobolo-wood handle, and was hypnotized by the reflection of its surgical steel. On a stakeout he could content himself for hours simply sharpening the blade as it glimmered in the moonlight. For a kill, he favored the knife over other weapons—it was more surgical, more reliable, more personal, more precise.

With a swift, familiar movement he brought the blade whistling down onto the martyr's wrist, severing the right hand with a practiced expertise. Since Yarik was confident that his adversary was a military man, he knew that his prints would be on file. If he had not been so sure, he would have taken the head as well.

Time to move on. Yarik could still see Alex's tracks heading into the woods, although the north wind would soon erase them.

As the corpse deflated through the severed wrist like a fly in a spider's mouth, Yarik slipped his trophy into the cargo pocket on his left thigh. His fingers came into contact with a plastic tube as he did so, and he smiled. The tube had a fourteen-character code stenciled to its side and "Ferris" penciled in below. One way or the other, the American was his.

CHAPTER 33

Siberian Outback, Russia

Alex heard the plane explode and looked up with satisfied eyes to watch it plunge to earth. *Andrey's booby trap had worked!* As he watched, pointed questions bombarded his head like fallout from the explosion: Would the KGB be chasing him? Where was the closest village? Was his number up in smoke?

For a moment the elation of regained freedom took Alex's mind off the profound sacrifice his mysterious new acquaintance had made, and added fuel to his pumping legs. But only for a moment. It would take a while for Alex to get his mind around all of the ramifications of that heroic act, but one conclusion was inescapable: what had begun as an investigation for truth and evolved into a fight for justice, was now also a quest of honor.

Despite the shock that numbed him and the danger that surrounded him, Alex found it hard not to dwell in disbelief on the way events were evolving, colliding, cascading around him. It was like the scenes of a Schwarzenegger movie without the cuts and cameras. He had followed the twisted path of a clever murder to the discovery of a diabolical device. Then he had uncovered the connection between that device and a grand scheme for international industrial espionage. Now that scheme had brought him to the heart of Russia, where invisible, opposing forces were going to extraordinary lengths to either ruin or rescue him. Where would it end? His investigation was snowballing by the hour, the pool of blood was spreading by the minute, and the only conclusion that seemed completely clear was that he must not fail.

Alex's elation over the explosion extinguished like a storm-blown candle as he caught sight of another parachute. A hulking figure had just dropped below the tree line a couple hundred yards away. *Yarik.*

Alex was glad he had taken the time to strip Andrey of identification. Now he could use it, and Yarik could not. It was too bad his fallen comrade's pockets had contained little more than papers. The pocketknife was a pitiful weapon, although he was very pleased to have it as a tool. Of course this tool could create weapons, and Alex knew all about doing that, but improvisation took time. Time was another thing that Alex did not have.

The dormant reflexes developed during Alex's relentless training had kicked in the moment he "hit the wind" jumping out the back of the doomed plane. Uncle Sam's finest had honed his predatory habits and sharpened his survival senses. Now that he was back in the wild, Alex let the animal in him take control. *Never mind the pitiful knife*, Alex mused, *he was a weapon*. Then his inner voice retorted, *Yeah, but Yarik is practically an army.*

Alex knew he had two opposing forces to contend with: the Siberian predator behind him and the Siberian winter before him. In addition to the extreme cold, he knew that death's two other daughters, wet and hungry, would soon be knocking on his door if he did not take the appropriate measures to fend them off. His was a grim scenario, but it was also invigorating in a primitive kind of way.

In the back of his mind, Alex knew that Peitho might render all his past investigative actions and future survival efforts pointless. If Yarik still had his number, then escape would require more than simply running away.

In the back of his heart, Alex maintained hope that Yarik had not passed along his number to anyone not on the plane, and that as a result, his number was now up in smoke. After all, Yarik did not know that the airplane would explode, so it was likely he had left both the number and the transmitter onboard the doomed craft. Unfortunately, Alex could not count on that hope. His acting assumption had to be that Yarik had the code but not the means to transmit it. If that were the case, then Alex would be safe until Yarik reached civilization. And that meant that while Yarik was trying to prevent Alex from escaping, Alex had to prevent Yarik from doing the same.

The hunted was also the hunter, but only Alex knew that. He was comfortable with the assumption that a man with Yarik's personality would never consider the option that he, too, might be prey. It was Alex's only advantage, and he intended to leverage it.

Alex had not been able to take in much geography during his descent—there had been a few other things on his mind at the time—but he knew that the airplane had taken off from Irkutsk. He also knew that he needed to head east from Irkutsk to get to that crescent-shaped lake near Academic City and the headquarters of the enemy. The airplane had also been heading east and Alex guessed that was its destination since HQ would be the natural choice of location for an interrogation. He wished he had paid attention to that as he jumped. Of course in the end the precise trajectory didn't really matter. Siberian distances were so great that a couple dozen miles this way or that were insignificant. What mattered now was that he had a meaningful bearing. He looked down at his compass-watch, and smiled.

Alex set a pace he knew he could keep up all day and then put his body on autopilot. The natural impulse was to sprint full-out for a few miles, to put some quick distance between himself and Yarik, but he couldn't afford to get winded or sweaty. Fortunately he had a head start. *Yippee.*

Alex spent the first ten minutes going northwest so as not to give the giant a straight azimuth on him from the landing site. Then, as soon as he reached a place where the combination of wind and rocky terrain camouflaged his footprints, he turned east. He hoped this would work, but knew it probably would not. Alex had the distinct impression that Yarik was at home in the elements. Alex would act accordingly.

With autopilot on and senses alert, Alex diverted his mind to strategy. The first thing he needed was an inventory. He started with the most important thing, his own body. He was not injured. He was hungry but not ravenous. He had no food, but knew from experience that he could last a couple exertive days without it.

Keeping warm was the next challenge. In addition to pocketing Andrey's documents and money, he had salvaged his coat and gloves. He would wear the second coat while sleeping and would be saved by a second pair of gloves when his own inevitably got wet.

Alex had also saved his parachute, bundling it back up as quickly as possible and securing it in the pack. The silk would provide both a blanket and a tent, and the parachute cord would have myriad uses if his stay in the wild became a protracted one.

In the hardware department, Andrey's pocketknife had large and small blades, screwdrivers, a can opener, a file, a saw, an awl, scissors, a toothpick, and tweezers: very nice. He was especially happy to have the toothpick; caribou tended to get stuck between his teeth.

The last little bit of paraphernalia Alex had was his watch. The face of the titanium IWC Porsche Design compass-watch flipped up to reveal a compass below, complete with luminescent markings. Given the low cloud cover and the limited daylight hours Siberia enjoyed in late November, his favorite possession would save him both nerves and guesswork.

The good thing about running was that it kept him warm. The bad thing was that he couldn't go on forever. Of course, the same applied to Yarik. Alex wanted to take comfort in the fact that Yarik was considerably older than him, but after seeing Andrey fight, he hesitated to give Russian warriors discounts based on age.

Occasional flurries drifted down from the steel-gray sky as he ran, foreshadowing pleasures to come. Those that hit his eyes conspired to freeze his lids together when he blinked. Those that hit his face absorbed precious heat. Some melted and rolled down his neck to saturate the top of his T-shirt. Once he stopped running and cooled off, Alex would enjoy a collar of ice. *Just keep running* . . .

That enchanting thought reminded Alex of how important it was for him to keep mentally preoccupied, now and throughout his wilderness trek. He would be lost if he began to focus on fright, exhaustion, or the various aches and pains that were about to beset his body. Fortunately, he did have a lot to think about.

Alex spent the first couple of hours actively recalling his survival training: how to keep warm, what to do for food, when to rest and when to run. Then he focused on evasion, on rolling his feet to avoid leaving tracks and keeping his profile off the horizon. It came back more quickly and clearly than he would have anticipated. Perhaps it was the frosty, pine-scented air. Perhaps it was the two-hundred-and-fifty-pound giant on his tail. It didn't really matter why those neurons were firing, as long as he had their wisdom at his disposal.

Once he had finished dredging the depths of his survival-training memory, Alex began putting together a wish list. He would have to pilfer from cabins quickly as he came across them, if he were lucky enough to come across any at all. Alex wasn't feeling particularly lucky at the moment.

First on the list of necessities was food, followed closely by a sleeping bag or blankets, matches, a canteen, a map, and any camping, cooking, hunting, or ice fishing tools he could lay his hands on. A gun was probably too much to hope for, but hey . . . Of course he couldn't risk being seen, but if he were fortunate enough to come across a cabin, he also couldn't risk waiting around for just the right moment. He would have to be bold while relying on stealth and speed, thus the preprepared list. Yarik would also be drawn to a cabin like steel to a magnet. Perhaps Alex could use that force against him.

Alex tried to focus on the positive. He knew how to survive and how to evade, and he had the advantage of speed: Tracking takes time. Unfortunately, this line of thought just led him back to the same, sore, inescapable issue: Physical escape was not going to be enough. He was going to have to take the giant out. To do that Alex had to keep the giant on his trail until he found some means of gaining a tactical advantage. He would have to orchestrate their encounter so that the time and place worked in his favor.

As time went on and no helicopters appeared in search of him, Alex got more comfortable with the assumption that Yarik could not communicate with the outside world. Thank goodness for small miracles.

Day turned to dusk, and dusk threatened dark, and still Alex's legs pumped on. He checked his watch at the moment the sun blinked out behind the mountains. It was just after five o'clock. He kept going for another ninety minutes in order to make it to the top of the ridge he was climbing. Alex figured he had covered about thirty miles over the last ten hours. For a man on foot in this terrain and weather, it was an impressive feat. Compared to the map of Siberia, it was nothing.

Alex ducked under an enormous spruce tree's canopy of boughs, removed his pack, and sat down to drink his water. Andrey had kept his documents in a plastic bag. Alex had taken the documents out and routinely filled the bag with ice throughout the day, drinking it as it melted in the heat of his exhaust. He filled it one more time while he was still hot from trekking.

Alex forced himself to get back up before his muscles went on holiday and began to climb the Siberian spruce. The grueling trek had sapped his legs, so he used his arms to do most of the lifting. Fortunately the wind had died toward dusk, so the sways were not extreme. It was a strange feeling, climbing up into boundless darkness in a place like this. The stars shone as bright and low as he had ever seen thanks to the cold, clean air. Alex found the climb to be physically exhausting but psychologically refreshing, the former being unavoidable and the latter being something every endurance soldier knew to be crucial.

Once he was as high as he could safely go, Alex stopped, allowed his eyes to adjust, and soaked up the view. It was beautiful, but he found that the combination of his physical condition with the swaying of the tree and the serenity of the scene was lulling him to sleep like a siren song, so he refocused on the task at hand.

He began a methodical three-hundred-sixty-degree scan of his surroundings, from the foreground to the horizon. He was looking for three things: movement, light, and smoke. He saw . . . nothing. Then he spent a full five minutes scouring the route he had taken to get there. Again, nothing. *Amen.* He descended feeling like the only man left on Earth, and almost wished it were so.

Alex had planned to make his way down the ridge to spend the night in a less exposed, less visible location, but he could not bring himself to move any farther. It was time to bivouac.

He selected two adjacent boughs from the mighty tree's lowest ring and stripped them of their little branches. Then he tied the ends of the boughs together with parachute cord so they formed an ellipse about eight feet in length. Next, Alex used thick, fallen branches to prop up the distal end at the spot where the boughs were tied, making the makeshift bedrails more or less parallel with the ground. Finally he finished the bed by looping the parachute very loosely around the boughs twice and then tying it off to create what amounted to a layered tube that flanked the wind. It had been quick, and it would be comfortable. Rest was one of the few weapons he had. Alex intended to make sure it was fully loaded.

CHAPTER 34

Siberian Outback, Russia

Yarik awoke at three a.m. in the fork of a tree, stiff, sore, and smiling. He was on the hunt. Given the excitement, he was confident that his three-hour nap would suffice to power this pursuit to closure.

The tree's trunk had shielded him from the wind, and its height had protected him from the wolves, but as he sat there stretching out the kinks, he was not sure it was worth it. He pushed his chin up and to the left with the palm of his hand until his neck cracked, then repeated the exercise on the right. *Better than a cup of coffee.* With a quick roll of the shoulders, he dropped to the ground like a gladiator entering the ring.

Alex had stayed ahead throughout the previous day, expertly camouflaging his trail as he went. Yarik had been able to follow easily enough, but Alex's unusual ability to maintain a constant speed hour after hour had kept a steady gap between them. His quarry's endurance had also changed the chase from child's play to man's sport—Yarik's favorite sport.

Yarik took a deep breath of the fresh mountain air and set off over the moonlit landscape in a rapid trot. Given his druthers, he'd string this match out for a week, but he could not allow that to happen. He had to catch Alex before they reached a city and Alex vanished into the masses. He could still kill Alex using Peitho in the city, but he needed to interrogate him first.

Karpov's orders were to take Alex alive and leave him unblemished. The general had not explained his intentions, but he did not have to. Yarik knew that everything Karpov did was calculated. He did not make strategic errors. For this reason, Karpov was the only man to whom Yarik ever truly deferred. Yarik found that he actually liked to please Karpov. Pity about the unblemished requirement, though. Still, there were many ways to inflict pain and suffering without leaving marks.

Yarik stopped running for a moment to inspect the ground more carefully and drink some water. Sniffing the air, he could tell that it was going to be getting even colder. If Alex didn't find clothing or reach shelter, he would be a meatsicle within forty-eight hours. Technically frozen was unblemished, but . . .

Yarik worried that there might not be any shelter to find. There were only about three million people in rural Siberia, a territory roughly the size of the continental United States. Everyone lived in the cities. Alex was headed toward Novosibirsk, which was the largest and closest and the obvious destination. It housed a US consulate, a major airport, and a million places to hide.

Knowledge of the destination removed risk and made the pursuit that much faster. Even if he lost Alex's trail, he could proceed with confidence, knowing he would pick it up again once the mountainous terrain narrowed the breadth of navigable options. But Yarik didn't expect to lose Alex. After a day of pursuit, he now understood his quarry's technique well enough to anticipate.

By waking at three a.m., Yarik expected to catch Alex in his sleep. That would make it easy to comply with Karpov's request. He suspected that Alex would have been too afraid to stop last night and would have run until he dropped. If that were in fact the case, it would be his first mistake but a fatal error.

The moon had risen while he had slept, augmenting Yarik's advantage. He found it easier to follow a fresh trail in bright moonlight than broad daylight because the moon highlighted the subtle reflections that result when someone dislodges a pebble or puts the pressure of a footfall on a dusting of snow.

To his credit, Alex had confounded Yarik's tracking by sporadically changing his heading five or ten degrees this way or that without impacting what was proving to be a relatively straight and efficient course. Alex's overall strategy seemed to be one of speed, probably because he had chosen a destination that was easy to guess. Instinct told Yarik that Alex would change course radically once they neared Novosibirsk in an attempt to both throw him off and to intersect one of the approaching tangential motorways. It was a good strategy, but it would be at least a day before he could deploy it. Alex would not last that long.

Forty minutes after starting out that morning, Yarik came to the tree on the ridge where Alex had slept and cursed the darkness. *Was it possible that Alex was not afraid? When would he stop underestimating this man?*

He quickly inspected the campsite before continuing. There was no sign that Alex had eaten. Yarik would have been surprised if there were, but it was reassuring to be certain that they were on the same diet.

As Yarik resumed the trail, his thoughts shifted back to the man who had freed Alex. Who was he and how much did he know about the Knyaz? Yarik was very concerned by the implications of the Knyaz being blindsided that way. For decades, they had led an invisible existence. For that to change now was unthinkable. The timing was just too critical. The bulge slapping against his left thigh reminded Yarik that he would get his answer soon enough; he had a helping hand.

Yarik cracked his neck. He shouldn't overreact. While this incident might indicate a major strategic complication, it could just as easily be nothing at all. They had kept the lid on it for a decade now. Karpov had everything brilliantly camouflaged in plain sight under the cloak of the KGB. No Russian was going to poke around there. Of course, one corner of the Knyaz operation lay beyond their circle of secrecy and control: the United States. Once again, Victor's territory appeared to be the most likely cause of their security breach. He would certainly have words with the boy the next time they met.

Yarik followed Alex's trail for a couple of hours along a ridgeline and then steeply downward into a snow-filled valley. That was when the first chink appeared in his quarry's armor. The first sign of fatigue. Alex began moving rapidly, even recklessly, taking advantage of gravity and keeping to the snowy grooves rather than the rocky ridges so the powder would absorb the shock of his descending bounds. And bounding he was. Alex's footprints were spaced nearly two meters apart. He was tiring and becoming desperate.

Of course Alex's desperation became Yarik's necessity. Predator had to keep up with prey. Yarik wasn't just keeping up any more; he was gaining. He had halved the distance between them. Alex was now less than thirty minutes ahead.

Bounding down the snowy mountainside, Yarik felt the freedom and exhilaration of the slalom skier. Perhaps biathlete was more appropriate. He would likely be shooting once he stopped. Raising his nose to the wind, he could almost smell his quarry. He certainly sensed the American. *It would not be long now.*

With that thought crossing his mind, the groove he was descending took a jagged turn, and Yarik caught sight of the valley below. It was a long, narrow valley, no doubt carved in eras past by a raging river. Only a meandering stream remained. He could just make out its frozen, silvery face through the dusting of windblown snow. He could also make out something else, something bobbing along a willowy thicket parallel to the bank. It was Alex.

CHAPTER 35

Novosibirsk, Siberia

Every eye in the restaurant was on them as Karpov pulled out Anna's chair. He was famous and powerful, and she was unknown but beautiful. That was enough to turn heads in New York or Paris, to say nothing of the middle of Siberia.

His future was on the line tonight, but he was far from his top form, and that coincidence had him cursing the gods. Just an hour before leaving for this all-important date, his personal aide Major Maximov had shown up at his apartment to deliver devastating news: The plane bringing Yarik back from Irkutsk had exploded in flight. Cause unknown.

Awash in grief at the loss of one of his oldest friends and with his mind still reeling from the potential impact on his grand plan, Karpov now had to woo the one woman who seemed immune to his usual charms.

Stepashin had been right about her on both accounts. As a first lady, Anna fit the bill perfectly. As a woman, she bewitched him like no other. Karpov had found himself captivated at a carnal level the moment they'd met. He had been yearning to possess her ever since. He was used to having his career on the line, but tonight his happiness was also at risk.

"What drew you to medicine?" he asked.

Anna raised her eyebrows. "No 'Have you been here before?' or 'What are you in the mood for tonight?' but straight to the main course." She left it there like a question, without answering his.

He liked her style. "A couple hours is not a lot of time to get to know someone more than superficially, especially someone so complex and multifaceted. I want to know you more than superficially. I thought the biggest decision of your life would be a good place to start."

She just looked at him, obviously expecting him to say more. He couldn't remember the last time someone had pushed back rather than rushing to please him. He found it refreshing, and he could use it to draw her in. "I'm a pretty competitive guy," he added, "and I think I know the answer. I'd like to know if I'm right."

A flicker of surprise crossed her amber eyes, followed by the hint of a grin. "It's not a trivial question, but I'll answer it if you'll agree to do the same. Will you answer a meaningful question for me?"

He held out his hand, eager to initiate physical contact. "You've got a deal, doctor."

She shook it across the table, surprisingly firm and businesslike, reminding him that despite their beauty, hers were a surgeon's hands. "I thought a career in medicine would allow me to maximize my contribution to society."

"Go on."

"I thought I'd enjoy both the analytical challenges and the interpersonal dynamics, and be good at them."

"Has that proven to be the case?"

"So far."

"What part of the job do you enjoy the most?"

"Outreach programs. One in particular. A nurse and I drive a stocked ambulance to remote villages on the last Sunday of every month. We take treatment to those who can't come to it. It's always the toughest, most rewarding day of the month.

"But enough about me. Did you pass? Were my reasons the ones you'd expected?"

"They were."

"So I'm predictable?"

Karpov wasn't completely sure that she was playing with him, and found his blindness disconcerting. After a lifetime in the KGB, he could usually read people's emotions like menu entrées. Anna was proving immune to his charms and impervious to his powers. "No. To be honest I'm finding you charmingly unpredictable. But as I had sensed the first time we met, your motivations parallel my own." He held up two fingers side by side. "The reasons you gave for selecting medicine are the very same reasons I chose my career." He paused to allow her time to run the comparative analysis. Then he asked, "So what's your question?"

Before she could answer, the waiter approached with a silver tray holding a bottle of French champagne, two crystal glasses, and a bowl of black caviar with toasted baguette slices and pats of butter. "As requested, general: Veuve Clicquot and Iranian Beluga."

Karpov had weighed the pros and cons of going modest versus extravagant. In the end he decided that the winning combination would be modest behavior coupled with a glimpse at the lifestyle that could be hers. Tonight's food and drink would be the best she had ever tasted. He wanted to leave that positive association imprinted on her senses. "I'll take it from here, Roma," he said, reaching for the bottle.

Karpov popped the cork and poured two flutes, fogging the glass and adding a yeasty aroma to the air. As he raised his with the intention of toasting their acquaintance, she beat him to the punch. "To sharing," she said, "beyond the superficial. With all the benefits it brings."

It had been a long time since Karpov had sat across a chessboard, literal or metaphoric, from someone who surprised him, someone who left him feeling unsure about what would happen next. For the first time he understood the moth who had spotted a flame. With some trepidation he asked, "What's your question?"

"My brother Kostya died five years ago during the radiation accident at the complex where you now work. I know there's no way a man of your intelligence and means would work anywhere near that site without first learning the details. My question is this: What really happened?"

CHAPTER 36

Siberian Outback, Russia

The sight of the American brought a Mona Lisa smile to Yarik's lips. He was glad to catch Alex before the wilderness did but sorry that the hunt was ending. Of course, he would still have the interrogation . . .

Alex was about half a kilometer ahead, moving through a thicket. He did not seem to be making much progress. Could it be that his foot was stuck in a hunter's snare? Or was it just deep snow slowing him down? Actually, from this distance Yarik couldn't even be certain that it was Alex, but who else could it be?

Yarik felt the adrenaline kick in and further increased the speed of his rhythmic, downward-bounding strides without taking his eye off the mark. *Hrunk . . . hrunk . . . hrunk . . .* his footfalls crunched the snow. *Scratch . . . scratch . . . scratch,* his trigger finger began to itch.

An arctic hare scurried from the side of the path a few meters ahead, the first Yarik had seen. It had been nibbling on . . . something. Instinct flashed a warning. Yarik thudded to a stop on both feet, sending a spray of snow surging forward like a braking skier.

He drew his Stechkin pistol and crouched at the spot where the hare had been. Then Yarik brushed aside the powdery snow with his left hand. He found a piece of taught rope. It was a length of white parachute cord. Alex had strung it out across the crevice beneath the snow.

Yarik directed his full attention to the ground at his feet. He brushed aside more snow and found another trip-cord an arm's length further down, and then another. Scattered throughout was a series of concealed stakes, each pointing viciously upwards beneath loose white powder. Alex had lured him into a deadly trap. If it had not been for the hare chewing the rope, he would have uncovered those stakes with his chest, rather than his hand. The nesting critter had saved his life. Yarik would have to rethink his hunting habits.

This, however, was no time to dwell on what might have been. The hunt was about to end. Alex had sacrificed his lead for a trap that had failed. He was just a couple hundred meters in front now, struggling, stuck, and unarmed.

Yarik felt like whistling as he resumed the chase, but he could not afford the noise. He still had to take the American unharmed. As he came to the top of the last small hill before the stream, Yarik got a better view of his prey. Alex was weaving and bobbing, not struggling and receding. Humiliation smacked Yarik in the face. He had been chasing a scarecrow.

A minute later, still shocked by the thoroughness with which Alex had duped him, Yarik reached the object that had made him reckless. It was the liner of a coat, strung up to bob in the wind between the branches of two birch trees. *Cunning bastard.*

This was a disappointment, but not a defeat. Alex had sacrificed half his lead to make the trap and its accompanying decoy. Yarik considered abandoning his measured pursuit to sprint after Alex. The American could not be that far ahead. Once he caught sight of him, it would all be over. It was a tempting prospect, but again instinct flashed caution. Alex was proving to be a proficient hunter himself. It would not be out of character for him to anticipate that reaction and plant a second trap to take advantage of his rage. Hell, it was even starting to seem conceivable that Alex might be planning to attack him. No, Yarik decided, he would not change his tactics. He was a bulldog, not a greyhound. *The bastard even has me second-guessing myself.*

For hour after hour Yarik kept on, swift and steady, knowing that Alex was just beyond his visual reach but not managing to close the gap. Ferris was the best he had chased, ever. Accepting that, Yarik recovered from his near-fatal stupidity and found sport in the chase once again.

There were times when he went for extended periods without a single sign that he was on the right trail. Those were intriguing tests if not agonizing trials, but a scuffmark or a fractured twig inevitably vindicated his instincts. It seemed that Alex was getting better at concealing his tracks as time progressed. That was unusual. Usually people got worse over time as they fatigued and the lack of nourishment diminished their power of concentration.

Yarik crested the fourth rise of the day around noon. On three prior occasions he had sprinted the last hundred meters to the top in anticipation, and all three times he had met with disappointment. Would this one be any different?

He reached the top and found the woods were thicker than before. He couldn't tell if his quarry was now within visual range, so he climbed a tree to survey the ground ahead. Halfway up he found the spot where another climber had torn away a piece of bark within the hour. *They were thinking alike now.* He would remember that.

Yarik finished the ascent and quickly scanned the countryside ahead, searching for movement rather than color. Nothing in the foreground attracted his trained eyes, but he saw smoke coming over the top of the next rise. He drew a mental azimuth to the point and picked out a few landmarks along the way. He descended quickly, using arms rather than legs. Snapping branches and smearing sap. Yarik knew that Alex might not be the source of the smoke, but he was confident that the American would at least head in that direction. Smoke meant food.

It took twenty minutes at top speed to get to the crest of the next ridge. The smoke was still visible—not a good sign—making it possible for Yarik to get an azimuth from the ground and saving him the time and energy required to climb a tree.

Five minutes later, he emerged from the woods into a picture postcard. The pristine valley floor boasted a beautiful frozen lake, and was surrounded on three sides by steep evergreen foothills. This was just the type of place Yarik would eventually choose to retire: lots of fish and game, but no people. Somebody else apparently had the same idea, as there was a large cabin on the other side of the lake, situated at the edge of a pebbly shore. The smoke that brought him here was billowing from one of the cabin's two chimneys.

If I were in Alex's place, Yarik thought, I would sneak up on the cabin and dispatch the occupant. Then I would wait, sated and warm, seated back behind a curtain with one of the dead hermit's rifles, watching for me to walk out of the clearing.

Yarik had survived nine bullet wounds in the course of his career. None of them had been bad. In fact, aside from the inconvenience, he had not minded them much at all. There was something romantic about the whole experience. But Yarik could not allow that to happen here. The stakes were too high.

He surveyed the surrounding area thoroughly before beginning a slow circle around the house. He did not see any movement through the back windows, and he could not get a good look in through the front without exposing himself. Nor could he wait around watching for movement. If Alex was not there, he was gaining time. It was maddening. A stalemate. He had to create a third option. He had to provoke a reaction.

Yarik found a large oak that had a view of the front door and concealed himself behind the trunk. He was about eighty meters out and set the Stechkin's sight accordingly. Keeping the tree trunk between himself and the cabin, he removed his coat and draped it over the forked end of a fallen branch. Then he pushed it up to shoulder height, swayed it back and forth so the movement would catch attention, and waited for the rifle crack. Nothing. He propped it up with a full shoulder and arm exposed. Again nothing. If Alex was watching, he was not taking the bait. Time to up the ante.

Yarik stood up and put his coat back on. Still concealed by the tree trunk, he fired a single shot through the upstairs window where he guessed Alex would be perched, and then switched the Stechkin back to fully automatic. Ten seconds later he heard the front door open. Yarik stole a quick peek at the front porch. Alex had come out holding a rifle. So much for Karpov's wish to keep him unblemished. Just keeping him alive would be a stretch. Yarik decided to aim for the legs and unload on full auto. It would take less than two seconds for the Stechkin to launch the nineteen remaining rounds.

Yarik spun around, brought his clenched fists to rest on a supporting branch, took quick but careful aim, and . . . it wasn't Alex. The man was Alex's height, and he was wearing the same military camouflage jacket as Alex, but the nose was too big and the face was too old.

Yarik dropped his pistol to his side and walked out of the woods.

"Good afternoon," Yarik said.

"Afternoon . . . ?"

"Are you alone?" Yarik asked, closing in quickly.

"Who's askin'?" The man still had his rifle pointed skyward, but he looked ready to rock and roll. Anyone living out here would certainly be an expert with his weapon.

"General Yarik, KGB. I am chasing an escaped prisoner. Have you seen anybody lately?"

"Didn't see him, but he was here not more than twenty minutes ago." The hermit had the slow-speak of country folk.

"Damn. How do you know he was here?"

"I put some fish out to smoke over the fireplace while I was checkin' my traps. When I got back them fish was gone."

"Did he take anything else?"

"That's what I was checking when I heard the shot. I thought you were him, but I don't smell the fish on you so I know it wasn't."

Yarik ignored the implied insult. "You mind if I get some food while you finish looking?"

The man did not look pleased with the request, which was understandable since Alex had just robbed him of his catch, but he nodded and motioned toward the door.

The hermit had a nice place. The main room was reminiscent of a hunting lodge, full of leather, fur, and hardwood furnishings. *Yes*, Yarik thought, *he had a lot in common with this guy*. The man brought Yarik a pitcher of water, a bunch of raw beets, half a spit-roasted hare, and some strips of dried venison. Then he went back to his investigation. Yarik tucked into the food like a man who had run a couple marathons but not eaten for twenty-four hours. All but one beet was gone a couple of minutes later when his host returned.

"As best as I can tell he took a blanket, a canteen, a reel of fishing line, and some hooks—don't know how he plans to use those without an ice drill, he didn't get one of those—a hand ax, some old snowshoes, and a couple cigarette lighters."

"No guns missing?"

"Nope. I keep those locked up, and he didn't get in. I got the impression he was in a mighty hurry, which was a smart thing 'cause I'd a shot him if I'd a caught him."

"How close is the nearest town?"

"Depends on what you mean by town."

"The nearest telephone?"

"Over in Krasnoe, which is about twenty kilometers southeast of here."

"How far are we from Novosibirsk?"

"A hundred and seventy kilometers."

"Also southeast, right?"

"Yep."

"You don't happen to have a two-way radio, do you?"

"Nope."

"What would you do if there was an emergency?"

"I'd use Vanya's two-way. He lives about three kilometers to the north."

"I didn't see a road or any kind of vehicle outside. How would you get there? How do you get here?"

The double question seemed to have confused the hermit. "An old service buddy flies me in and out on his seaplane. I spend January through April with my daughter in Novosibirsk. The rest of the time I'm here."

Yarik borrowed a pen and paper and wrote a quick note to the regional KGB chief. In it, he ordered a roadblock to be set up on the highway from Krasnoe to Novosibirsk, and any other roads along that vector. He included a description of the American Alexander Ferris posing as the Russian Alexander Grekov. Yarik needed to send a message to Karpov as well. He needed to let him know that somebody was on to the Knyaz. He also wanted to give him Alex's Peitho code as a precautionary measure. But there was no way to do that without exposing secrets that could never be revealed. To this day, the Knyaz's power depended on keeping the relationship among its members secret.

"Okay, listen. I have got to continue chasing after the prisoner, so I am heading toward Krasnoe. You have another task to perform for your country. Read through this and make sure you understand it."

The man took his time reading the note.

Yarik tossed the baseball-sized beet back and forth between his hands while he waited.

At last, the hermit looked up.

"You are to take this to Vanya's and call it in on this frequency." He circled the number. "Use my name and they will be most cooperative."

"But there's a storm coming in. It's going to get down to fifty below. Colder in the wind."

"Well then you better get moving. Take along a bottle and plan to spend the night. And lest you think of turning back before you make that call, you remember that I know where you live." The man paled. Yarik crushed the beet to a pulp in his palm. A pool of blood-red juice spread over the table. "Now, I need a pair of snowshoes, a sleeping bag, and some more of that venison."

CHAPTER 37

Novosibirsk, Siberia

Karpov was experiencing déjà vu. He had been sitting in his apartment pondering his precarious relationship with Anna, when once again a knock on the door disturbed his thoughts. Once again it was Major Maximov bearing unexpected news.

Karpov still blamed the major, unfairly he knew, for throwing him off his game with Anna the night of their big date. He had managed to keep her on the line even without revealing the secret of her brother's death, but on the line was not in the boat. That vexed him.

Looking his aide in the eye, Karpov sensed something unusual. Something good. As always the major's uniform was immaculately pressed, and his gray hair was perfectly coiffed, but tonight there was evidence of exuberance beneath his crisp military demeanor.

"Pardon the intrusion, sir. But I thought you'd want to know right away. Yarik's alive."

"Yarik's alive," Karpov repeated. "How is that possible?"

"Three people parachuted from the plane before it exploded. They found tracks and harnesses."

"Is he okay?"

"They think so. They can't be sure because they don't know where he is. The team investigating the crash site found parts of eight bodies, none of which was his. Therefore they're assuming Yarik was among the three jumpers. One of the jumpers had a problem with his parachute and didn't survive the fall. We don't know who he was—the wolves didn't leave much—but he had hair."

"Where do they think Yarik went?"

"He ran off in pursuit of the other survivor. The details are scant. According to the senior officer at the scene, the few remaining tracks indicated that a heavy jumper set out in pursuit of a lighter one. Judging by the tracks, both men appeared healthy. That's all they know."

"How's the search and rescue going?"

"There isn't one. The trail was already a day old when they got there. The terrain was too rough to follow them in a jeep. What's more, the location is too remote for helicopters to service it efficiently—there's no place to refuel. The government is not going to make that much fuss over one man, even a general. Yarik is on his own."

"So we just sit tight and wait for him to call?"

"That's all we can do."

"For how long?"

"Could be days. There's nothing out there. But you know Yarik. He's no doubt enjoying himself."

"Yes," Karpov said. "No doubt."

CHAPTER 38

Siberian Outback, Russia

The first gust of the storm front swept in like a big broom from the sky, nearly knocking Alex off his snowshoed feet. This was what Siberia was known for. Alex shifted his gaze from the heavens to his watch. It was two thirty in the afternoon, and dark as dusk.

He promised himself to keep going for another hour before holing up. He was still feeling good from the smoked fish, and his legs were holding. Minutes later, it became clear that he would not last an hour. Half that would be a stretch. His eyelids were freezing together every time he blinked, and the storm had cut his visibility to near zero. Threatening as the weather was, Alex knew it might be more dangerous to stop. Yarik could be ten meters behind him now, and he wouldn't know it. Fear was a great motivator, but it could also be blinding.

Alex had not caught sight of the giant since he had spotted the descending parachute. He had no objective way of knowing that Yarik was still on his tail. But he sensed it. He had been coddling the hope that Yarik had fallen hard on the trap he had spent valuable time preparing. That hope had vanished an hour earlier. Before the wind kicked in, he heard a shot from the direction of the cottage. *So much for getting lucky.* There was a chance that the hermit was just hunting, or even that he had killed Yarik, mistaking him for the man who stole his supplies. But Alex was far more inclined to believe that if someone was shooting, it would be Yarik. And there had only been one shot. It would take more than that to kill the hulk.

Alex put the maddening range of possibilities aside and continued to press on. He briefly considered trying to set another trap. In the storm it was getting difficult to see your own feet, much less spot a snare. But he now realized that it would be redundant. The weather was a trap, and both of them were already in it.

Alex wrapped both his pilfered blanket and the parachute around himself and trudged on. A few steps were all it took him to figure out that this system was not going to work. With his hands thus occupied, he could not move and check his compass at the same time. That was unacceptable. Now that the weather had cut his visibility to an arm's length, he had to check the compass constantly. He cut a slot in the middle of the blanket and donned it like a poncho. Then he cut eyeholes in the center of the parachute and a slit to breathe through and draped it over his head. He secured the new ensemble at the waist with parachute cord. Alex finished the transformation off by laughing at himself and that gave him strength: He was now a ghost in a snowstorm.

The new outfit worked for a while, but the whipping wind forced him to stop and adjust it every quarter mile or so, exposing his freezing fingers and further slowing his pace. Where the wind worked its way through, it licked at him like an icy flame and burned his flesh. The outfit was awkward, too. He was wearing a T-shirt, a shirt, two winter coats, a blanket, a fur hat, and a parachute. He worried that any moment Yarik would bump into him, and he would be as helpless to fight back as a kitten in a sack. Still, he pressed on.

After half an hour, he concluded that Yarik was no longer the most immediate threat to his life. Despite Alex being dressed like the Michelin man, the cold was killing him as surely as any bullet could.

There was no way he could live through the night exposed this way. He simply had to find shelter.

Alex struggled on and on, investigating every dark shadow in hopes of finding a grove of tightly packed trees or a rock formation that would shelter him from the wind. There was little around. Although ice and snow caked his face and choked his view, he was painfully aware that his labored steps were leaving Yarik a trail as plain as a furrow in a field. It was no longer a game of hide-and-seek. It was an endurance test.

After trudging for a while across a particularly barren stretch of landscape, Alex realized he was out on a frozen lake. *Perfect.* If the lake were more than a mile across, he would not live to see the other side. He would freeze to death midstride. When the spring thaw came, the ice would melt, and his body would be interred with the fishes. No, no, nothing that romantic would happen, he rambled on, distracting himself from the pain with his ghastly tales. Wolves would feast on his carcass long before the fish got him. Mother Nature was exerting her presence and her power. She seemed determined to put him in his place. The man who had once been Alex Ferris, International Private Investigator, was now just so much red meat, a protein link in the great food chain.

With that joyous thought, he felt the gradient change. Two steps later he bumped into a low-hanging branch, and fell backward into the snow. He had made it across the lake! And, wait a minute, it wasn't a branch, it was a railing covered in snow! Alex was standing in front of a cabin, a cabin more glorious than the Taj Mahal.

He followed the railing until it ended, and then he climbed two steps up onto the porch. He tried the front door without knocking and found it locked. He wanted to ram it with his shoulder, but there was a big bear spike set in the middle to prevent exactly that move.

Alex looked for a pregnable window, but found them all small and shuttered. Panic began to close in. He shed the ghost suit, retrieved the hermit's hand ax, and began working at the aged oak surrounding the door's lock. Time and again he swung vicious blows powered with wild desperation. But the door was made to withstand a bear attack, and the job was maddeningly slow.

After about fifty whacks, the wood around the latch looked sufficiently splintered. Alex tried kicking the door. It gave a little. He took a couple steps back and aimed a lunging side-kick just below the spike. The wood screamed in protest and then surrendered. Alex crashed into the cabin and onto the hardwood floor. *He was saved!*

The wind came in with him, disturbing the thick layer of dust like a tomb raider's brush. Stale air had never tasted so sweet.

By the time Alex managed to regain his feet, there was already a mat of snow on the floor. It had rolled in after him like winter's hungry tongue. Alex had to expend some effort to push the door closed against the blustering fury, but he managed, grateful the latch still found something to cling to. "Feast on the giant if you're so hungry!"

Frozen and exhausted, he collapsed right there onto an inviting bearskin rug. For the brief moment he remained conscious, Alex felt himself melting, draining, soaking into the warmth of the fur, and he was happy.

It seemed only seconds later that the door crashed open in the wind. Was he dreaming? No, the icy gale was very real. It took a strength of will far greater than that required by the earliest Monday-morning alarm for Alex to roll over and get up to close it.

Halfway to the door, he stopped in his tracks. Something was there. The light was dim, and at first he didn't understand the sight that met his eyes. Alex found himself hypnotized by the muddle before him, his starved mind slow to engage. He watched with abstracted noncomprehension as Yarik struggled to extract himself from a snow-encrusted cocoon. Apparently, he had cut arm, eye, and leg holes in a brown sleeping bag and then zipped it up around himself.

As their eyes met, Alex saw that Yarik, too, was surprised. The eye-to-eye contact carried the force of a cattle prod, giving each the electric adrenaline surge necessary to tap into reserves neither knew he possessed. Siberia still wanted her sacrifice.

CHAPTER 39

Siberian Outback, Russia

Time slowed for Alex as Yarik sloughed off his sleeping bag to rise like a demon from the mire. His adrenal glands were going for broke, heightening his senses, and speeding his thoughts. He could feel the individual chambers of his heart contracting—*bu-bum, ba-bump, bu-bum, ba-bump*. He could see twitches and tweaks as clearly as signals and flares. But this final confrontation wasn't going to be about observation. It was going to be about action.

Alex needed a weapon. Preferably an elephant gun, hand grenade, or howitzer. He scanned the room and spotted the hand ax on the floor to his left, lying where he had dropped it when bursting through the door. He spun down, snatched it up, and continued spinning around, wielding the ax in a wide clockwise arc, a helicopter with one blade. He whipped his head around faster than his body so his eyes could fix on an appropriate target—a head, hand, or throat—and saw Yarik bringing his hand cannon to bear. Alex adjusted the arc, and a split second later the hand ax and the Stechkin flew out the door and into the snow along with Yarik's forefinger.

Yarik seemed unfazed by his loss, and dove at Alex. Alex dodged with a diving roll and jumped back to his feet with a couple yards between them. So much for the opening salvos.

The two veteran combatants faced each other, like a boxer against a wrestler. Alex knew he couldn't let his opponent get hold of him or it would all be over. He backed away to gain some time to think and saw the giant's hand go back down to his side. *Another gun or a hunting knife?* Alex's heart wavered, but whatever it was that Yarik had reached for was not there. His hand came back empty. Death was demanding a fair fight. *Fair?*

They circled each other like contenders in a ring, studying, calculating, anticipating. Alex used his peripheral vision to survey the room, seeking areas of tactical advantage, searching for improvised weapons. A homemade end table drew his eye, with wooden legs the size of baseball bats.

He lunged for the table, flipping it and kicking off two legs as Yarik jumped atop a dusty couch and yanked a moose rack off the wall. The enormous antlers were joined together without the head in the middle.

Yarik jumped down off the couch to land squarely on both feet with a thump that rattled the windows. His eyes gleamed with satisfaction as his mouth crinkled to the right with confidence. His weapon was an awkward one, but very deadly. The beast's rack also provided Yarik with a formidable shield. Alex's weapons were far less menacing, but they left him more quick and nimble, accenting his only natural advantage.

With a devilish grin on his face, Yarik began backing Alex into a corner, swinging the rack before him left to right to left like a prickly pendulum. Alex watched as if in third-person, mesmerized by the approaching kaleidoscope of death. Yarik was getting a feel for the new weapon in his hands, and he began to swing it faster and faster until the wind whistled and the points disappeared from view. He moved a small step closer with each deadly swing, swoosh step, swoosh step, swoosh step, obviously savoring the climax of their whirlwind romance. Speak now, or forever rest in peace.

Alex's mind raced, then locked on a plan. One shot, do or die. He waited for a swing toward Yarik's right and then shot forward and crouched down on his own right knee. He used the bat in his left hand to block the rack's return while channeling all his own momentum through his right arm into that club as it crashed down on the giant's leading left shin. Even as he heard the crack of snapping fibular bone, Alex felt the searing pain of moose prongs ripping into the back of his skull. Fortunately, he had preprogrammed his moves and continued his planned combination without hesitation or loss of momentum. Ducking his head, Alex dropped the left blocking club and brought that hand down to join with his right on the thick end of the offensive club. Then, still crouching on one knee, he spun his shoulders 180 degrees and brought the thin end of the club up and around to impale the giant's stomach with the force of a cavalry lance. Alex felt the gust of exhaled breath, heard the sickening mortal squish, and rolled aside to see what happened next.

Yarik doubled over, blood erupting from his mouth while his eyes bulged like balloons. He toppled forward, fell hard onto the rack, twitched twice, then relaxed. Like a puppet with cut strings, Yarik never made a sound.

A dozen wounds wept blood onto the hardwood floor. Alex averted his eyes. Regaining his feet, he staggered over to the door and pushed it closed. His head was pounding mercilessly and the room starting to spin.

CHAPTER 40

Siberian Outback, Russia

With Yarik dead, fire was Alex's immediate priority. He needed to absorb energy. The hearth and kindling were right there, so he managed to get a healthy blaze going in no time. That done he staggered around the cabin looking for a source of water, but of course there was none. There would be a hand pump outside for use during the warmer months, but nothing for the winter. This was a seasonal place.

His head wounds were next on the triage list. He found a mirror in the kitchen cupboard, and brought it back in by the fire to survey the damage. He could not see the entire wound on the back of his head, but the portion the mirror exposed was a scary sight. His head and shoulders were covered in blood, and part of his scalp seemed to be hanging there like a hairy red Post-it note. If he did not immediately tend to his injuries, he would likely succumb to them.

He found a dishrag and bound his scalp as best he could to stanch the bleeding. Then he turned his attention to the grisly task of searching the whale of a corpse that was beached and bleeding in the foyer. Alex was delighted to find some strips of venison in one pocket, as he was craving meat. Then he found what he thought was a frozen fish in another, but recoiled in disgust when he saw what he had pulled from the corpse's pocket. It was a human hand. *What kind of a sick creature had he killed? Did Yarik collect hands the way Indians had collected scalps?* A moment later Alex understood, and he looked down on the relic in a very different light. Andrey. Fingerprints.

He set the hand reverently aside and continued the search. One pocket contained a couple of clips of ammunition. Alex retrieved the bloody pistol from the porch but found that the ax had ruined it. You couldn't win them all.

Returning to Yarik's pockets Alex extracted a plastic tube that looked like it would hold a long cigar. It bore a stenciled fourteen-character sequence with "Ferris" written just below. As he read his name, Alex felt a huge weight lift off his shoulders. *Now he had his own number*. He took a minute to memorize it and then tossed the tube into the fireplace. He started to smile but then winced at the pain this caused. Man, did he have a headache.

Alex kept searching the dead giant's pockets. He found a wallet, a plastic bag, foreign and domestic Soviet passports, and a ring with a plastic identity card and three sophisticated metal keys. He pocketed everything. Then, leaving two large snow-packed jars to melt by the fire, he began searching the cabin.

One of the first treasures he uncovered was a bottle of aspirin. *Thank you, God!* And then, as if in a personal answer to his other prayer, he found the prize he needed most: a map of the surrounding area. Stored in a box of fishing tackle, it was large in scale and showed little but mountains and lakes. There was a star to the side of one lake, presumably marking his present location. Many of the other lakes had notes penciled in on them, references to the type of fish and the best fishing locations. Alex could not care less about that. Fortunately the map also contained one thing that might save his life: a road.

At the closest attainable point, the highway to Novosibirsk appeared to be just ten kilometers away. In good conditions on flat land, he could run ten kilometers in forty minutes. But the land wasn't flat, the conditions were as bad as conditions could get, and he was two steps from death's door. Alex reckoned it would take him anywhere from two hours to eternity to get there.

He returned to the fire and inspected his head. The external bleeding had stopped, but internally a hematoma could be growing. Given his depleted condition, if he gave in to his overwhelming desire to sleep before receiving medical attention, he would probably never wake up. That road was his best shot at survival.

He used a freshly-melted jar of water to wash his wound and then rebound it with a fresh towel. His external repairs complete, Alex threw a few tea bags in the remaining jar and sat down to eat some dried venison while the tea steeped by the fire. He studied the map as he ate, knowing full well that it would probably be his last meal but trying to remain optimistic.

Despite the gravity of the situation and his resolve to complete his quest, Alex found his head bobbing on his chest. He desperately needed to sleep, and he could not fight it anymore. Maybe just a few minutes . . .

Alex pulled the bearskin rug before the fire and collapsed onto it. No sooner had he closed his eyes than they sprang open again in shock from a mighty crack. It was just the fire. Sap in a log. His eyelids had begun dropping again, along with his adrenaline and life expectancy, when his eyes came to rest on Andrey's hand. First it shocked him one way, then another.

The strength and dedication of his fallen comrade seemed to flow into Alex, and he heard Andrey's final words once again: "Don't you fail me, Alex! Don't you let my children down!"

Alex found the means to force the Reaper's sleep to wait. He propped himself up and drained the jar of strong, tepid tea. Then he stood up and re-dressed, choosing the best of the clothes from his and Yarik's wardrobes. With that accomplished there was just one thing left to do.

Alex threw more logs on the fire, arranging a couple of them on the top like a platform. Then he took Andrey's hand and consigned it to the flames with a prayer of thanks and a blessing for his friend's soul. Andrey had given his life to the mission; Alex could do no less.

Fully aware that this was either the bravest or most foolhardy thing he would ever do, Alex bid farewell to the warmth of the fire, screwed determination firmly to his heart, and strode back out into the stormy Siberian night.

CHAPTER 41

Novosibirsk, Siberia

"Sir, I've just received word that General Igor Stepashin was killed in the line of duty."

Karpov felt his aide's words like a blow to the stomach but resisted the urge to double over. "What happened?"

"The chief justice caught him just after the Peitho implant. Apparently the anesthetic didn't work properly. He woke up and saw an unfamiliar male silhouette by his bed. In light of the recent threats, and being the paranoid bastard that he is, he shot Stepashin without a word."

"Fatally?"

"Yes, sir. Stepashin died instantly."

Karpov's next question came out as a whisper. "Was anything discovered at the scene?"

"No, sir. Major Luchenko saw to that." Maximov placed an empty Peitho syringe on Karpov's desk.

Stepashin had accomplished his mission, but it had cost him his life. Looking up at his aide while a torrent of emotions whipped him to and fro, Karpov did something he hadn't done since childhood: He surrendered to his need for release. "I sent Stepashin."

"I assumed as much."

"We need the chief justice on our side. He's a hard target. Stepashin was the only one who could get close enough."

Maximov nodded, but remained silent.

Karpov didn't dismiss him. Maximov was a Knyaz confidant and borderline friend. Karpov was weighing the risks and benefits of bringing him closer into the fold. For two full minutes he left the major standing there, still and silent like a guard at Lenin's tomb. Then he spoke. "His job wasn't done. Gaining control of the chief justice was just a precaution. A means of ensuring our desired ends."

"Yes, sir."

"You know what that ultimate end was, but have you guessed how we plan to achieve it?"

Maximov, true to his style, didn't mince his words. "I assume that if you want Gorbachev's job, you first have to eliminate Gorbachev."

Karpov nodded and gestured for Maximov to take a seat. "You make assassinating a head of state sound like a simple math problem. I like your sense of clarity. It was to have been Stepashin's crowning achievement. He was going to be the triggerman. Of course he wouldn't have made the history books, that honor will go to the fall guy, but he would have known.

"Stepashin was perfect for the job. Highly skilled. Completely dedicated. And virtually invisible. His job gave him the ability to hide in plain sight without question. Nobody questions the presence of the head of the Guards' Directorate in places where there are security concerns. The very fact that Gorbachev was killed would justify Stepashin's having been there."

"Sir, it would be my honor. Just say the word."

Karpov met his aide's eye and shook his head. "Thank you, major, but I'm just thinking out loud."

"Really, sir. I could do it."

"I'm sure you could. But putting a bullet in the president's brain is only half the battle. The real trick is getting the Americans blamed for it."

Maximov's disappointment showed. "If you don't mind my asking, sir, why is that important?"

Karpov didn't mind. He welcomed the distraction. "Three reasons. First, by focusing the investigation outside our borders, which of course is what every Russian will want to do, nobody will be looking inside. That will ensure our safety. Make sense?"

"Perfect."

"Second, this extreme act of foreign aggression will bring Russian patriotism to the highest levels we've seen since the Great Patriotic War. That will prime the country to rally behind the man of the hour."

"General Vasily Karpov and his economic miracle," Maximov said with pride. "First you stir up emotion, and then you focus it. Politics as usual."

"Correct. And third, with the world believing that the Americans have just assassinated the Russian head of state, they can hardly choose to quibble over intellectual property rights. Russian corporations will be immunized against charges of American patent violation."

"Brilliant." Maximov spoke with admiration in his eyes. Clearly he understood why Karpov was the general. Then a question crossed his countenance. "Why will everyone think it was the Americans?"

"Because the killer will be caught in the act. Too late to save Gorbachev of course, but right there on the scene with the rifle in his hands. That American is on his way here now, a trained Special Forces soldier and CIA agent who snuck into the country on a false passport."

"The man Yarik is bringing in? Ferris?"

"One and the same."

"Brilliant!" Maximov was no longer attempting to mask his excitement or admiration. "How are you going to get Ferris to go along? Peitho?"

"I don't think even Peitho has that power. No, we'll just have Ferris in the right place at the right time. First drugged and then dead."

"So who will have the honor of actually pulling the trigger, then?"

The answer came to Karpov then and there. "I've got just the boy for the job."

CHAPTER 42

Siberian Outback, Russia

Alex felt a sudden rush of cold. Oh, and he had been so warm, so blissfully warm. Then something began pulling at his face. There were voices, too, but they were far in the background.

His memory was returning slowly, as though his brain were thawing. He had walked and stumbled through snow and over ice and then . . . and then there was this beautiful angel and her helper. She had given him tea—yes, he remembered the tea. He had never been so grateful for anything in his life. Then the grand revelation struck: He was alive. He had survived the storm and found the road.

A contentious chord penetrated the fog, disrupting his thoughts. A noise . . . what was it? Was it . . . screaming? The next time he heard it, his conscious senses jolted back to life like power returning after a blackout. Alex opened his eyes and saw the low ceiling. He looked left and right and remembered that he was in an ambulance. He tried to sit up but found that he could not move. He began to panic. He took a deep breath and then looked down at his bonds. He was strapped to a stretcher. The restraints were tight, but nothing compared to Yarik's knots.

The screams came again, frantic and piercing. A woman's screams. His angel's screams. Alex tried to look out the windows. They were fogged. *Relax and focus, Alex. Medical restraints are designed for precaution, not confinement. Work it; don't fight it.* He sucked in his gut and pulled one forearm up across his body to freedom. The rest was easy. A moment later he was on his feet.

Ignoring the head rush, he looked around for anything that he could use as a weapon—a scalpel, a trocar . . . Nothing. He could probably fill some syringes with tranquilizers, but there was no time for that. The doctor who had pulled him from the snow was in grave distress so he was counting milliseconds. Half-loaded or not, he would have to be the weapon.

Alex burst out the back of the ambulance like a bull from its pen. The only living person who had been kind to him in this country was now suffering, probably on his account. He was determined to make it stop.

The scene was simple enough to comprehend, even in his distressed state. They were at a makeshift KGB checkpoint on a desolate stretch of highway. Two bored soldiers had found themselves in possession of a beautiful woman, and decided that, given the circumstances, they didn't need to resist nature's calling. Now the big male nurse was spread-eagle in the snow with blood was streaming from his nose, and the good doctor was receiving their full attention.

From where he was behind the jeep, Alex could see her kicking, clawing, and screaming at two men in KGB uniforms. One soldier was standing in the left doorway pulling her into the backseat of their jeep by the arms, while the other one worked in the right doorway to pull down her pants. The good news was that neither held a weapon. The bad news was that he couldn't attack them simultaneously. He'd have to take the first out with a single blow to avoid attack from both sides.

Alex ran and jumped at the soldier on the left, delivering a double-kick to the side of his head and cracking it hard against the doorframe as he let out a mighty, "Hoooaahhhh!" for shock value. The soldier dropped like a bagged duck.

The instant the fallen soldier released his hold on the woman, she rolled over and began pulling herself out through the jeep's doorway, pummeling the startled soldier behind her with kicks as she went. Alex used the distraction to climb over the roof and drop in from above. He planted his feet firmly on the doorsill, grabbed the soldier from beneath the arms, and blasted upward, crushing the back of the soldier's head into the frame with the force of a launching rocket. The soldier lost consciousness to the sickening sound of metal on bone and then collapsed back onto the woman.

Alex ran back around the jeep while the woman wriggled out her side and then into her pants. She kicked the back of the first fallen soldier a few times and then stopped, sobbing and shaking.

"You better have a look at your friend," Alex said, gesturing toward the man lying spread-eagle in the snow.

"Vova," she screamed, snapping out of her own hysteria and running over to him.

Alex checked the soldiers to be sure they were out cold. They were. Both would be sporting nasty bruises and nursing concussions, but neither was bleeding.

He picked an AK-74 off the front seat and shot out a tire before piling both agents into the back of their jeep so they wouldn't freeze. He considered shooting a second tire, but even one would take quite a while to change in this weather. He didn't want to overdo it. There was no sense in provoking a vendetta.

He emptied both rifle magazines into the drifting snow. The rapists were now unconscious, immobile, and unarmed. He needed to add incommunicado to the list. With a grin that was painful but satisfying, Alex yanked the microphone off the radio and then hurled it into the woods.

Confident that they were safe for the moment, Alex turned and walked toward his two new friends. He found himself staggering like a drunk and then felt hot blood trickling down his face. The adrenaline was wearing off quickly, and his head was throbbing like a jackhammer.

The woman was using smelling salts to wake her friend. "Vova! Vova, wake up!"

Vova shook his head and opened his eyes with a nasal grimace.

"Thank you, darling."

With the woman safe, the soldiers dispatched, and Vova recovering, Alex felt the energy draining from his body like water from a flushing toilet. First he felt dizzy. Then he felt nothing.

CHAPTER 43

Grand Cayman

Victor could hardly believe where he was, or what he was doing. It was such a radical shift in course, such an unexpected turn of events. His was a long list of sins, but heretofore defiance was not among them.

Karpov's words still rang in his head. "With Stepashin gone I'm counting on you to step up. I'm counting on you to put everything into motion, to make all our work pay off. Victor, I need you to be the triggerman."

And so began the roller coaster that ended in the tropics. After the initial shock had run its course, the valley of fear had yielded to a mountain of pride. This was the culmination of decades of work, its single boldest stroke, and father was entrusting it to him. To him!

Gorbachev was scheduled to spend a couple days with the governor of Novosibirsk, shoring up his support. They'd be staying at the governor's home, a large country estate Karpov knew well. Gorbachev would spend the early mornings plowing through the leading newspapers, devouring them with cups of strong coffee before the dawn's quiet yielded to the controlled chaos that ruled his days. That habit would put him before a known window at a known time. Everything a competent shooter with the right access and equipment would need. Father had even arranged for Victor's personal nemesis to take the fall. Yes, Victor thought, that last point alone almost made it worthwhile, but—

"Mr. Rembrandt? Mr. Rembrandt, are you all right?"

"Yes, yes, I'm fine," Victor said, shaking his head.

"Well then, I believe we're all set."

Victor looked across at the banker, and smiled. "We are, indeed," he said, rising from the burgundy armchair. "I think we're going to work well together, Mr. Mulberry."

"'Twill be my pleasure."

"Until next time, then," he said, and sauntered out into the buttery glow of the Cayman sun.

Victor had kept his contingency funds at Cayman First National for three years now. They were registered under the favorite of his false identities. Pierre Rembrandt's signature-access safety deposit box contained a million dollars cash, four different passports, a silenced Desert Eagle .50AE, and a supply of Medusa. Everything a man on the run might need.

Victor's line of work required a man to maintain the kind of insurance even Lloyds of London couldn't offer—although to be honest, he never thought he would need to use it. He didn't need to use it now; he was choosing to leave.

Once the initial thrill of his father's "offer" wore off, Victor found himself questioning some of the assumptions that grounded his life. He was going through what philosophers would call a paradigm shift. Looking down the long, wide beach, Victor realized that a mile of white sand was all the philosophy he would ever need.

He slipped off his loafers, rolled up his Dockers, and began walking his cares away. As the hot sand burned the bottoms of his feet, Victor remembered a similar situation in a similar location, many years ago. He had been sixteen at the time. The Crimean beach was similar, although the sand was not as fine. His mother watched from afar with tears in her eyes. Beside him walked a man with a vaguely familiar face and a startling revelation. Victor had experienced a delayed reaction to Karpov's words then, too, but eventually he had ripped his gaze from the waves to look up at his father for the first time. "So, why wait until now to tell me?"

"You have to understand, son, I got accepted to the KGB Academy the same week your mother learned she was pregnant. I was very lucky to get in, and would have lost my slot if word got out. Fortunately, your mother and I were able to come to an agreement. As a result, everything else has been possible. I've so much to tell you . . ."

Victor had never really questioned Karpov's choice. At the time he had just been thrilled to learn that he had a father. Then Karpov had told him about operation Immaculate Conception and the potential to serve Russia in the United States. In one afternoon, Victor had been given both a father and a purpose. Thank goodness he had learned about both when he did. Those moorings kept him afloat a few months later when his mother died.

Victor's plan had always been to leverage his secret status to his favor. Once his father assumed Russia's helm, he would ask Karpov to appoint him Minister of Foreign Affairs, the Russian equivalent of the US Secretary of State, and the good life would be his.

He had spent many a stakeout daydreaming about being MFA, flying around the world on his government jet, being wined and dined and sexed like a VIP everywhere he went. The rulers of foreign, exotic lands would kiss up to him as the emissary of the world's most powerful nation—and their ladies would take it from there. They would lay their best before him, and then ask if they could do anything more. He would have a prestigious, powerful position, and an excuse to spend the winter months abroad.

For a long time that dream had seemed perfect. But now, Victor was starting to see the cloud that lay within the silver lining, the tarnish on the crown. He began to question his desire to ever return to Russia.

The Minister of Foreign Affairs was a member of the president's cabinet. Victor's life would once again amount to a struggle for his father's approval. *Thanks, but no thanks.*

With Karpov's latest assignment came the realization that switching to the high-profile life of foreign minister would also be very dangerous. He had never really worried about getting caught before, not until the Ferris brothers revealed his mortality. Now he was questioning everything. He even found himself suspecting Elaine Evans of working in cahoots with Alex. Did he need to eliminate her as well? Would her name soon appear on his ethereal tab? Victor already carried around a wad of secrets that could choke a hippopotamus. Of course the peril they evoked paled in comparison to what Karpov was now asking of him. If he were to add the assassination of President Gorbachev to that list, he would forever live his life on the edge.

An idea that had been building up in the back of Victor's mind over the years like crustaceans on a breakwater. With Karpov's grand revelation, that idea began to solidify into the foundation of an alternative lifestyle. As Victor pondered fresh possibilities, a real estate advertisement in the *Wall Street Journal* caught his eye. The Island of Emily was a mere forty-six nautical miles from the sand where he now strolled. It came fully equipped with a six-bedroom mansion and a fifty-eight-foot yacht. The cost was a mere thirty-two million dollars.

Now, Victor didn't have thirty-two million dollars, but he did own a twenty percent stake in Knyaz AG, the Swiss umbrella corporation that owned Irkutsk Motorworks, SovStroy, and RuTek. Karpov had given twenty percent each to Yarik, Stepashin, and him, retaining forty percent for himself. Victor's shares were only worth about half the cost of Emily now, but in a year or so, after the Knyaz had successfully launched all the new product lines, they would be worth billions.

There was one big problem, however. Victor did not yet have physical possession of the shares. He had not been to Russia since the companies had privatized.

Standing there on the scorching sand, watching the waves pound endlessly away like his father's scorn, Victor weighed his options, and made his decision. He would find some excuse to go to Russia. He would take possession of his shares, one way or the other. Then, before Karpov knew what had and had not happened, Victor would be off to Emily in a puff of green smoke. Let the old man find someone else to kill Gorbachev.

CHAPTER 44

Novosibirsk, Siberia

Alex opened his eyes to a familiar face, a kind face, his angel's face. Yes, yes, the doctor from the ambulance, now he remembered. "Where am I?"

"You're safe. Don't push it; let yourself come out of it slowly."

Alex took a long, deep breath and propped himself up on one elbow.

"How do you feel?"

"I feel like I was rolled down a mountain in a rusty barrel. A big improvement. What's your name?"

"Anna."

"Where am I?"

"You're in my apartment. Tell me, what's *your* name?"

What's your name: three mundane words, one tricky question. It got his mind going. Alex didn't have his own documents anymore, or even Alexander Grekov's. The last time he checked he had Yarik's and Andrey's passports. *Could he pass for either of them? Should he try? Was it possible she had staged the rape?*

"You're hesitating."

"I'm sorry. Your simple question got me thinking about a lot of things; I've been through quite a bit lately. My name is Alex, Alex Ferris."

"What kind of a name is Ferris?"

"My mother was Russian. My father . . . American."

Anna exhaled slowly. "How about I give you some tea, and you give me your story."

"That sounds like a fine plan. One question first, please. How long was I out?"

It was her turn to pause and his to exhale. "Five days."

Five days. Alex looked at his wrist. His beloved compass watch was still there, but it had stopped so he could not verify the date. Perhaps that was a good sign. A mastermind might well have wound the watch and set the date to reinforce a ruse.

Anna smiled and got up from the edge of the bed. "I'll make tea."

Once she left the room, Alex flopped back down and stared at the ceiling. He wanted to absorb and process what had happened before moving ahead, but he did not have the time. He had to decide if his surroundings were real or staged, if Anna was an angel or an actress. She passed his intuitive test—he was naturally relaxed in her presence—but he had been fooled before. Playing the long game, sending in a beautiful doctor, a vulnerable soul eager to save and be saved, was classic KGB.

Alex tried to distance himself from his emotions so he could run objectively through his options. He had four basic alternatives: he could delay, he could lie, he could tell her part of the truth, or he could tell it all. He only had a couple of minutes to decide while Anna waited for the water to boil. If this was all a clever interrogation—the ambulance, the rape, Florence Nightingale's apartment—giving him time to think was their first mistake.

As he began to dissect the scenarios, Alex realized that his initial calculation had been wrong. He did not have four alternatives; he had two. If Anna was an actress, then he was a prisoner and nothing he said or did would get him anywhere but dead. Conclusion: lie to the liar. But if Anna was what she appeared to be, then the truth would set him free.

Images began flashing through his mind, ranging from Clint Eastwood's *do-you-feel-lucky* line, to the logic problems of his youth. He never expected that he would actually have to make this decision, but he had been preparing for it all his life. The big difference between this puzzle and those: no eraser.

Alex was still chewing when Anna returned with two teacups and a basket of Russian chocolates. He accepted his cup with a smile and flashed back to the scene where she had found him staggering along the side of the road. She had given him tea then, too. Alex looked his benefactor in the eye. He saw nothing but kindness and concern painted there, in beautiful amber strokes. He smelled and then tasted the tea without breaking his gaze. Nothing peculiar registered. It occurred to Alex that he had been in a similar situation ten days earlier, sitting on a park bench with a woman no less desperate than he was now. Elaine had chosen to trust him. She had chosen wisely. Alex wanted to trust Anna, but would it be wise? With that thought Andrey's image flashed before his eyes, and Alex made up his mind.

He could only imagine what thoughts were going through Anna's mind as she listened to the crazy American with the bandaged head. Yet she listened without a skeptical crease or a judgmental twinge. She listened attentively even when Alex himself found it hard to believe. So he told it all. The only thing he kept secret was Elaine's involvement and identity, and by the time he finished, he even felt guilty about that. He left nothing out, factual or emotional, from Frank's death to Andrey's to Yarik's. Walking through it sequentially it struck him that each chapter concluded with a headstone. Would "Alex" soon be but another chapter of someone else's larger story, or would he get to author the book?

For the first time in his life, Alex understood what drew people to counselors and psychiatrists. Perhaps they weren't only for the weak. He had refused such services twice in his life: once when his father's chain of mistresses came to light, once after the bomb in Rome. Perhaps if he had been more open-minded . . . But probably not. They had been sterile professionals in staged settings. By contrast, Anna was truly engaged, and likewise exposed. She was a partner rather than a third party.

After two hours of catharsis his story was complete. Alex leaned back on the couch, and Anna broke her silence. "I've got a few questions, if you don't mind. But first I'll make us some more tea." As she rose, Alex knew that what she really needed was a few minutes alone to decide if she believed in him. Either that, or he was about to have another very bad day.

CHAPTER 45

Novosibirsk, Siberia

As soon as the kitchen door closed behind Anna, Alex crept across the room to see what she was up to. He crouched down so his shadow would not appear at eye level and then peered through the crack.

He couldn't see much of the room, but the glass on the oven door reflected enough. Anna was sitting sideways on a chair with her back to the wall. She had tucked her knees up beneath her chin and wrapped her arms around them as though she were minding a nest. The pose wasn't quite Rodin, but close enough. She was for real.

When Anna returned to the main room a few minutes later, she had a serious look on her face, but it melted when she looked his way. "What?" she asked.

"Nothing."

She gave a shrug and sat back down across from him. Then she took a deep breath and dove right in. "You really don't have any idea who Andrey is or why he was helping you?"

Those were questions Alex had pondered more than once. "No, I don't, although I'm sure those answers lie at the heart of the mystery.

The only things Andrey told me about himself were that he worked for a cabinet minister and that his friend's death was related to Frank's."

"And you believe him—a man you just met, the man who called you to the murder scene—when he tells you that a guy you went to four years of college with, your brilliant brother's friend and confidant, is really a murdering Russian spy?"

Alex had gone over that one again and again while trekking through the wilderness. "As naïve as that may sound, I do. I have to admit that part of the reason I believe Andrey is that I want Jason to be the guilty one. But at the end of the day, I buy his story because the one thing I do know for certain about Andrey is that he was a man with a profound sense of duty, and honor.

"Mind if I ask a question now?" Alex said.

"Sure."

"What's been going on these last five days?"

"Well, as you might imagine, Vova and I have been concerned that the KGB rapists would track us down for personal revenge. We assumed, apparently correctly, that they would not report the embarrassing incident. We guessed that their most likely course of action would be to search the hospitals in their off hours for you."

"So you didn't take me to a hospital . . ."

"Right."

"I've been here the whole time?"

"Right again."

"There were some documents in a pocket. And some keys . . ."

"They're in the end table."

"Was I in a coma those five days?"

Anna flushed. "No. You were exhausted, depleted, and critically wounded. Your body needed quiet time to heal, but I couldn't stay with you, and I couldn't risk involving anyone else by asking them to stay with you . . . so I kept you drugged." She looked up to meet Alex's eye. He gave a reassuring nod while his hand found the spot on his arm where the IV had entered. "That way I knew you wouldn't wake up while I was away during the day," she paused, "and I felt safe at night. Today is Saturday, so I let you wake up. That's why you've been able to keep talking these last few hours."

"I can't thank you enough for your kindness, your courage, your resilience. You're an amazing woman, and I owe you my life. I won't forget that."

Anna blushed and looked relieved. "So, Mr. Private Eye, what's next?"

Alex cleared his throat. "Good question. Can you get your hands on a map of the area surrounding Academic City?"

"I think I can manage that."

"Excellent. There are some people I have to find."

CHAPTER 46

Novosibirsk, Siberia

Two meals, eight hours, and a long nap after Alex's story, they were in her kitchen, finishing off the cheap bottle of Moldavian wine she had uncorked with dinner.

Acting in the interests of her patient's recovery, Anna had cajoled Alex into a day of rest and relaxation with the promise to procure him the map he wanted—tomorrow. Once he acquiesced, the pressure came uncorked, the wine began to flow, and a refreshing exchange bubbled forth. Anna did not usually drink or prescribe alcohol to her patients, but she knew that the sweetest memories were born in life's exceptions, not its routines. She ran with her instinct on this one.

Their conversation eventually turned to the topic of Alex's implant and the deviant power it represented. Soon they were slogging through a quagmire of conundrums, moral and political, but Anna felt uplifted despite the weighty words. She found it rejuvenating to enjoy an enlightened conversation with an attractive man, a man who wasn't looking for anything from her but common kindness. "Do you think the axiom is true, that 'all is fair in love and war'?" she asked.

"Of course not," Alex said. "That's the antithesis of the Golden Rule. The precipice of a very slippery slope. The universal justification for lowering the bar."

"Go on."

"I accept that 'turnabout is fair play,' but would assert that there is a 'right' side in most conflicts. You can identify it by looking for the side that doesn't lower the bar. Morals are meaningless if you can suspend them at whim—and 'love and war' can encompass just about any whim." Alex paused and rolled his shoulders. "I don't mean to preach, Anna, I've just been thinking about this stuff a lot since Yarik Peithoed me."

"It's got to be terrible for you, the not knowing."

"Pardon?"

"How do you handle not knowing if Yarik gave your number to someone else? It must be terrifying."

Alex nodded. "It's the pits."

"If I were you I'd be spending every waking moment frantically trying to figure out a way to rid myself of that thing. How can you remain so calm and nonchalant with that time bomb in your body?"

"What are the alternatives?"

Anna wasn't sure where he was going. "Alternatives?"

"The alternatives to being calm and nonchalant."

"Are you saying you have a choice about how you feel?"

"It's more of a question of control. When you can't control a situation," he nodded toward his hindquarters, "your best move is to control how you feel about it. In situations like that you're almost always better off forcing vibrancy than feeling vulnerable."

"Easier said than done."

"Agreed. But I usually manage. More wine?"

"Uh-huh." His tone was turning playful. She was ready for a little of that. "Is there some Zen technique they teach you in the CIA? Do they bring in a Tibetan monk to spend a day with you at orientation?"

"No, it doesn't work like that." He paused and grew the mischievous smile she had already come to know as his trademark. "In my case it was a Turk named Mehmet."

CHAPTER 47

Novosibirsk, Siberia

"So a Turk named Mehmet taught you to be vibrant when vulnerable?" Anna said. "Is that another one of your American movie references like—what did you use earlier when you told me about your decision to leave the cabin—'Yoda in the cave.'"

"Well, yeah. I mean yeah I did learn it from Mehmet, not yeah it's a movie reference."

"Go on. Tell me about it. I want to learn your secrets."

"My partner Mehmet and I were in Turkey, near the Iranian border, looking for men of, shall we say, anti-American sentiment. After six weeks of dead ends, we had gotten a tip about a man who was willing to talk to us. He was a man whose son had been a member of the terrorist cell we were after—right up to the day they killed him. It was the first real break of the investigation.

"Mehmet and I were given a place to go and a time to be there. The site was an old abandoned monastery at the dead end of a dirt road ten miles from civilization. When we got there in our old Mitsubishi Pajero, a shiny, new black Range Rover was waiting. Four men wearing ski masks got out, two with AK-74s, and two with metal detectors. The leader yelled over that we should leave all our equipment in the Pajero. We did. Then his boys gave us the once-over with callused hands and metal detectors. They say you never really know the Middle East until you've been patted down by a fanatic, and I would have to agree."

Anna choked on her wine and began to cough. She hadn't opened a second bottle since medical school, and it showed. "Excuse me."

Alex plowed on. "Anyhow, once mister feel-good was satisfied, the leader raised his AK and pointed a couple hundred meters to our right, and said, "The small building."

"You weren't afraid of a trap?"

"Of course we were afraid of a trap, at least at first—working these kinds of jobs you're always afraid—but we figured we were clear when the fantastic four didn't use their AKs to improve our Pajero's ventilation. So, Mehmet and I made the trek over the rocky terrain to the cliffside plateau that housed the abandoned monastery.

"The small, windowless stone building to which we'd been directed looked like the sheltered entrance to a cellar, presumably the larder where the monks kept their food protected from the merciless sun. As we got close, we heard the pounding of feet and turned to see two enormous dogs barreling toward us with the ferocity of starving tigers.

"Mehmet and I ran to the building and jumped inside to put the door between us and those murderous fangs, only to find ourselves falling into darkness. The building didn't cover a stairwell, but rather a water well. We splashed down after a five-meter drop. By the time we surfaced, the Caucasian wolfhounds were barking above, furious that we had denied them instant gratification.

"Can you picture it, Anna? There I am, treading water, shocked, scared, demoralized, and likely seconds from death. Then my eyes adjust, and I look over at Mehmet to see that he's smiling. He looks back at me, and his smile turns to laughter. I'm thinking that he hit his head, or had a stroke. "What's funny?" I ask. And do you know what he says?"

"Surprise?"

"No, but that's a good guess. He says, 'Alex, we're in the middle of nowhere, trapped five meters down an abandoned well, with night falling and a couple of the meanest creatures on God's green earth waiting above to devour us if we miraculously find a way to climb out of here before we drown. Absolutely nothing is funny.'

"'So why are you laughing?' I ask. And then Mehmet gave me the power to change my life. He said to me, 'Alex, we're probably going to die today. I want to enjoy myself while I still can.'"

Anna stopped to stare at the faux lace tablecloth and think about what she'd just heard. Alex let her think. Finally, she looked up at him and said, "Better vibrant than vulnerable."

"Exactly. Of course, I didn't get it at the time. There in the well I thought Mehmet was crazy."

"What did you do? How did you get out?"

"Doesn't matter. The point is that Mehmet didn't get out. But he did get to die on his own terms. He died laughing. He found the strength to enjoy the bitterest of ends, and has been my role model ever since."

CHAPTER 48

Novosibirsk, Siberia

Alex looked up to see Anna enter the kitchen with a triumphant stride. "I got your map."

"That's great. How did you manage it so early on a Sunday morning?"

"My neighbor is a geologist. One thing we have plenty of in Russia is scientists." Anna unfolded the top of her tiny kitchen table, turning it from a two-seater into a four-seater. Then she rolled the map open, securing one end with the saltshaker, the other with the pepper.

Alex took a minute to get oriented. He wanted to be sure of himself. It was not the same type of map he had seen scanned onto an acetate in the Irkutsk Motorworks boardroom, and the scale was different, but the distinctive landmark gave him his bearing nonetheless. "That's where I have to go," he said, pointing to the right of Lake Banana.

"That's not going to be easy. That complex is a KGB facility, the regional headquarters. It's also within the same fence line as an abandoned nuclear power plant, so it's doubly dangerous. There's lots of security—a high fence and patrols."

"But people do go there to work?"

"Hundreds work at the KGB complex. The power plant, however," she traced her finger a couple kilometers north to another complex, "Nobody in their right mind would go there."

"Hum," Alex thought. The words "nobody goes there" smacked of a clue, but before he could process it, he noticed a sadness in Anna's eyes. "What's wrong?"

Anna blinked, and a silent tear dropped onto the map. Then she told him about her brother Kostya, and the others who lost their lives to the radiation leak. "Sometimes people still climb the fences, ignore the radiation signs and wander back there to hunt or scavenge. They end up dying in my hospital if they don't go straight to the morgue. If you wander into the wrong place back there, Alex, it's . . . it's beyond horrible."

"Why would the KGB keep its office so close to a radiation zone?"

"They had just finished building it a month before the accident, a beautiful new facility. I thought it was strange myself that they didn't move it, but apparently the radiation is very contained. There are a couple of kilometers of what they call a green shield between it and the offices. It obviously works since none of the employees has had a radiation problem. We monitor them closely."

"Green shield?"

"A forest."

"I see."

"Let's talk about something else," she suggested. Alex smiled, and before he knew it they were back in chitchat mode again while Alex's mind processed in the background. The hours flew by.

After lunch her eyes began to sparkle with a hint of intrigue, and she said, "I want you to take a nap now."

"Why?"

"Well, for starters, you're not fully recovered yet, but the main reason is that we have a big evening ahead of us."

"Big evening?"

"It's a surprise. Now get some sleep."

CHAPTER 49

Moscow, Russia

Foreign Minister Sugurov was worried. That wasn't like him. Worrying was wasted energy. Better to spend your time fixing a problem than fretting over it, he always said. And there was the rub. For the first time in his life, Sugurov was at a loss for how to fix a problem.

It had been one week since he had heard from Andrey. One week since his chief of staff had gone into Chulin Air Base to pry Alex from Yarik's clutches. And one week since an airplane had exploded. That was all Sugurov knew for certain. Everything else was just conjecture.

It was possible that the escape had gone awry, and the plane had blown up with everyone aboard, but Sugurov didn't think that was likely. Andrey was too good. He was also the most likely cause of the explosion. Sugurov clung to the assumption that Andrey and Alex either never got on the plane, or had jumped off before it exploded. This optimistic hypothesis gained credence when Sugurov got word that Yarik had survived but was missing in action. But a week had passed, and there was still no word from Andrey. Sugurov's optimism was waning.

It was time to take action, and unfortunately, that action would have to involve other organizations. Sugurov composed his thoughts and then got his assistant on the intercom. "Natasha, I need to make two calls . . ."

CHAPTER 50

Novosibirsk, Siberia

As he walked the long central corridor at SovStroy, Karpov tried to meet everyone's eye, if only for a second. He was ostensibly at the Knyaz's photovoltaic plant for a dress inspection. His actual intention was just the opposite. Karpov had come to SovStroy to be inspected.

He had been spending a lot of time there lately, a fact that was not lost on the workforce. They were proud that General Karpov, a man who had dozens of factories under his purview, chose to spend so much of his precious time with them. It must be personal, they reasoned. All they made were bricks. *If they only knew.*

Karpov picked up a freshly cast brick, a Karpov brick, and felt himself begin to glow. He held the future of the world in the palm of his hand. For now, however, he was the only person at SovStroy who knew it. Unlike Irkutsk Motorworks and RuTek, where sophisticated product lines forced him to bring management into the Knyaz loop, here at SovStroy ignorance remained his asset.

That was about to change. Soon the whole world would know that you simply needed to connect Karpov's bricks with Karpov's mortar to transform your building into a power plant. Be that as it may, the electrifying secret would remain grounded until he was ready to flip the switch. To figure out that Karpov bricks were solar cells and Karpov mortar a conduit, you would need to see the other half of the puzzle.

That other half was located six hundred kilometers away at a Knyaz-owned factory in Krasnoyarsk called RuTek. There, one manufacturing line over from the latest microchip out of Seattle, a group of skilled workers was cranking out *Karpov Controls*. Karpov Controls were the power-management and storage systems that would harness and direct the energy collected by his bricks. Bill Gates might control computing power, but Vasily Karpov would control the power of the sun. Russia was about to become the source of the cheapest, cleanest, most revolutionary power source on Earth.

The billions he would earn personally were but a means to an end for Karpov. He was put on the planet to raise Russia to its proper place at the very top of the global food chain. To make that happen, he needed the power of the presidency. To attain that, he needed the support of the people.

The workers and families at Karpov's factories would form a core political base that spanned three major metropolitan areas. They would seed a swell of grassroots popular support that would blaze across the country. In no time, everybody in Russia would know that people who worked for Karpov lived better and felt better about themselves. At the end of the day, that was all anybody required of a politician.

All he needed now was a dead president, and Victor was about to create one.

Chaos would break out when Gorbachev died. The prime minister was not popular. Presidential wannabes would come out of the Moscow woodwork, and a nasty battle would ensue, further dividing the country and adding to the mayhem. After a month or three of that, after the people and the reporters tired of the speculation and the mudslinging, Vasily Karpov would launch his product lines on the market, and spring onto the world stage. By the time the constitutionally mandated elections rolled around a few months later, he would be the very symbol of Russia's future. A living legend. A favorite prince virtually forced to be king. If the people got their way.

With the economic miracle arranged, and the Supreme Court in the bag, the only thing with the potential to derail Karpov now was the assassination itself. Framing the Americans was the perfect solution. Like his bricks, it was simple, elegant, and easy to understand. That was why he was so keen to have Ferris under lock and key. Where was Yarik? It had been a week.

Maddening though it might be, and since there was nothing he could do to make them appear faster, Karpov turned his attention to the issues he could influence. With all the ups and downs surrounding Yarik's disappearance and Stepashin's death, he had dropped the courtship ball. It was time to pick it back up and run for the goal line. Perhaps he could leverage the death of his friend. Stepashin would surely approve. He could go to Anna in his grief and play to her heartstrings.

Karpov looked at his watch. It was eleven thirty already. In an hour he would have lunch in the SovStroy employee cafeteria and then make a motivational speech for dessert and have a coffee with the employees of the month. He would be out of there by three and back in Academic City by four.

As he pondered his next move, Karpov found himself feeling romantically inspired. Perhaps he should just drop in on Anna. He wouldn't even need to change. She had not seen him in full dress uniform except on TV. His thick stack of medals and gilded general's trim always impressed women. Yes, it was time to show Anna his softer, spontaneous side . . .

CHAPTER 51

Novosibirsk, Siberia

The surprise Anna had teased him with was dinner at her mother's, a fine rendition of chicken Kiev for which he had so far complemented his charming hostess no less than three times. The actual surprise was Anna herself.

She had disappeared into her simple bathroom only to emerge fit for the cover of a French magazine. Her long brown hair beautifully coiffed up in a spirited tangle. Her strong Slavic features made up to accent her sparkling amber eyes. Plump lips painted red to match a dress that relentlessly funneled his gaze beyond polite conversation.

"I understand your mother was Russian?" Mrs. Zaitseva said, her voice warm and comforting. A handsome woman in her mid to late fifties, she looked nothing like her daughter, but she shared the same disarming manner. He'd felt at ease from the moment she first cracked the door.

"That's right."

"Where did your parents meet?"

"Geneva. My father was there on a banking internship the summer before he graduated from Wharton. My mother was working at the Soviet consulate. Mom got pregnant and they got engaged. When Dad graduated, he moved to Geneva and they got married. My twin brother and I were born a few months later."

"Did you grow up in Geneva?"

"Primarily."

"Are they still there?"

"No. They died years ago."

"I'm sorry. Were you close?"

"To my mother."

"But not your father?"

"Mother!" Anna said.

"It's okay," Alex said, still looking at Mrs. Z. "Probably do me good to talk about it. It's been a pretty healthy week in that regard. Your daughter has quite the bedside manner. Now I know where she got it."

Mrs. Z just smiled and took a sip of the wine they had brought.

"My father never took much interest in Frank or me. We just seemed to be the obligatory two kids he needed standing next to his beautiful wife in the family photo on his desk at the bank."

"I don't understand."

"That's a good sign. Nobody should. My father was all work. He was a banker, like his father. Climbed the ladder all the way to managing director before . . . before he died."

"Did he love your mother?"

"I'd like to think he did, at least at first. As my mother explained it, babies are tough; twins are tougher. It was too much for dad, so first he dove into work. Then he dove into other dalliances."

"Sounds tragic, but not that unusual. How did your mother react?"

"Not the way you would expect. Her nonchalance was always a mystery to me."

"How about Anna's father? Where did you meet?" Alex asked.

Mrs. Z gave him the family history, peppered by Anna's colorful anecdotes. By the time dessert was over, Alex knew as much about Anna as anyone else in his life. The only standard topic they did not discuss, the one conspicuously absent from all their other conversations to date, was relationships. Alex appreciated their discretion. He was single, but for a reason. Nobody ever left it at that, though. You couldn't just say, "I'm not fit to be a husband" and switch to the weather. Everyone had to know why, so they could convince you that you were wrong. It was as if they wanted you to join their religion. So eventually he would have to tell them the story of his father's philandering ways. He hated telling the story. People always smiled reassuringly and nodded with understanding, but they never really understood. To be perfectly honest, neither did he.

"Are you bringing Alex to church?" Mrs. Z asked Anna while pouring cups of fragrant jasmine tea from her samovar.

"I don't think he would find that particularly interesting, Mother, and we don't want him to be seen."

Alex surprised himself by saying, "Actually, I would like to go."

Mrs. Z gave him an approving nod and said, "We'll say that you're Anna's cousin from Vilnius."

Anna looked back and forth between him and her mother with a bemused smile on her face. Alex was pleased to have Mother as a coconspirator. Because his looks and accent weren't pure Russian, saying that he was from Vilnius, the capital of the distant Soviet Republic of Lithuania, would work just fine. Making him a relative would further diffuse the speculation that would undoubtedly arise in their small village if Anna suddenly produced a foreign suitor. *Two points for Mom.*

As the three walked slowly through virgin snow, Anna explained, "It's not a regular church service. It's a memorial service that has evolved into something of a community social event. We have it every Sunday night at eight o'clock. You remember I told you about Kostya being killed along with twenty-four other villagers from a radiation leak?"

"Yes, I remember."

"Well, you can imagine the staggering impact a tragedy of that size would have on a small village like ours. Everyone lost a relative or friend. Five years later we're still mourning."

Alex knew about loss, but he did not want to turn the discussion in that direction, so he just reached out to hold Anna's hand. They walked on in silence.

They arrived thirty minutes early for the service, as planned. Anna wanted to show off their beautiful church. "It was built nearly six hundred years ago," she explained while tying on a scarf to cover her head, "back when our annual fur fair was a major regional event."

European dates always amazed Alex. To think, this building was three times older than his country. It really put things into humbling perspective. His curiosity aroused, Alex pulled enthusiastically on the brass handle of the massive door. It sprang outward with surprising ease and brought the scent of burning beeswax to their noses.

"It's perfectly balanced," Anna said with a knowing smile.

The nave of the church was a semicircular dome. At the front was an assortment of ornate gilded icons behind a hand-carved pulpit. For a town of this size, it was magnificent.

Although the first to arrive, they walked around quietly while Anna pointed and explained the history and architecture in a whispered voice. It was as though the church itself was not to be disturbed. Nevertheless, as they approached the pulpit, Anna said, "It's okay to go up; we're all family here."

Alex mounted the pulpit and found himself looking at an enormous ancient Bible. After an approving nod from Anna, he flipped delicately through a few pages of the beautiful book. The printing was done mechanically, but the illuminations were delicately wrought by hand. It must be worth a fortune, he thought, but not to anybody within a thousand miles of here.

"Alex," Anna whispered.

He looked up, but she wasn't there.

"Alex."

Where was she? Had she slipped behind an icon? Into a secret antechamber? Through a trapdoor? He looked around with bemused curiosity. Then he heard her laugh. A moment later he saw her approaching from the rear of the church, wearing a big smile.

"What was that?"

"Did you like it? It's because of the dome." Anna gestured upward with her head. "The nobleman who built the church set it up so the peasants could sit quietly in the chapel off the back of the nave and listen to the service out of sight of the gentry. Some say he did it so the peasants wouldn't feel ashamed of their common clothes. Others think he just didn't want to have to look at them. Now we're all peasants so it doesn't really matter." She gave a carefree shrug and reached for his hand. "Actually, the chapel is kind of cozy; come have a look. It's where we hold the memorial services."

Alex walked to the back of the church and ducked through a narrow, arched tunnel into an ancient, windowless room with a low domed brick ceiling. "You were whispering from here?"

"That's right."

"Amazing," he said, thinking of the church, the girl, and the dress.

About thirty people filtered in over the next ten minutes as Alex admired the enduring architecture. Then, promptly at eight, Father Nikoli came through the entryway clad in an antique gold-and-silver robe. He walked slowly, ceremoniously, to the front, where he stood between two enormous candles. Once in place he spread his arms wide to gather the crowd's attention and then slowly brought his palms back together to focus it. After a thick moment of silence, he invited them all to bow their heads in silent prayer for the souls of their lost sons.

Alex found it an amazing experience, standing there in the ancient, candle-lit chamber, praying in silence amidst a crowd of mourning villagers. As the priest circled them in silence, waving the smoking censer, Alex felt as though the tiny tunnel had transported him back through the ages to the days of parchment and apostles. He knew he was standing among God's people, and felt he finally understood what was meant by "the meek shall inherit the Earth." It was a feeling he would never forget.

Ten mystical minutes later the priest began speaking a language that Alex did not understand, interspersed with words that he did. Regardless of the language, Nikoli's rich baritone voice seemed to pour out of the rocks and into Alex's soul. He began to understand how some cults attracted more than just the feebleminded. He mouthed along as they recited a collective prayer, and then Father Nikoli concluded the service by reading the names of the twenty-five victims, including Anna's brother, Konstantine Anatolievitch Zaitsev.

Anna turned to Alex. She seemed about to speak but stopped to look at his face instead. Alex realized it must be fraught with emotion. Her eyes lit up, and she leaned close to whisper in his ear. "We can go now. Mother will stay here chatting with her friends, perhaps for hours. They'll walk her home."

Alex thanked Mrs. Zaitseva for a lovely meal and a touching evening, and left the church with Anna on his arm—a Russian norm among friends. Her apartment was a good kilometer away, but the sky was clear, the air was dry, and they were warmly dressed in wool *dublyonkas*, so it was a pleasure despite the hour. He enjoyed walking with Anna, although they didn't speak much. She was obviously lost in thought, and he did not want to disturb her.

"You're leaving tomorrow, aren't you, Alex?" Anna asked, as they hung up their coats, and she locked the door behind them.

"Or the day after," he said softly.

She gave him a long, sad look, and then he saw the sparkle he had grown so fond of. "You've changed me, Alex. I find myself looking at the world and my life differently after sharing your foreign perspective for a few days. I'm aware now of something that was missing, and I feel better equipped to deal with the challenges I'm facing. You've inspired me to find the courage to take the chances required to live life without regret. I want to start doing that, right now." She reached back to unzip her dress and let it drop to the floor.

For the second time that night, Alex found himself having a religious experience. Anna looked as divine as any form that had ever graced his eyes, and the sight of her nearly naked body was enough to turn his throat dry. He stood motionless for a moment, stunned and silent as he drank her in with his eyes.

While moonlight streamed through the curtains to illuminate her heavenly body, Anna glided over and placed her hands lovingly around his neck. Her touch was warm and gentle, and it convinced Alex that, despite the fantastic nature of what was happening, this was not a dream.

CHAPTER 52

Novosibirsk, Siberia

Anna felt a quiver of pleasure run down her body when she heard the knock on her door. Coming this early, it could only be Alex. He must have rushed through his work and run back to her bed. She was all for that.

"Helloooo—" she said in mock-romantic tone, opening the door with a flirtatious grin. "Karpov," she swallowed the name and stepped back in shock, pulling her bathrobe into place as she did so. Further words would not come so she just stared in shock.

Mixed emotions crossed the general's face like lightning on a thunderhead. "Good morning, Anna. These are for you," he said, extending an enormous bouquet of roses. "I apologize for such an early arrival. I wanted to get you these while they were still fresh. I brought them by last evening, but you weren't here . . ."

Anna blinked a few times, forcing her mind to switch gears before responding. "Yes, yes, I had dinner with my mother, and then we went to church."

"I see," he said, flashing one of his trademark smiles and clearly waiting for an invitation to enter.

"Thank you for the flowers," she said, trying to sound genuine. "Now I must get ready for work. Mondays are our busiest days at the hospital."

"I see. Well, I hope—"

"Have a good week, and thanks again for the roses. You're very thoughtful." She closed the door and turned the lock.

Anna stood with her back to the door for a moment, digesting this startling twist. She could feel Karpov on the other side of the door doing the same thing, so she moved quietly to the kitchen. She put on tea and nestled atop the kitchen chair to think with her knees tucked up beneath her chin.

Karpov's visit had doused her with a cold shower of reality. Despite the roses, his appearance was an unwelcome reminder of the world she actually lived in. Anna had been getting used to the thrill of living a secret, double existence with a handsome American spy. Now her old life seemed not only mundane but frightfully so. When she left for work this morning, she would be walking back into her old life, which suddenly seemed cold and stale and gray.

She missed Alex. With him there, she had been living in a retreat, a hideout. Now all she could see were the walls of a prison cell, and she felt condemned to solitary. Adding to her list of frustrations was Vasily Karpov. How did you get rid of a KGB general? She had been foolish to think that she could get him to reveal the secret of her brother's death. Was Karpov out there right now, guarding her like a jealous stalker? Probably not, but possibly. What would Alex think of that situation? As she drank the last swallow of her tea, Anna decided not to mention this morning's incident to Alex. Vasily Karpov would remain her little secret.

CHAPTER 53

Novosibirsk, Siberia

Karpov's eyes sprang open as a shocking thought jolted him from sleep. Only in the calm of the night with his mind freed from the labors of a conquering general's daily grind, had his processor found the wherewithal to make the subtle connections that sounded the alarm. The clock read five a.m.

Now he lay there staring at the ceiling, chewing on his latest insight while the sharp taste of bile grew ever more bitter in his mouth. *Anna was seeing Alex Ferris.*

Karpov would normally have figured it out as soon as he heard the old lady's words—"You're too late. She's already fallen for that handsome foreign patient of hers"—but Anna's rebuff, coming just thirty seconds earlier, had him feeling like James Bond's martini.

The babushka had needled Karpov from a bench by the entrance to Anna's building, much to the amusement of her peers. He had hurried past rather than inquiring, embarrassed for the first time in ages and eager to put the incident out of his mind. It was a scornful, puerile mistake.

Before berating himself further, Karpov decided to dissect his subconscious conclusion. On the surface it seemed farfetched. *What were the odds of Anna and Alex meeting?* He tossed this question around a bit until he came to the conclusion that it didn't matter. He wasn't a gambler. *Forget the odds. Look at the facts.*

Karpov knew from an obsession-driven background investigation that Anna had never been swept off her feet. This was clearly not due to a lack of opportunity on her part, but rather to her exceptionally high standards. Therefore, Karpov reasoned, it would take somebody extraordinary to win Anna over, somebody like himself, or, he spat out a surge of bile, perhaps an American.

Yesterday Karpov had been caught up on the word "handsome," and had let "*foreign*" fly right by. Chinamen and Mongols were the foreigners that first came to mind in Novosibirsk, not Americans. As a handsome American, Alex embodied one thing that Karpov did not: the appeal of an exotic, forbidden fruit. That and a much narrower age gap.

The babushka had also called the man Anna had fallen for "her patient." How would the old lady know that, unless Anna had treated him at home rather than in the hospital? Plus the babushka had obviously seen Ferris; the word "handsome" made that clear. Her wording further implied an ongoing relationship, which in turn implied that his condition had been serious. But if Anna's patient were seriously ill, he would be treated in the hospital, unless he couldn't go to the hospital. Who but Ferris couldn't go to the hospital?

That was one long chain of supposition—and the longer, the weaker—but there was more. There was the news from Yarik, news that had taken a week to filter up. Yarik had sent word through a hermit that the KGB should establish checkpoints to look for Alex on the roads leading into Novosibirsk from the south. So Karpov knew that Alex was headed this way. But neither Yarik nor Alex had surfaced, and eight days had elapsed.

Karpov now realized that he had handicapped Yarik when he gave him the order to bring Alex in unharmed. He had not considered it a factor at the time. A general normally wouldn't worry about straining Yarik's combat skills any more than a billionaire would worry about buying beer. But suppose he had gravely underestimated Alex's power. Was Alex the David to Karpov's Goliath? Karpov had to admit that the facts on hand—a wounded foreigner and a missing Yarik—fit nicely with that nasty conclusion, unbelievable though it may seem.

Karpov knew his conclusion might not be particularly robust, but it wasn't flimsy either. And somehow, as tenuous as it all seemed, it still felt right. Rather than feeling pleased with himself for figuring this out, Karpov found himself getting angry. He was not sure why. Welcome or not, catching Alex at Anna's would be a victory. Of course he was angry with himself for being slow to catch on, but the emotion he felt was different; it was more primitive. Eventually he got a handle on it. Finding Alex there would confirm that the American had both bested Yarik and seduced Anna. Karpov wasn't angry; he was jealous. It was the first time in thirty years that emotion had crossed his cortex.

A smoldering fury began to burn within him. Karpov had caught the look in Anna's eyes and seen the drape of her robe when she first opened her apartment door, confident that the knock had come from another. That look had quashed his composure and caused his pitiful oversight with the babushka. He had been blocking the image out ever since. Now it was back, as painful and distressing as a dagger in his side. Like the thought that Yarik could be bested in combat, the idea that he might have serious competition for a woman had simply never entered his mind. Karpov had always enjoyed his way with women. Always.

Then Karpov realized that he could still possess Anna. Her affair with Alex did not rule that out. By consorting with a spy, Anna had committed a serious crime. That gave Karpov a hold on her he might otherwise never have had. Perhaps that dagger in his side was really a double-edged sword. Did he still want Anna? A resounding "yes" came without hesitation.

Karpov was systematically finding the answers, but the questions kept coming as well. He took them to the shower. Where was Alex? What was his plan? Did he know about the Knyaz? What about Yarik? The answers, he realized, were all in one place. He would confront Anna—now, this morning, immediately.

As Karpov toweled off, a wonderful, terrible thought occurred to him. He should take Medusa with him to Anna's. There was a chance that Alex would be there. If he was, then Medusa would help him bring Alex in unscathed. A little paralysis would also add the perfect touch of poetic justice to that historic occasion. After all, it was Alex's search for his brother's killer that brought him to Russia. The least Karpov could do was explain it to him firsthand.

Taking Medusa would require a trip to The Complex—Karpov didn't dare to keep something so incriminating in his apartment. Could he afford the time? Might that extra delay allow Alex to slip through his fingers? There was no way of knowing. He certainly *liked* the idea . . . Then Karpov remembered Victor and Yarik, and the decision was made. They had both underestimated Alex. He would not.

CHAPTER 54

Novosibirsk, Siberia

It was a quarter to six in the morning and Alex was half frozen before the first set of headlights approached his snare. It was a jeep, and a general's jeep no less. Clean cars were a rarity in Siberia in the winter, but this one shone in the starlight, and its flag was easy to spot.

He dropped flat to lie motionless beneath the white sheet borrowed from Anna's bed. As the wind began concealing his cover beneath freshly blown snow, he wondered if a VIP vehicle would stop. Alex supposed that depended on who was driving. He hoped it was just a chauffeur.

He held his breath as the headlights illuminated the large cardboard box he'd placed in the middle of the road. The jeep slowed . . . and stopped. As the lone occupant got out and walked toward the front, Alex scurried to the back and slid underneath. He wriggled toward the front axle, sliding quietly on the cardboard strapped to his back like a sleigh. His heart was trying to pop out of his chest, and his lungs were protesting the noxious exhaust, but still it felt good to engage.

The driver kicked the box and shouted "undisciplined fools" loud enough to be heard above the rumbling engine. Alex strained his neck to see his host but could only see his feet. Spit-shined shoes, and sharply creased pants with an officer's stripe. Alex slipped a leather belt around the filthy front axle and then wrapped one end around each wrist as the officer opened the door. *Forgive me if I don't salute.*

As the jeep lurched forward, the picture of two bloody stumps clutching a belt flashed through his mind. Did he really know what he was doing? Whether he did or not, he was now committed. If he got caught now it would be a capital offense, and potentially a national embarrassment. He was an ex-CIA operative breaking into a KGB compound.

The officer seemed to listen to Alex's telepathic command, and slowed but did not stop while passing the gate. Excellent. From this side of the gauntlet, all Alex had to hope for was that they weren't headed for covered parking. He did not relish the idea of being dragged over bare asphalt. Regardless, he could not let go for fear of being spotted in the rearview mirror.

The jeep neither stopped nor drove over bare asphalt. This puzzled Alex, and it wasn't helping his back either. The main entrance to the KGB headquarters was just fifty meters or so from the guardhouse. Surely a general would have priority parking, especially at this hour. What was happening? *Anybody got an aspirin?*

Alex felt the road beneath the snow turn from asphalt to gravel. Should he release there, away from the guards and lights? Or should he hold on to see what it was that pried a KGB officer out of bed at five thirty in the morning? Alex decided to give it two more minutes. After that, the hike back would be too long, and he would be in trouble with his dentist.

It took five minutes, but as soon as they stopped Alex knew he had chosen wisely. That was two gambles that had paid off today, and the sun wasn't even up yet. He wished he were in Vegas.

Alex looked up at the mammoth chimney silhouetted against the starry Siberian sky and enjoyed one of those deep smiles that warms you from the inside out. The officer had parked before the abandoned nuclear power plant. This virtually confirmed a suspicion he had been harboring ever since Anna told him the story of her brother's death. Another piece of the puzzle slid smoothly into place.

He waited motionlessly while the officer entered the building. Unarmed and under a jeep was no way to engage the enemy. That line wasn't from Sun Tzu, but he was sure The Master would agree. Besides, if his hunch were right, there was no great hurry.

Alex watched the red second hand on his compass-watch make one full sweep, and then he rolled out from under the jeep. It took just twenty seconds for him to brush over his tracks with a branch and hide behind an evergreen that yielded good views of both the entranceway and the approaching road. In the distance to his left, Alex saw the moonlight reflecting off the lake that had guided him to this place, and felt a rekindling of something that might actually be pride. He had come a long way.

Reflecting on the current situation while the wind further obliterated his trail through the snow, Alex figured there were three likely scenarios: one, the officer had come to the complex this early to retrieve something; two, he had come in to meet someone who, given the absence of any other vehicles, had not yet arrived; or three, he had come in early to work. If it were either of the first two, it would be a mistake to move now. So Alex decided to wait for ten minutes and see what happened. *Where could he get a cup of coffee?*

As it turned out, he was still warm from the under-jeep adrenaline rush when the officer emerged. He had been inside just four minutes. As the officer walked briskly to the jeep, Alex caught sight of the star on his shoulder board. *Thank you, general.*

Seconds later the jeep's taillights were fading fast down the gravelly road, and Alex found himself with only the ghosts of the past to keep him company. *Time to rock and roll.*

Alex caught himself holding his breath as he swiped Yarik's card-key through the reader. He had moved from craps to roulette, and now he was betting big on green. What would he do if an alarm sounded? His only option would be to run across the surrounding field of virgin snow. Yes, he was betting big indeed. But his color came up, there was a click, and he was in. Too easy? He wasn't home yet. *Let it ride*.

As the door swung open, the stench of stale air greeted his nose while nothing but the blackness beyond met his eyes. Had there been a doormat, Alex would have expected it to give way at this point, dropping him into a pit or a moat, but all remained as still and silent as the crypt everyone was supposed to think it was. Alex stepped in decisively and closed the door behind him. As the latch clicked, dim, emergency-level lighting switched on to reveal a corridor with a dozen doors each on the left and right. Which way to go? The dilemma reminded Alex of the Dungeons & Dragons games he had enjoyed as a child. Fortunately, Detective Ferris did not have to guess.

He followed the general's trail along the dusty floor to a door at the left end of the corridor. There was another card reader there. Once again, he bet his only chip on green—and won. As this door opened, the scent of chlorine assaulted his nose, and a concrete stairway greeted his eyes. It led down into darkness with no end in sight.

As he descended through the dark, a dozen horror films, mystery novels, and detective shows assailed his imagination and ripped at his resolve. None of them had happy endings. This was not the eccentric neighbor lady's basement that had frightened him as a kid. This was the KGB, and the fright was man style.

Thirty-eight steps later, his sweaty hand came into contact with a door. This was it. He had gone one-on-one with Yarik, and Andrey had given his life, all to learn what was on the other side of that door. He found the handle, gave it a firm twist, and walked into wonderland.

In sharp contrast to the dusty abandon above, the subterranean suite surrounding him matched his image of the White House Situation Room. It was not a large setup, but it was an extremely well equipped one. He would have liked to take the tour, but could not risk the time. For all he knew, Yarik had a twin, too.

Alex crossed the common area to what appeared to be the executive offices of the clandestine organization whose headquarters he had infiltrated. There were no names or titles on the doors, but the suite was obviously equipped to service a triumvirate. He assumed Yarik was one of those three, and wanted to find his office. The odds were best that no one would discover him there or notice if he disturbed anything. That might be splitting hairs, but his victories on this case had all been razor thin, so split he would.

He had three doors from which to choose. Once again, he was living a logic puzzle. Despite the giant's intelligence, Alex was intuitively certain that Yarik was not the top dog, so the central of the three offices was out. That gave him a fifty-fifty choice between the two flanking suites. What else could he infer? Yarik exhibited an underdeveloped sense of right and wrong, and displayed an unabashed disregard for society's rules. He was a man of passion, of instinct. That indicated right-brain thinking. Right-brained people prefer the right side of the room. Conclusive? No. But Alex played it conservative nonetheless, and went right.

He went straight to the computer and began the boot sequence. If he could not hack his way in, his backup plan was to take the hard drive with him. He hoped it would not come to that. Actually, "hack" was not the right word. Alex hoped to walk right in the front door. He was betting on human nature.

It took fifty-two seconds for him to find the password cheat sheet taped to the bottom of the pencil holder. LuV2KiL confirmed that he had selected the correct office. Although there is nothing so frustrating as being denied critical information by an unresponsive computer, the opposite is also true. Alex was feeling good. Once inside the system, he ran a search for the fourteen-character sequence that was "his number." *Nothing!* Alex let out a long, slow sigh of relief and then performed a second search. This time he used "Kimberly Evans," and he got a hit. The file was titled "Peitho." He should have searched for that in the first place. Three minutes later Alex tucked two printed copies of the Peitho victim list into his pocket.

The Peitho list was a long one, but it was not outrageous. Relieved as he was to learn that there was not an army of forced combatants out there, Alex was nonetheless overcome by a wave of pity for the hundred or so souls laid raw before him. Then a second wave struck, only this time it was inspiration.

It took two minutes for Alex to change a random character in each of the 116 Peitho codes. It was one of the simplest things he had ever done, and yet undoubtedly the most significant single event of his life. *One small mouse click for man . . .* For kicks, he destroyed Yarik's cheat sheet and changed his network password to "Ferris1" before logging off.

Now Alex had a new priority in life: getting the list of Peitho victims out of Russia. He spent ten minutes packing the list of names into his brain as a type of insurance, hoping it would be sufficient for passive recall if disaster struck. What else could he do? Within a few feet of where he was sitting, there was probably equipment that could compress the data onto a microdot he could swallow or implant beneath the skin of his forearm, but there was no time for that. A swift retreat was clearly the winning wager at this point.

Alex had one more thing to do before leaving. He needed to find a uniform. His own clothes were a wreck after riding beneath the general's jeep. He would be a fool to attempt marching out the front door looking like a hobo, and marching out was exactly what he planned to do.

A quick search of Yarik's office was unproductive, but he struck pay dirt in the office to the left of center. Three minutes later Alex Ferris was a general in the KGB. The rank of general was much too conspicuous for his tastes, but there was nothing he could do about that, so he pressed on. It was time to get the hell out of Dodgenik.

CHAPTER 55

Novosibirsk, Siberia

Karpov couldn't believe the twist of fate that had him arresting the woman he'd been wooing just hours earlier, the woman he had hoped and conspired to make his wife. But Russia was his first love, and Anna had been harboring a spy. "Take her away, major. Confine her at The Complex and wait for my arrival."

"The Complex. Yes, sir."

Maximov's tone was obedient for Anna's benefit, but Karpov caught a questioning look in his eyes. All Karpov said was, "I'll be there in a couple of hours." He had shown weakness once before. He would not show it again.

"Very well, sir."

Karpov shut the door, tucked the Medusa pen back into his breast pocket, and sat somberly on the edge of Anna's bed. Whatever he'd been expecting, it wasn't her complete defiance. She had completely stonewalled him, but her bed said everything there was to say. It was obvious that two people had slept there. The woman he loved was sleeping with the man he hated. Alex had made it to Novosibirsk a week ago. That meant Yarik had not. One week to bag Yarik and bed Anna. Yes, hated.

Karpov had pushed Stepashin to Peitho the chief justice, and now Stepashin was dead. He had pushed Yarik to bring Ferris in alive, and now Yarik was dead. Had he gotten too cocky? Too greedy? No. Both were required to complete the plan. The three had committed to that decades ago—whatever it took, and despite the risks.

And they were so close, so very close. And he still had Victor. Karpov felt his blood pressure rising unexpectedly as he thought of his son. A moment later he understood why. Victor's incompetence had brought about this mess. If Anna didn't cooperate, if she didn't give him Alex, he would summon Victor back to Russia immediately. Let the boy clean up his own mess.

Despite this morning's setback, the Knyaz were still on course. His overall strategy of using Alex as a lever to pry Anna into the Kremlin was still sound and salvageable. In fact, he might still be able to win Anna's heart and have Alex in jail by nightfall if he played the interrogation just right. That was why he instructed Major Maximov to take Anna to The Complex.

Maximov would not take Anna there by way of the gravelly road Karpov had used an hour earlier when he went to retrieve Medusa. Maximov would walk Anna through the main lobby of the KGB headquarters, where Karpov had his official office. This would give her a false hope he could later snatch away. He would walk her past the lobby elevators and down the long hallway that ran the length of the first floor and continued along the back. Once they reached its far end they would board a service elevator, which, according to its buttons, would take them either two levels higher or two levels lower. Major Maximov would push and hold both the "-1" and the "-2" buttons long enough for the computer to identify his thumbprints. Then the doors would close, a special light would illuminate, and the elevator would descend to a secret level. When the doors opened, Anna would find herself looking into the mouth of a long tunnel blasted from bedrock. This was the back entrance to the Knyaz headquarters, the one they almost always used. It virtually cried out, "All hope abandon, ye who enter here."

Karpov was proud not just of the tunnel and the headquarters at the other end, but of the clever means by which he had acquired them. Like most everything else of note he owned, they were the spoils of a strategic campaign.

If there is one constant that applies to leaders and governments throughout the world and across time, it is this: whatever they do well for their people, they do even better for themselves. When the Soviet government built the peoples' bomb shelters in preparation for the nuclear war their strategists thought inevitable, they created metros, deeply buried metros, in all of Russia's first-strike cities. When they built the party leaders' bomb shelters, they found the hardest location within fifty kilometers of the city center, and then built themselves an escape tunnel to reach it.

Novosibirsk's elite bunker was located beneath the ten meters of hardened concrete that formed the foundation of its nuclear power plant. When Karpov built the new KGB office a few kilometers from there, he ensured that it rested directly above that escape tunnel, presumably so that the top KGB brass would also have access to it. Then, as soon as the building was completed but before anyone had moved in, he faked a radiation leak at the nuclear plant, Peithoed the children of a couple government inspectors, and voilà, the bunker became the Knyaz's invisible headquarters.

This morning, Maximov would whisk Anna to The Complex through the last three kilometers of the forgotten tunnel in a glorified mining cart. He would know to leave the headlights off, making the silent five-minute commute feel like an endless journey to the depths of hell. By the time she reached the other end, she would feel like she was buried alive. After a couple claustrophobic hours alone in a dark cell, she would be thrilled to see him. Then the fun would start . . .

CHAPTER 56

Novosibirsk, Siberia

The road or the woods? Alex was facing a dilemma. His exit strategy from the KGB compound was bold and simple; out the front door. The dilemma was selecting the route that gave him the best chance of getting that far.

It's hard to judge distance while riding beneath a jeep—kind of like judging descent when falling from a plane—but he figured the KGB complex was no more than three miles from the nuclear power plant, and probably closer to two. That fit with his recollection of the map. If he took the road he increased the risk of encountering a patrol, but he would probably reach the building before daybreak. That would increase the odds that he could slip in the back door unobserved. On the other hand, if he went through the woods, he wouldn't need to worry about patrols, but then his last hundred meters would be fully exposed.

He looked to the heavens for guidance and chose the road. Eighteen breathless minutes later he arrived undetected at the back of the central building. Whether the patrols were infrequent, or he was just lucky, Alex did not know or care. Freedom was but a few feet away, and conditions were favorable. He tapped the Peitho printouts in his breast pocket with a sense of profound satisfaction.

Once he passed the front gate, he would take the bus to the metro and the metro to the center of Novosibirsk and the US Consulate. There he would work with the officer-in-charge to get himself on a plane home. Then he would team up with a couple of Agency friends and pay a visit to his old friend, Jason Stormer. *Yes, just a few steps more . . .*

Alex took a moment to catch his breath, and then held it again while sliding Yarik's card through the reader. The red diode turned to green with a friendly click, and he slipped inside. You couldn't get much closer to the fire than this.

Alex found himself standing near the toe end of an L-shaped hallway. There was an elevator a few yards farther down the dead-end hall to his right. To his left the hallway ran about ten yards and then turned right. Alex did not want to risk taking more than a moment to shake off the cold and get his uniform in order. The elevator doors could open at any time.

The hallway lights were still working on their nighttime dim setting, indicating that not many people had arrived yet, if any. *Excellent.* Now he had to work his way to the front of the building undetected and find a window from which he could watch the front gate. There he would wait for either a changing of the guard or the arrival of a large group of people before attempting his bold frontal retreat. Just a walk in the park. Nothing to be nervous about.

Alex had a general's uniform and a colonel's ID. That wasn't perfect, but at least the Soviets didn't share the Americans love of nametags. *No reason to worry, Alex, guards never pay much attention to people leaving, right?*

No sooner had Alex turned the corner into a long corridor and begun his homeward march than the hallway lights brightened. Had he tripped a motion detector? Activated a surveillance camera? Neither. Two other people were walking his way from the other end.

It was a long corridor, probably fifty yards or so. He continued walking at the same pace while his mind raced ahead, trying to get an early read. They did not look like a security detail. One was in uniform; the other was not. Alex began willing them to turn into an office before they reached him, and he slowed his pace to improve those odds.

Natural, natural, try to look natural. What! Holy shit! It's Anna.

The KGB officer with Anna had his right arm tightly around her left bicep. It was not a gentlemanly escort. The sight flipped a switch in Alex's brain, releasing chemicals and reactivating the predator within.

The pair was ten yards away and closing with no one else in the hallway. Alex turned to the doorway on his right and pretended to fumble in his pocket for keys. Then, as the couple walked past behind him, he whipped his right elbow back and around and smashed it into the man's nose with all the fury he was feeling. The crack was sickening, but only Anna was there to hear it. Fortunately she didn't scream. Alex continued his pivot and caught the KGB major by the throat as he dropped. Squeezing hard and moving fast, Alex used his free hand to open the door. Then he propelled the stunned officer inside.

"Close the door, Anna."

Alex had planned to pinch the man's carotids until he passed out, but now he saw that this would not be necessary. His elbow had punched the cartilage from the major's nose up into his brain. He was dead. *Wow.* Alex knew that this was possible, but he had never done it before—it was hard to find volunteers for practice. His drill instructors would be proud.

He looked up at Anna and felt a rush of affection.

"Are you okay?"

Anna nodded. Her eyes were wide as saucers.

He took her arm and led her to a chair. "Why don't you sit down for a second?"

Alex looked around. They were in a storage room full of dusty metal desks and filing cabinets and other odds and ends. *Someone was watching over him.* He grabbed the major's corpse by the heels and dragged it to the back of the room, where he stuffed it into the foot-well of a desk.

Then he paused in thought, nodded to himself, and ducked back under the desk for a demotion. A moment later Alex was a major. Now he was underranked versus Andrey's identification—he couldn't use Maximov's ID since the guards almost certainly knew him—but at least he was less conspicuous.

He walked over to where Anna was sitting and crouched in front of her.

"What happened?"

"They came looking for you," she began, sobbing. Then Anna pulled herself together and told him everything.

When she got to the scene where she stood her ground against the general, Alex added *toughest* to the list of superlatives he could use to describe Anna. When she had finished Alex took both her hands and said, "I'm so sorry to have gotten you into this, Anna. All I can do to make it up to you is help you to get out of it safely. Do you trust me to do that?"

"Of course I do."

"Good. Here's what you need to do . . ."

After Alex finished he made her repeat everything back, twice.

Anna seemed stunned, but then who wouldn't be. Her life might never be the same again. It certainly wouldn't be anytime soon. Although they needed to move, he gave her a minute to breathe deeply and let his instructions sink in. He needed the minute himself to figure out one last problem.

When at last Anna looked up, Alex handed her a copy of the Peitho list. "Anna, on your way out of town, I want you to go to the church and hide this in the spine of the big Bible when nobody is looking. It's my backup."

"Okay. Why there?"

"Your apartment is clearly out, as is your mother's. And you can't entrust it to friends without endangering them. The US Consulate isn't an alternative because they will have it watched the moment they find you missing. Actually the KGB probably has somebody permanently inside."

"Okay. But Alex, how will you find me?"

He felt a surge of emotion but pushed it aside. There was no time for anything but action. "We'll use a simple code. Leave a note in the care of Father Nikoli, a message for him to pass to Father Fyodor Fedin."

She nodded again.

Poor girl. He had dragged her into the deep end of his dangerous world. It was time to change the subject. Alex looked at his watch: ten to eight, time to get moving. "All right now, you need to compose yourself. You've got to walk out that front door looking calm and relieved."

"I don't understand why you can't go with me, Alex."

"We have to get at least one copy of that list out of here. Splitting up doubles our chances. Besides, together we would draw more attention than alone, and we need to leverage every advantage we can find. Don't you worry. I'll be watching. If you get stopped at the gate just tell them Major Maximov released you. If that doesn't work, I'll show up and try to bluff us both out."

She didn't look convinced, and Alex didn't blame her. He wasn't either.

"And you'll be right behind me?"

"Once I see you catch the bus back to town, I'll be walking out the door myself. Believe me, I want out of here just as badly as you do." Alex sounded so confident he almost convinced himself.

Five minutes later Alex felt the weight of the world slip from his shoulders as he watched Anna board a bus. She had passed through the exit booth wearing the perfect combination of righteous indignation mixed with fear and relief on her beautiful face. Now the Peitho victim list was out, and Anna would be okay—as long as she followed his instructions.

Alex had read the bus schedule the day before. It ran to and from the metro every ten minutes weekday mornings and afternoons, bringing workers in and out. And there was one now. *Alex Ferris takes on the KGB, and wins!* His daily billing rate had just doubled.

The next bus approached as scheduled, exactly ten minutes later. He had felt all six hundred seconds but had not doubted that the bus would come. There were advantages to the precision of a military economy. Alex was pleased to see that there was also a jeep on approach. It would add to the confusion. Ironically, it looked like the same one he had ridden in, or rather under, a couple of hours earlier. The ships that passed in the night had come full circle.

Like the entry, the compound's exit was an intimidating gauntlet. It was a glass booth with magnetically sealed doors at both ends. With the combined distraction of a busload of passengers and a jeep seeking entry, Alex stepped into the exit booth. His timing couldn't have been better.

Standing there before the guards, his mind screaming, "Just buzz me through," while his face struggled to remain indifferent, he waited for the clicks that would set him free. *Was this what restaurant lobsters felt like?*

As the first door locked behind him, Alex began silently singing to himself. *One hundred bottles of beer on the wall, one hundred bottles of beer . . .* But instead of hearing the second click, the one announcing his freedom, he heard a car door slam. Alex followed the guard's gaze and turned around to see a man in a general's uniform running toward him. This couldn't be good. *His* uniform was probably real. The general stopped before the door and stared in at him. Alex met his eye and saw a flash of recognition. *Again?* He was feeling more famous than Michael Jackson.

Then the booth began filling with gas.

CHAPTER 57

Palo Alto, California

Victor lay on the guest room bed and busied himself by tossing Elaine's antique teddy bear up into the air, playing chicken with the ceiling fan. Two doors down, Elaine was reading *Dancing Shoes* to her sleepy-eyed girl, as oblivious to her impending fate as a fish to a hook.

Victor had weighed the decision for a week, the risks and rewards of another murder. In the end, the possibility that Elaine had assisted Alex tipped the scale against her. That pissed Victor off. They had a deal, an arrangement, a *quid pro quo*. He didn't kill Kimberly, and she was his bitch. If she had reneged, all bets were off.

Victor's change of plan, his decision to disappear, had toppled the first domino. Once he oversaw the remaining sabotage at United Electronics and MicroComp, his Knyaz job would be complete. He would have assured Knyaz AG's position at the forefront of three booming industries. His twenty-percent interest would be worth billions. He could buy his island, have women flown in and out with the groceries and trash, and enjoy the rewards of his life's labor. It would be perfect—unless someone was looking for him.

The way to avoid that, of course, was to tie up every loose end. Yarik had taught him as much. The only person left in America who might suspect his identity was Elaine. Alex's meddling had frayed the knot. She could be the difference between a carefree life in a bungalow, and a cowering life in a fortress, between breathing easy, and holding his breath. He gave teddy another toss. No, not that tough a decision after all.

The time to act was now. Completing the sabotage would take a week, ten days at most. Then he would pay daddy a surprise visit to deliver the news, pick up his Knyaz AG stock, and vanish. Once comfortably and anonymously ensconced in his new island life, he would contact his KGB boss and inform him of his decision to retire. Victor was still three years short of twenty years of service, and his action would be highly irregular, but they would let him go. Since his KGB boss had no knowledge of Peitho, Victor's results had appeared miraculous. He had allowed his boss to take the credit for those miracles in Moscow, and that put him in Victor's debt big time.

Victor had spent two prior evenings in and around Elaine's house, studying her from the shadows and learning her routines. After putting Kimberly to bed, she would change into her bathrobe and slippers and begin drawing a bath in her deep Roman tub. Then, while the tub filled, she would zip down to the kitchen to pack Kimberly's lunch and flip through a magazine over a cup of tea. Tonight, Victor would slip from the guest bedroom into the linen closet in the master bath while she sipped her tea, completely unaware that she only had minutes to live. Her god had nothing on him.

Once Elaine finished her tea, she would come back upstairs and hop in the tub with the water still running, waiting for it to hit the perfect level. When she moved to turn the faucet off, Victor would slip out behind her and release Medusa. Even if she should happen to see or sense his approach, there would be little she could do. One paralyzing puff and it would be over. While she lay paralyzed in the tub, he would slit her wrists with a razor blade.

Her death would look like a cut-and-dried suicide to the investigating detective. There would be no struggle, and she would be in the bathtub of her own accord, as was her normal routine. Lord knew the police were gullible enough to lap that easy explanation right up, at least if the Frank Ferris murder were any indication. Victor was not pleased that the kid would find her mother that way. It would be traumatic, to say the least. But in the end, Kimberly was going to lose her mother anyway, so what did it really matter?

The only tactical downside to the plan was that there was no way for him to work sex into the equation. He had thought about using one of the killer condoms Yarik had sent him. Thought about, hell, he had racked his brains for a way to use one. Unfortunately, the evidence of copulation would raise too many questions. Given all the other events that had happened, the police might not buy into the heart-attack scenario that the condom supported. Such a shame. Victor still remembered the note that Yarik had attached with the shipment—for use in sexecutions—and laughed. It did have a ring to it. He launched the teddy bear again.

The sound of a filling tub snapped Victor out of his fantasy. It was like the starting gun at a sporting event. As he rose from the bed, Victor realized that he had an erection.

A minute later he heard Elaine's soft footfalls going down the stairs. They were music to his ears. He felt like a maestro conducting a symphony of one—until his pager chimed a dreaded note, and the music stopped. Oh, how he hated that thing. He snatched it from his belt and read the unwelcome text: 001-111 SU326 SFO-SVO 2300 !!! "Nnnooooo," he mouthed a long, silent scream. It was a message from his father, urgent, priority one, drop everything else. He was booked on Aeroflot flight 326 for Moscow departing San Francisco in, he checked his watch, less than two hours. He would have to leave immediately. The "!!!" was clear enough: Drop everything and get to the airport at once. There were to be NO excuses.

Victor looked at his watch again. The tub took close to ten minutes to fill. There would not be time to dispose of Elaine properly. Victor refused to make the amateur mistake of deviating from his plan. That was how fools got caught. He would just have to pick up where he left off when he returned. Oh, but how he wanted to do her now. The juices were flowing, the plan was in place, and he was ready for action. Suppose he were to disobey his father . . .

CHAPTER 58

Novosibirsk, Siberia

Bloop . . . bloop . . . bloo-bloop . . . God, he hated that sound. Alex couldn't see, or smell, or taste, so the maddening bubbles were all he had. Bubbles and pain. Was that laughter in the background? Or was his mind conjuring phantoms, desperate for some diversion from the sound of his own ebbing life?

Bloop, bloop, bloop, bloop . . . When he was nine, he had overinflated the back tire of his Schwinn Sting-Ray and blown it up by mistake. Though his hands had stung, it was the "POP!—hiss" that scared him. He had dropped the bike and run home from the gas station with tears in his eyes . . . His lungs felt like that tire now. *Would they make the same POP!—hiss?*

Bloobloobloobloo . . . With his lungs at their limit, his carotids began thrashing like shackled snakes, and his neck began to crawl. Then the vipers latched their fangs on his optical nerves, and his eyes began to swell. Alex could take no more. *I'm sorry, Anna . . .*

Icy water sluiced his sinuses, sending shock waves surging through his skull. As their reverberations tore at tissue and bone, cascading flashes of searing white pain climaxed in an electric crack, and then—

♦ ♦ ♦

Alex jolted back into consciousness and a screaming headache. This was the third time he had gone through this. Or was it the fourth? It was tempting to pray for it all to be over, but Alex refused to let it come to that. He still had a mission to complete. People were relying on him. One hundred and sixteen names on a list.

As his world of pain came into focus, Alex realized that he was not hanging upside down this time. There was no barrel of icy water below. That was progress. The second environmental factor to break through the fog and fire to register on his bewildered mind was the horrible smell of sewer gas. Then the events of the past few—hours?—began to come back to him: the dunkings, the beatings, the blackouts.

Alex sat up. He was in a dark, damp box with crumbly concrete walls and a rusty iron door. He heard water dripping behind him but did not have the energy to turn around and inspect the source. He did not want to move at all for fear of bumping his tortured feet again. Tortured feet, that was it. That was what had awakened him. He had rolled in his delirium and slapped a raw foot against a rough wall.

As he sat there in the dark, images of the torture sessions began flashing through his mind like a medieval slide show. *Stop it, Alex. Don't think about what they've done to you, or what they might do to you next. Focus on how you're going to beat them.* He would have liked to say those words aloud, if for no other reason than to confirm that he could still speak, but he knew they would be listening, so he kept the pep talk to himself.

He heard footsteps and felt his heart begin to race in response. Then he heard a stubborn dead bolt scrape aside. The door groaned open, and Alex saw the bottom halves of two beefy soldiers.

"Get out here," one soldier said.

Alex took a meditative breath and crab walked out of the cell trying to keep the weight off his wailing feet. As soon as his shoulders cleared the door, the soldiers lifted him off the ground by the arms and sat him down on a small triangular stool in the middle of the room. They cuffed his hands behind him.

"Do not move."

Alex was in a round room with eight doors. Six of the doors were similar to the one that led to his own suite—short iron portals with heavy rusted hinges. Misery had company here. The six looked toward the center of the room like so many hopeless eyes, gloomily awaiting the answer to the question that now taunted Alex: Who or what would be coming through the main door?

It was time to find out. The soldiers opened the main door and took flanking positions outside. Then a man in the uniform of a KGB general walked into the room. He wore an appraising look on his handsome face that seemed to say, "So you're Alex Ferris. Let me have a look at you," but he said nothing. He just stared.

Alex recognized the general as the man who had captured him in the exit booth, but this second glance also gave him the impression that he knew the face from somewhere else. The plot was thickening.

The general took a long, slow walk around Alex's stool, then grabbed a chair from the side of the room and sat it down a couple of feet in front of Alex. "I am General Vasily Karpov of the KGB. You are Alex Ferris of the CIA. It's time we got acquainted."

"Yes," Alex said. "I've come a long way to meet you, Vasily." Alex saw a flash of displeasure cross his captor's face at the disrespectful use of his first name. There was something in the gesture that Alex found familiar. Perhaps their paths had crossed when he was with the CIA. Alex decided to put the momentary imbalance to work in his favor. "I know you from the Middle East, don't I, Vasily?"

The guards tensed in the doorway like bulldogs on leashes. They wanted a sign to attack, but none was forthcoming. "No, you don't. Tell me, Alex, why are you here?"

Karpov was offering him the choice between a pleasant conversation with a general and immediate return to the company of Frick and Frack. Smart guy.

Alex realized he was about to play a game of high-stakes brinksmanship with his hands bound behind his back and half his cognitive power tied up with pain suppression. Lovely. "I'm investigating a murder. What did you think I was doing here?"

"Whose murder?"

Alex knew it would be foolish to push for answers to his own questions, or to refuse outright to answer Karpov, but by asking questions himself, he was rewriting the rules. Perhaps he would find the right button and provoke an unscripted response.

Alex saw Karpov pulling at the hair on the backs of his fingers and realized he wasn't the only one under stress. Fancy that. "My brother's murder. Did you kill him?" Alex was not sure where he was going with this. He'd had no time to analyze or to plan. He was flying blind on intuition, hoping he didn't crash into a mountain or stall an engine. It was dangerous, but he would be in danger no matter what he did. Intuition was all he had.

"Of course not," Karpov said. Then he smiled. "My son did."

"Your son?"

"My son, Victor. Why—"

"Oh, you mean Jason?" Alex interjected, hoping to rattle Karpov. The general just nodded, appearing nonplussed.

"Why were you looking for your brother's murderer here?"

"My brother left a note. Was Yarik a friend of yours?" This time Alex got a flinch, and this time he recognized the face. Tumblers began falling into place, freeing locks in his mind and opening doors that Alex did not know were closed. As they swung open, his situation fell under a completely new light. Was it possible?

There was a buzzing in the background, but Alex ignored it. This was too big. His mind was sprinting, his pores were sweating . . . the noise came again.

"Answer me! What did the note say?"

With some effort Alex brought his eyes back into focus. "Have you ever been to Geneva?"

"Your brother left you a note that asked if you had ever been to Geneva?"

"No, Vasily, I'm asking you: Have you ever been to Geneva?"

"Not in your lifetime. Now—"

"The note said, 'The problems come from Irkutsk.' Alex's voice was shallow—not the best for this sort of game, but it was all he could muster. He looked up to watch Karpov's face while he asked the next question, and saw that the general was giving him a funny look. "When?" Alex asked. "When were you in Geneva?"

"Nineteen fifty-seven."

Karpov kept talking, but Alex did not hear. He could not process any more information than what his own mind was throwing at him. If he weren't a professional investigator . . . if it hadn't been bothering him for so long . . .

Even as the soldiers picked him off the stool and wrapped the rope around his ankles, Alex hardly noticed what was going on outside the confines of his mind.

CHAPTER 59

Novosibirsk, Siberia

As Karpov stood before the armored entrance to the interrogation suite, he found himself remembering the rumpled bed in Anna's apartment and picturing what had happened there. He was a professional interrogator, but this one was going to be personal. Alex had crossed the line.

Alex had now enjoyed a full twenty-four hours of Knyaz hospitality. According to the professionals, it took that long for a prisoner's new reality to sink in. Alex had already endured a rough stay, but now Karpov would really start turning the screws, Spanish-Inquisition style.

Karpov was secretly handicapped as to how far he could turn. Because he was going to frame Alex for killing Gorbachev, he could leave no traces of torture or coercion on Alex's body. That meant no chemicals, no cuts, no scrapes or holes, or even significant bruises. It was a shame, and it was a challenge, but Karpov was always up to those.

Alex's round-the-clock torture began with a dark, damp, decrepit old cell that was too short to stand up in and uncomfortable to lie in. Water dripped constantly from a small hole in the cell's ceiling down to an open sewer pipe on the floor, one just large enough for the rats to use. The trickle was Alex's drinking water, his washing water, and his toilet. Aside from the drip . . . drip . . . drip, the only other attractions in the cell were the Judas peephole and a trough bolted to the door. The trough caught the tasteless slop that a custodian poured in through a pipe once a day to keep Alex alive. The pros said holding cells were supposed to dishearten, humble, weaken, and drain their occupants. Surely his version would rate a ten.

To further Alex's mental destabilization, Karpov was making every effort to remove all psychological grounding. He established no routines, except for the lack thereof. He scheduled feedings, beatings, and interrogation sessions to take place at odd intervals and to last different lengths of time. Last night, for example, after one four-hour session, the guards returned Alex to his cell for just twelve minutes before coming to get him again.

The physical tortures Karpov selected for Alex were classics, tried and true. Bastinado, beating the bottoms of his feet, caused blinding pain without leaving marks. As a fringe benefit, this torture also made it very painful to walk, thereby furthering Alex's sense of helplessness and dashing his hopes of escape. Karpov was pleased to receive a report that before the third session, just the sight of the cane was enough to make Alex whimper. *Try and take my girl, will you . . .*

Then there was the water torture. Karpov would have dreaded this one himself most of all. To begin with, the guards hung Alex upside down by a rope with his hands bound to his sides. Then, after a random interval, they dropped him headfirst and waist deep into a barrel of icy water. There Alex thrashed about like a fish on a line until he passed out. Then the guards pulled him out, revived him, and did it again. Wash, rinse, repeat . . .

Water torture was a great conditioner. Each dunking was nearly the psychological equivalent of dying, and the headaches it caused were blinding. Yet, like the bastinado, it left no marks when properly administered. Karpov would toss in a few other favorites as the week progressed, but for now it was an acceptable repertoire. He kept a defibrillator on hand just in case.

Excruciating though these torments were, the physical part of the regimen was mundane enough. For the most part, Karpov left it to the guards. The psychological tortures, on the other hand, Karpov conducted personally.

Oddly enough, he felt a connection with Alex, an intuitive understanding of his gestures and moods. Perhaps it was the side effect of a mutual love for the same woman. Perhaps it was the intellectual parity Karpov rarely shared. In any case, that connection facilitated his ability to hone in on Alex's pressure points.

The unwelcome corollary was the fact that Alex seemed to have the same read on him. From what Karpov could gather, Alex had known someone like him either in Geneva or the Middle East. Karpov had never been to the Middle East. He had spent a summer in Geneva during his Academy years, but that was before Alex was born. It occurred to Karpov that Alex might have cracked during the six-hour warm-up session that preceded their first chat. It was time to find out.

The interrogation suite had a large round room at its center with eight doors around the perimeter. The one Karpov had just walked through opened to the tunnel that connected the KGB offices with the Knyaz command center. Six of the other doors led to holding cells. The seventh was directly across from the entrance. That special door had the international sign for radiation boldly painted on its thick leaden surface and looked as inviting as a coroner's slab.

As Karpov passed through the interrogation suite, he admired the props: the knives, the cables, and the dunking tank. *Medieval* was the adjective that leapt to mind, but it was inadequate. The dark art had progressed a lot in six hundred years. He walked to the storage cabinet and selected a revolver.

Karpov opened the leaden door to find Ferris placed as instructed. He was alone in the room, sitting on a special small stool with his arms bound behind. The stool's tiny surface sloped forward, forcing Ferris to hold himself upright with either his feet, which were in agony from the bastinado, or his hands, which he had to twist painfully against the ropes to gain a hold. Alex did not have the option of falling to the floor, as a taught noose ran from the ceiling down to his neck.

Karpov found it effective to let his prisoners contemplate suicide. It distanced them that much further from their god. Of course, he would not allow Alex to kill himself, but Alex didn't know that.

Karpov walked over to his prisoner and removed the noose. Alex looked at him with an expression that resembled pity. *Where was that coming from? Perhaps Alex really had cracked. Or perhaps that's just what he wants you to think. Ignore it.*

Karpov began with the words that would henceforth start every session: "Perhaps we are meant to talk, Alex, perhaps we are not." Then he held up the revolver for Alex to see. With some ceremony, he placed a single bullet in the chamber, closed it, and gave the revolver a long spin. When it stopped he nodded with satisfaction, placed the barrel against Alex's forehead, looked him in the eye, and said, "Remind you of Frank?" Then he pulled the trigger. *Click.*

There was that look again. Ignore it! "All right, Alex, we talk," Karpov said, putting deliberate indifference in his voice. He removed the bullet from the gun, placed it back in his pocket, and set the gun down on the floor.

As with everything that took place during a professional interrogation, the Russian roulette served a purpose. Karpov had designed it to shatter any hope Alex might have that he or anything he had to say was particularly important. Of course since Karpov needed Alex alive, there was no gunpowder in the bullet, but Alex didn't know that either.

The room they were in was a very special one. The sign on the door was for real. This was the anteroom of a radiation chamber. The army had used the machine in the adjacent lead-lined room during the 1950s to conduct experiments on the effects of radiation. Stalin had wanted to know how long his men could continue to fight in a nuclear hot zone, and several hundred political prisoners had given him the answer.

Karpov discovered the machine in 1983, gathering dust in the basement of one of the research centers under his purview. A very different use for the machine had sprung to his mind, and he had it moved to this location beneath a veil of secrecy.

Acting on Karpov's orders, the guards had seated Alex so he faced the lead-shielded door and its radiation warnings. He wanted his prisoner's imagination to run wild with the possibilities. It helped set the mood.

He sat down so that his lips were just a couple centimeters from Alex's ear, and began whispering a story that would convince the Devil himself not to trifle with Vasily Karpov. "We're ten meters below ground, Alex. Above our heads is an abandoned nuclear power plant. I'm sure you've seen it. It is abandoned because people believe that flawed engineering led to the accidental release of dangerous amounts of radiation. The locals also believe that accident caused the death of twenty-five of their own."

Karpov leaned back in his chair and pulled a cigar from his pocket. He took his time trimming the end, letting Alex's imagination plow forward before lighting it with a long cedar match. "Have you ever seen a man die from radiation poisoning? It's not a pretty sight. Kind of like a severe sunburn that runs all the way through the body. It's horrible to see the macerated skin peeling off on the outside, but worse yet is the realization that the same process is taking place throughout the body, on the inside."

Karpov could tell by the stillness of the air that he had reached Alex with that image, so he continued. "I'll let you in on a little secret." He paused to exhale a long stream of smoke. "There was no accident here. The reactor above our heads had no leak. I used the machine behind that door to create an illusion." He brushed the smoke aside with a magician's wave.

Alex whipped his head around to strike at Karpov with a venomous look, but Karpov just smiled back. "You see, I needed to be sure that I would have a place to work in absolute secrecy. Fences and pass codes only go so far if a man is determined to get around them. You proved that yourself just yesterday. The only foolproof way to keep people out is to make them want to keep out. And want to keep out they do. The locals would sooner visit a leper colony than poke around my headquarters.

"Unfortunately even the worst of memories fade, so every year I stoke the legend by disposing of a bothersome chap or two," he gestured toward the leaded portal, "In most cases, I leave the scarecrows in until they're, shall we say, fully cooked. It takes about twenty minutes. It is the humane thing to do, you see. But those who have particularly offended me . . . well, I leave them *al dente*.

"Using a file prepared for Stalin, I determined that seven minutes is the optimum exposure for such people. It takes them twelve to twenty-four of the most agonizing hours imaginable to die. Here, I've brought along a few photos that I thought might amuse you." He spread a series of grotesque body shots out on the floor and then stood up and moved aside to leave Alex with nothing but the photos to focus on.

Alex squirmed at the sight of the horrific images. People always did. Karpov paced behind him, continuing in the same, nonchalant monotone. "We immediately take the irradiated trespassers back to the city so they can spend their final hours refreshing the memories of the locals on the dangers of climbing the fence."

Karpov saw hope flash across Alex's face, right on cue. "I can see what you're thinking, Alex, but you're wrong. There is no chance that you would be able to reveal anything during your final hours. After that much radiation the human mind is not capable of focusing on anything but the pain." Karpov took a long draw on his cigar. "Are you beginning to see where you could fit into all of this, Alex?"

♦ ♦ ♦

Karpov sat in his KGB office, enjoying his lunch and reflecting on what he had learned during the three-hour session with Alex. He was concerned that Alex had help inside Russia. The surprising thing was that although Alex admitted to receiving assistance from a man named Andrey Demerko, he truly knew almost nothing about why. Of course, it had not been easy for Alex to convince Karpov of that fact, but in the end Karpov had to accept it. No man would have endured that pressure if the release valve were at his disposal. All Alex had was a name—backed up by the identity papers they had found on him—and a description.

Karpov had run Andrey Demerko's name through the computers while Alex was unconscious. The result was both startling and concerning. He was the foreign minister's chief of staff. Why would such a man want to help an American private investigator? Karpov would mull that one over tonight, scotch in hand, before his chessboard.

Karpov knew precious little about Foreign Minister Sugurov. He was the one member of Gorbachev's cabinet who refused protection from the Guards' Directorate, preferring instead to use troops from his own alma mater, the army. Enter Demerko. Karpov used to have one of Sugurov's deputies in his pocket, Leo somebody, but the man had died a few months earlier when a small plane collided with his helicopter, on a Knyaz errand, no less. Karpov had not gotten around to replacing Leo yet. Apparently, that was a bad move. He made a note to plant someone in Sugurov's camp ASAP.

CHAPTER 60

Lake Baikal, Siberia

Victor was pissed. He had been in a perpetual state of pissedoffness for five days now, ever since the pager ripped him from Elaine's execution and brought him to this frozen wasteland.

He had come close to blowing off his father and going through with the kill. He had been so psyched up, so excited to see Elaine's helpless, naked body, to explain the price of betrayal and look into her eyes as she understood what was happening. Ooh, how he had yearned to whisper it all in her ear while she watched her own life ebb away into crimson waters.

He had hesitated there in her closet, torn between that desire and the fear of his father's wrath. Then he focused on the big picture, realized that this trip to Russia would give him the chance he needed to pick up his Knyaz AG stock, and made the decision.

What was the reward for his obedience? Life in the freezer. He felt the way a TV dinner looked before you zapped it. This doubled his resolve not to be Karpov's triggerman and potentially forever out in the cold.

As much as he hated to admit it, Victor did understand his father's logic. Victor's slipup with Alex had initiated the chain of events that first killed Yarik and now jeopardized the whole Knyaz operation. Of course, part of his father's choice of action was probably just venting his frustration about not having Yarik around anymore to do this kind of thing, but Victor wasn't about to bring that up. He was looking forward to venting some of his own frustrations on the Zaitseva woman.

Victor was still stunned at the news that Alex had bested Yarik. Victor would miss the old bulldog. There must be more to the story than what Karpov reported Alex had revealed, but who knows? Of all the secrets to try to conceal during an interrogation, why would you choose that one? Regardless, Victor was glad not to be the only Knyaz member Alex had outmaneuvered.

Although Victor left San Francisco Tuesday night, he had not arrived in Academic City until Thursday afternoon, local time. A lot had happened while he was in flight. Karpov had ordered an intense, systematic search of the whole region for Anna Zaitseva when only one of the two printed copies of Peitho victims was found on Alex. "Find her! Get the list! Bring them both to me, intact!"

Karpov had stationed agents at airports and train stations. He had them set up roadblocks and search hotels. KGB agents had interviewed all Anna's friends and relatives. Victor knew "interrogated" was probably a more appropriate term, but nonetheless it had produced nothing. Anna and her mother had vanished.

By the time Victor arrived on the scene, most of the agents were standing around scratching their heads, trying to avoid the general's flaming gaze. Their predicament was a tough one. Siberia was a big region, bigger than the continental United States, and it offered a lot of remote nooks and crannies to hide in. Without discovering a trail, uncovering any clues, or receiving a big break, the search was a hopeless cause—at least in the short term.

Victor brought a fresh mind to the search and grasped the essence of the problem almost immediately. He then took a more deliberate, delicate approach than his predecessors had employed. It wasn't easy. He felt like Sherlock Holmes working on the heels of the Gestapo. A lot of dust had been kicked up, and the resulting cloud worked to conceal any clues.

Victor proved his genius on the evening of his second day in Siberia, but only to himself. He kept his discovery a secret. He liked to present things *fait accompli* whenever possible, and especially when his father was involved. It was the only way to avoid being wrong.

The genius was the insight to go through the photo albums at Anna's mother's house. The *Gestapo* had already done this when they ransacked the place, but they were looking for the Peitho list and people to squeeze rather than clues. They had left the photo albums strewn among a pile of books on the floor. Victor noted that most of the latter were in English, and filed that fact away for later reference.

After an hour of relatively thoughtful perusal, Victor had yelled "Bingo!" The KGB soldiers responded with a clueless look. "Guess you guys don't play that here yet. Give it a couple of years." They still looked confused, but to hell with them. He had found a cottage, a dacha that appeared and reappeared in photos from different years, even though there was no dacha currently registered to anyone in the Zaitsev family.

Victor knew the Zaitsevs had owned a dacha when Anna's father was still alive, but had sold it years ago after his death. The KGB had searched it anyway before Victor's arrival. They had interrogated the whole surrounding village as well. That had proved to be a waste of time. But this was a different dacha.

This dacha was on a large lake, a lake that the locals subsequently claimed could only be Lake Baikal. That was when Victor got an ecology lesson. Although Baikal's surface area wasn't anything out of the ordinary in the global sense—each of America's Great Lakes covered roughly the same geography—Lake Baikal's depth was extraordinary. Baikal was so deep, they explained, that it held more than a quarter of the world's fresh water supply. While none of this meant more than a *Jeopardy* question to Victor, the fact that the geological anomaly gave rise to thousands of species of flora and fauna that didn't exist anywhere else, was golden. Victor had found his big break.

He rounded up the appropriate experts. From the position of the sun, the view of the shorelines, and the date stamps on the photos, they were able to determine the region of Baikal where the photos were shot. That gave Victor a grid square on which to focus. Of course, there was no guarantee that Anna had gone to the dacha, and for that reason he did not tell his father of this discovery, but Victor was certain that he would find her there. It was only a matter of time.

Victor, a KGB major by rank, immediately commandeered six two-soldier teams and a helicopter. It took them three hours to fly the seven hundred kilometers southeast to the appropriate section of Lake Baikal. That seemed to take forever. He was anxious to bag his victory, retrieve his shares, and head for the tropics. This was going to be it, he had decided. Once he delivered the girl, he'd make a quick trip back through California to eliminate Elaine and pack a few bags, and then he would vanish. He could manage the remaining sabotage by telephone.

Victor directed the pilot to land in the front yard of the small, centrally located hotel he'd picked out, and then proceeded to appropriate it as their field post. A dozen snowmobiles and a jeep were already waiting, compliments of the local KGB. He quickly assigned each pair of agents a zone to search, gave them photos of the dacha and instructions on what to do when they found it, and let slip the dogs of war.

"When you find the dacha you are not to approach it. Is that understood?"

"Yes, sir," they replied in chorus.

"You are to sit back out of sight and radio for me. I will join you to make the bust personally. Is that understood?"

"Yes, sir."

He knew it could take a while. There were trails rather than roads that connected many of the dachas to civilization, and the snow was deep. Victor paced for an hour, fantasizing about life on Emily Island as he waited for his radio to bring good news. Once he tired of that he sat down to perfect his interrogation strategy.

The photos of Anna had inspired the strategy Victor would use to crack her. He was busy refining the details when his radio sparked to life.

"Team Six to Base, Team Six to Base, over."

"This is the Base. What do you have, Team Six?"

"We've found the nest."

CHAPTER 61

Novosibirsk, Siberia

Alex was holding his own. After six days of captivity, he still had his wits about him and his brains within him. Furthermore, he had disclosed nothing of significance, at least not any of the five secrets he deemed most crucial. Ironically, he had obtained one of those secrets during his capture. That one was so poisonous that he not only had to withhold it from Karpov, but Alex had to keep it from himself as well. Doing so proved to be problematic. He found it possible to redirect his conscious thoughts, forcing them to focus elsewhere, forbidding them to scratch the itch. But he was helpless to hobble his dreams. They would wander where they wished.

The rancid facts swirled around his sleeping mind like chunks of fetid meat in a malevolent stew: the quick marriage, his mother's secret, his father's distance, the nervous habit, the facial expressions, Jason a Russian, Geneva in fifty-seven . . . Alex had traveled twelve thousand miles to find his brother's killer. He had found his biological father instead.

Looking at the facts en masse, it was clear to Alex that his mother had consummated an affair with Karpov shortly before her whirlwind betrothal to his father. Given the excitement of youth and the romance of a foreign land, Alex found his mother's *joie de vivre* easy to understand. Of course, people may not have been so understanding back then. Keeping the world ignorant—Frank, Karpov, and himself included—must have seemed to be a simple solution to a complicated situation.

Alex had not been expecting anything like this. He had never consciously questioned that his mother's husband was his biological father, but now he realized that the doubts had been percolating beneath the surface all along. It took a bizarre congregation of horrendous events to bring all the pieces together, but once juxtaposed they formed a perfect square. Perfect? Maybe not. But Alex knew it was a lock. And he knew how to prove it to Karpov. But he had decided not to.

This restraint was not his first impulse. To the contrary, restraint was quite the opposite. He would have spilled the beans on the spot if they had not resumed the water torture before he recovered from the shock. After the Brothers Grimm were done with his bedtime story, Alex had anxiously awaited his next opportunity to tell Karpov the truth, and when that meeting proved to be too long coming, he had even screamed through the door to "Bring me the general!" But when Karpov at last arrived, Alex found intuition holding his tongue.

It took him a while to grasp the intuitive with his conscious mind, but he eventually found a hold. Alex was dangling from the edge of sanity by weary hands. If he suddenly became someone else, if he allowed himself to be Alex Karpov, he was likely to lose his precarious grip on reality. To do anything other than to ignore this new information would be to lose the identity that grounded him—and then it would all be over.

Now Alex was back in the radiation room antechamber, waiting for his father—*stop it!*—waiting for Karpov to arrive.

To the best of Alex's knowledge, he had been there once a day, every day, for the past six days. He wished he were certain. Keeping track of time was crucial to his escape plan.

During his Special Forces training, Alex had learned techniques for tracking time. Studies have shown that POWs who keep track of time maintain a stronger bond with their previous lives and convictions than those who lose their orientation. Accordingly, those soldiers who know *when* they are, are also better equipped to withstand interrogation. No one can hold out indefinitely, but in war, hours can make a crucial difference.

Although his mind had become thoroughly disoriented during the early hours and days of his imprisonment, his body's clock was still working. He had been trained to pay attention to the fact that his bowels would know what time it was for a day or two, regardless of how many times he was knocked unconscious. Alex used that grace period to pick up on the other cues that would henceforth allow him to scratch hash marks on the wall. He studied the guards' five-o'clock shadows, sought patterns in the cycles of ambient noise, and tracked the appearance of nocturnal rodents.

Ah, the rodents. The living conditions were, to put it mildly, far from humane. Again, Alex's military training and experience with a Turk dying in a well had taught him how to cope. He definitely was not enjoying himself, but he was in reasonably good spirits, all things considered. He understood that it all boiled down to what he chose to spend his time thinking about.

Alex's first rule was to refuse to think about his present condition or to speculate on his future. Full stop. He knew that such thoughts would only stoke the fire that fueled feelings of longing and self-pity. At the end of the day, he might be stuck in the proverbial well again, but at least at this very moment he was not drowning, and the dogs that held him here were no less fallible than the pair he and Mehmet had bested.

One technique he used was analyzing the happenings around him as though he were watching a movie. Rather than sitting in dread, he made it a game to guess what would happen next and to coach the film's hero accordingly. When he tired of that, he thought back to the cases he had studied or the novels he had read, always third-person experiences with vivid scenes he could step into, thereby stepping out of his own. He did his best to carry those images over into his dreams, leaving that part of his life unchanged, except for the scheduling.

The other thing Alex did to keep his mind busy with disciplined thoughts was working to recall and repeat the names from the Peitho list. After five days of fishing the canals of his mind, he could recite ninety-four of the 'hundred-sixteen.

Then there was torture time. They attacked him physically, and he fought back mentally. When they beat his feet, he pretended he was an Israelite, wandering through the desert on burning sand: salvation just ahead. When they dunked his head it was a river baptism, bringing him closer to God. As for the radiation-room antechamber, well, that was the lion's den, so call me Daniel. In all cases, he convinced himself that there was a happy ending waiting. The technique kept him afloat. Alex had, after all, survived worse. He knew he would not be able to keep it up for long. Soon the sleep deprivation and lack of nourishment would turn his brain to mush. But he wasn't planning to be there long. Alex suspected that wasn't Karpov's plan either.

Regardless of his mind games, dealing with the pain was all but unbearable. Try as you might, it's virtually impossible to distract your senses when the pros go to work. But with creativity, faith, and a lack of options, he was adapting to it. Like any physical regimen, each day became easier. The toughest part was knowing he had that escape valve there in his hand. All he had to do was tell Karpov . . .

Psychologically, the Russian roulette was especially tough. Even the Dalai Lama would be pressed to disregard the business end of a revolver pressed to his head. Fortunately, Karpov's gun backfired, figuratively speaking. It backfired when it occurred to Alex that none of the other tortures they were subjecting him to were seriously life threatening or even physically scarring. That indicated to him that Karpov wanted him alive and unblemished, for some propaganda ploy, no doubt. Thus, he reasoned, the revolver was rigged.

Knowing that he had figured out Karpov's bluff somehow made Alex more powerful, and his captor weaker. It was a major morale boost. Of course, he still flinched every time Karpov pulled the trigger.

Alex had done something else to increase his power. He had generated it. He had leveraged the fact that they wanted things from him. They wanted the location of the Peitho list. They wanted the location of Anna Zaitseva. They wanted to know if Elaine had betrayed them. And they would want to know that he had changed the Peitho codes in their database.

The tactic he employed to generate that power and outwit Karpov was to bury those answers. Alex mentally filed them beneath a pile of potentially, seemingly, possibly valuable information, information that he could cough up instead of what was asked for when the pain was too much to bear. Alex built the disinformation pile wide, and he built it tall, filling his mind with elaborate stories, plans, and conjectures. Red herrings all, he generated them by mixing a healthy imagination with the few facts he did know.

"Tell me!"

"It's Krasnoyarsk."

"What?"

"Krasnoyarsk. They're on to you in Krasnoyarsk."

"Who's on to me?"

"The Canadians."

"What Canadians . . . ?"

Like all games, Alex did not expect it to go on forever. He was playing for time.

Time was what Alex needed. It was his worst enemy, and his best friend. When he concocted it, his escape plan had required him to endure another five days at the Karpov Hilton. It had seemed like forever back then. If one counted how much he aged during those five days, it was probably comparable to five years. But once he had made the plan, once he had decided on the timeline, he, Alex Ferris, was in charge. He was the one keeping himself in the cell, subjecting himself to the best the KGB had to offer, and taking it like a man. That perspective had made all the difference. Now he had almost made it. Now he only had to last until nightfall.

During his second day in captivity, they threw another prisoner into his three-by-five cell with him, some poor soul who was even more expendable than he. The boy could barely talk. Without his gold-framed glasses, it took Alex a while to figure out who he was.

Karpov gave the two of them a few hours to get reacquainted, then he ran Sergey over the coals for a day and a half, returning him briefly to Alex's side after each new adventure. On Alex's fourth day, they threw Sergey back in the cell with only a few minutes left to live. Henceforth, when he wasn't in session, Alex lived with Sergey's corpse and the sewer rats that enjoyed it.

Barbaric though it was, Alex recognized that the Sergey scenario was a solid tactic on Karpov's part. He was using Sergey's torture and death to elicit feelings of guilt, the one emotion that experts know can undermine even the toughest resolve. The unstated argument was that Alex had done this to Sergey when he deceived him in Irkutsk. Alex wasn't buying. He was here to save the likes of little Kimberly. There was no guilt to be found along that path.

During his tenure as Karpov's guest, Alex had enjoyed one brief glimmer of sunshine. The custodian who brought his food the second day smiled through the peephole. He smiled with kindness in his eyes, and Alex reckoned that his glance was more nourishing than a T-bone steak. But his friend never returned. Alex figured this had been just one more way of dashing hope, of making him confront the helplessness of his situation. He even began to wonder if it had been a hallucination—the first sign of madness. He would probably never know, so like all other speculation, he put it out of his mind.

Alex had also learned a few things about Karpov during those days. Interrogators try to avoid giving away information about themselves, but they can't work in a vacuum. Karpov was desperate to know where Anna had gone and what she had done with the copy of the Peitho list Alex had given her.

Alex had tried denying that there was another copy, but the printer server kept a record: two pages, two copies. It was a shame the exit-booth gas had overcome him before he could eat his own printout. Maybe they wouldn't have checked the server.

Karpov also made a mistake or two. He screwed up by pretending that his men had arrested Anna when she got off the bus, and that she was now enjoying a hospitality suite and recreational program similar to Alex's own. "We just need you to confirm her story. If your story matches hers, it will confirm that she told us the truth, and then her interrogation can stop."

It would have worked on an amateur, but Alex had studied the art. Karpov eventually had no choice but to backtrack; otherwise he could not inquire about where Anna had gone, or what she had done with the list. That slip-up bought Alex a day. He held out for another before admitting what Karpov already knew, that she had taken a copy of the list with her. Then Alex denied knowledge of where she had gone or what she had done with the list. It was half-true, and he knew Karpov could sense that. *Good.*

Yesterday, after a couple hours on the rack—the latest addition to *Karpov's Dark Ages Review*—Alex had finally admitted that Anna had stashed the list somewhere on his orders. Alex hoped this would take the pressure off the search for her, but knew that was probably wishful thinking. Today, Karpov would force him to reveal that location—right on schedule. What was in store for him before then? More of the rack? A man could never be too tall.

Alex looked up at the leaden entrance to the radiation chamber and smiled. This was the homestretch. It was do-or-die day, and his soul was prepared.

The door behind him slammed open as if on cue, and Karpov entered. The moment he came into view, Alex could tell that Karpov was thoroughly incensed. This time it didn't feel like a ruse.

Then Alex saw what Karpov held in his hand, and he knew it was going to be a very bad day indeed. This was not what he had been expecting.

CHAPTER 62

Lake Baikal, Siberia

Victor was pleased. Team Six had found the dacha in the photos at four o'clock on the first day of the search. It was his third day in Russia, Anna's fifth day in hiding. Father would be proud.

The cabin was only about fifteen kilometers from where Victor had set up base, so he decided to take a jeep rather than the helicopter. If it was Anna, he did not want the noise to give her any warning. Team Six reported that they had not seen Anna, or anybody else, for that matter, but they were sure that somebody was living there as the fireplace was in use and there were two sets of female footprints in the snow.

Per Victor's instructions, the leader of Team Six met him where they had parked their snowmobiles, down the road from the dacha. "There's been no activity since our call, sir."

"Good. Have your partner wait around back while we go to the door. I don't want to take any chances."

As they approached the front door, Victor said, "You wait back here, out of sight." He did not bother trying to explain to the man why a heavy hand could be strategically counterproductive. It was enough that Victor himself knew that the interrogation would start the moment he rapped on the door, and here again he wanted to be more Sherlock Holmes than Gestapo.

When no one answered his knock, Victor shouted, "I can see the smoke from your fire. Please open the door." He was sure the soldier behind him was rolling his eyes at his geniality, but Victor didn't care. He wasn't the ignorant thug.

A bolt drew back, the door opened with a squeak, and there she stood. Even scared and unbathed, Anna Zaitseva was breathtaking. The photographs had not done her justice. They didn't capture the glow of her skin or the sparkle in her eyes. Actually, at the moment it was more of a defiant glint than a sparkle, but her amber orbs were beautiful nonetheless.

Victor walked past her into the cabin without a word. It took less than a minute for him to determine that Mother wasn't there. It was just as well. He didn't want to waste time dealing with an old woman. Coming home to find her daughter gone would be penance enough for her sins. "Where's Mom?"

"She's gone for food."

Victor nodded. It made sense. You could hardly put out an APB for "old woman" but "tall, auburn-haired beauty with large breasts and sultry amber eyes" was a different story. So naturally, Mom made all the contact with the outside world.

In life, even more than in pictures, Anna reminded Victor of the actress Uma Thurman. Uma Thurman with an MD; this girl was in the wrong country. "Put your coat on, Uma," he commanded.

Anna looked at him inquisitively but didn't say anything. She did as he told her. He locked a pair of handcuffs around her wrists as though pinning on a corsage and escorted her from the hideout. Then Victor yelled, "Burn it to the ground" to the senior officer when the angle was right to give him a casual view of her face. He wanted to make certain Anna understood that her life had changed, permanently.

Victor did not speak during the ride back to the helicopter. It was part of his interrogation technique. Let her get uncomfortable. Let her mind run wild while waiting for the next blind lash. Make her want to speak just to fill the painful void of anticipation. He sat beside her on the backseat, opening walnuts with a big pair of rusty pliers, *crack, crack, crack*. He thought he detected a quiver with each new nut, but he wasn't sure—the ride was hardly a smooth one. They arrived at the helicopter ten minutes later. It was well below zero, but Anna was sweating.

The helicopter was an Mi-8, which boasted a relatively quiet salon and offered them plenty of room for face-to-face discussion or whatever else might strike his fancy. They boarded and Victor ordered the pilot to fly full throttle for Academic City. His team could take the train back.

Once they were airborne, Victor uncuffed Anna, removed her sheepskin coat and hat, and then put the handcuffs back on.

"Are you comfortable?"

She nodded.

"Alex told me where you were."

Anna gasped.

"Don't get me wrong. He did put up a fight, but . . ." Victor let his voice drift off as he shook his head slowly back and forth. Then he took her hand in his. "Tell me about the printout, Anna. Where is it?" he queried with a sickly sweet voice, rubbing one of her knuckles all the while.

Tears began to flow down her face. "I don't know where it is."

"You don't know . . . You don't know . . ." he said, keeping his voice low as he looked out the window. Then Victor turned so that his face was just inches from hers. "We've only been flying for ten minutes. It will take us at least three hours to get back to Academic City. Hell, if the weather gets bad, we may have to touch down and spend the night in this thing." He slipped the pliers around the middle knuckle on her index finger, waggled the teeth a bit, locked his eyes on hers, and then raised his brows in silent query.

♦ ♦ ♦

Victor was thrilled by how quickly his strategy had worked, but not surprised. He had not used the pliers on Anna. His father had ordered him not to harm her. Of course she had no way of knowing that, so his properly played threat had been enough. He kept the pliers out as a reminder anyway.

While walking her through the interrogation, he felt a flood of confidence begin to wash over him. By the time they were halfway to Academic City, he was sure he knew everything that she knew, and he was feeling better than at any other point in his life. Karpov would have to respect him now. Talk about leaving on a high note.

Although Victor was convinced that Anna had told all, he had to be certain. Meticulous. "You know, Anna, you're much smarter than Alex. He chose to go through days of the best my colleagues had to offer before telling us where to find you."

Anna did not respond, so Victor leaned over and lightly bit her earlobe. Then he whispered exactly what it was they had planned for Alex. Afterward, he sat back to appraise his work. Although she had been pale before, Anna was positively ghostly now. It was time for the coup de grace.

"If you've held out on me, I'll see that you get a one-way ticket to the Lubyanka. You know what happens to people at the Lubyanka, don't you? In the Lubyanka they have mastered the pain-to-damage ratio. The only result that counts for the scientists there is sustainable discomfort. It's a contest among those guys. If you've lied to me, I will probably visit the Lubyanka basement on weekends to watch you scream and squirm while I drink vodka and enjoy blinis with caviar."

"And what's to happen to me if you *are* satisfied with my cooperation?"

It was her first question, and an inevitable one. In truth he did not know what Father had planned for Anna, but he wasn't about to reveal his ignorance. Given that he shared Karpov's genes, Victor felt he could make a good guess. The only thing that was going to keep his pants on for the next hour was Karpov's order that she not be touched.

"Assuming you've been truthful, and completely truthful, all that has occurred will be chalked up to your being in the wrong place at the wrong time. We will consider you the victim of American subversion, rather than a coconspirator.

"Now, is there anything you would like to add?"

"No. You know it all."

Excellent.

CHAPTER 63

Novosibirsk, Siberia

Karpov was vexed. Despite a week of wrenching torture, Alex still maintained his annoyingly witty veneer. The unwavering persistence of his flippant remarks and use of his first name had gotten under Karpov's skin. How was he doing it? Karpov was in control, complete control. Yet somehow Alex seemed to be the one scoring points.

It had been so long since he had engaged a worthy opponent that he had forgotten what it felt like. Well, Karpov would beat Alex at his own game. Alex would die with no doubt as to exactly who had beaten him, who had bested him, who had won. Karpov owed that much to Yarik.

Time to shake things up a bit, he thought, removing a propane torch from the supply closet. He flipped it over twice in his hand, getting a feel for its balance and weight as he grabbed a sparking igniter from the shelf. Then Karpov flung open the door to the interrogation suite, rocking it on its hinges.

"No more games, Alex. Today you are going to tell me everything."

"What is it you want from me today, Vasily?"

Karpov felt himself going red. *No. Don't let him get to you. You're better than he is. Beat the boy at his own game.*

"Give me the list."

"Which list is that?"

"Do you really want to play games, Alex?" He squeezed the sparker twice.

"Actually a good game of chess sounds wonderful. You any good?"

"Perhaps later."

"After drinks, you mean?"

Karpov held up the torch and gave Alex a very serious look. "Left eye or right eye?"

"If it's up to me, I'll choose your left eye."

Karpov turned on the propane and gave the sparker another squeeze. Then he adjusted the flame to a small, blue cone. Satisfied with his tool, Karpov grabbed Alex by the hair on the back of his head and began pushing his face closer to the flame. He did it slowly, drawing it out, letting Alex feel his power.

"Okay, okay, gee whiz. Where's your sense of humor, Vasily? Give someone a big star for their shoulder board, and it's all work, work, work."

Karpov stopped pressing, but did not pull Alex's head back yet. He left it there until the smell of burning hair filled the air. Twenty seconds and Alex's eyelid would be gone. Another minute after that and his eyeball would come to a boil in its socket. *Cocky bastard.*

Alex would die, and soon, but not yet. Slowly, ever so slowly, he moved Alex's head back from the flame. "Last chance."

"I'd be happy to show you the list, Vasily, if you'll let me go afterward."

"Show me? Show me? Surely you're not in the mood for more games," he said, gripping Alex's hair even tighter. "I know you don't have the list stashed anywhere around here."

"Yes, your boys were quite thorough in their examination. My compliments. I mean I'll take you to the list."

"Take me to it?"

"That's right. Do we have a deal?"

"Sure."

"And once you have the list you'll drop me off at the US Consulate? Forgive and forget and all that?"

"Wherever you like." *Alex would have to be mad to believe that. Was it possible? Excessive humor was often the first sign of madness.*

"Deal."

"Let's go."

"Just you and me?"

"Don't push it."

"You afraid, Vasily?"

"Don't be silly."

"Well then?"

Karpov scoffed. It hardly mattered. He was a god in this town, and Alex could barely walk, much less run. He would defeat him, one-on-one. "Okay. Why not? Let's go."

"I need some time to clean up. Can't really go anywhere looking like this. I have my pride, you know."

"I'm not a patient man, Alex."

"Just a few more hours. The place we'll be visiting doesn't open until after dark, and I see by your shave that the sun's still shining. Besides, I've got to say good-bye to all my new friends."

Karpov kept a serious look on his face but smiled inside. After dark would be just perfect.

CHAPTER 64

Novosibirsk, Siberia

Alex liked riding in Karpov's jeep much more than under it. He told him as much. Provocation was part of the plan. Fortunately, a weak ego was not one of Karpov's shortcomings. Unfortunately, Alex was fading fast. Feigning cheerful indifference under these circumstances was draining a tank already on empty. *Just a few minutes more . . .*

Alex had been watching the jeep's mirrors as best he could and was relatively sure that Karpov's goons were not behind them. He had taken a few extra turns to help make sure, and to time his arrival just right. Twice Alex thought he heard a distant helicopter, but if Karpov was being that cautious, there wasn't a thing Alex could do about it, so he put that concern out of his mind.

Alex knew that Karpov had no intention of living up to their agreement to set him free. He would have been mad to think otherwise, but that was one conclusion he wanted Karpov to make. Anything that encouraged Karpov to drop his guard would help. Truth be told, Alex suspected that if this did not work, madness would descend. For all his tricks and mind games, this week had piled on more than a mind should ever have to bear.

Alex spotted the path he and Anna had used walking home from church. "Turn left here."

He was gambling big that Karpov wasn't a churchgoer. It was a comfortable wager. Alex had Karpov pegged as a man full of confidence but devoid of faith.

"Park in front of the church."

Karpov circled the building once and then parked on the side. After looking around to convince himself that this wasn't a setup, he said, "Let's go."

Alex held up his cuffed hands for Karpov to unlock them.

"Not a chance," Karpov said, draping a coat over them.

"How will I cross myself?"

"If you've come here for last rites, Alex, you're a bit early."

"Actually, I was hoping to convert you."

"You're getting closer to meeting your god with each minute you keep me from my list. If it isn't here, Alex, I will take you straight to the radiation chamber."

"Never fear, Vasily, salvation lies within."

Their footfalls echoed prophetically off the stone walls as the two made their way through the dark church toward the warm glow of beeswax candles. Golden icons reflected their flickering light back from the altar, giving Alex the feeling that he was walking into a Rembrandt. Which would it be, *The Raising of Lazarus*, or *The Sacrifice of Isaac?*

As he walked, Alex fought back the pain with the determination of a wounded soldier in a battle not yet ended. Unfortunately, he knew that mere endurance would not be enough. He had to remain witty and flippant. *How do you*—His eye caught the icon of Christ, nailed hand and foot and bleeding from the side, and Alex knew that he would find a way.

As they reached the base of the pulpit, Alex stopped in his tracks. He forced himself to don an admiring expression and then turned to face Karpov. "You know, Vasily, all jokes aside, before we part company, I really should congratulate you. You're the only man who was ever able to catch me. Back in my CIA days, I could dance around KGB agents all night long, and they would never detect a beat. But you, you're different. I can see why nobody ever caught you. You're always two moves ahead, aren't you?"

"Two moves is for schoolgirls, Alex. I work decades ahead."

"Decades! Decades . . . wow. Yes, I can see that. Faking that radiation leak was a brilliant move. But tell me, doesn't it keep you up late at night? Sending those twenty-five villagers to a horrible death has to be hard to live with."

"You Americans are so weak. History's great leaders have always been willing to sacrifice the proletariat when there was need. Generals all the more so. Stalin made his share of mistakes, but he got one thing right: the peasants are expendable."

Alex wanted to vomit and collapse, but instead he maintained a look of astonished admiration on his face. "I suppose you're right. Now that I think about it, it's practically part of the job description."

"Damn right it is. I took the worthless men of this village and turned them into something great. So what if they suffered a little from radiation? Their pain was short-lived, but their sacrifice will service generations to come. They will go down in history as martyrs, as founders of the great new nation of Russia. Without me, they would have died anonymously, having lived flaccid lives devoid of meaning or purpose."

"Yes, but—"

"Can't you see that what I'm doing here is so much more important than anything they could have ever hoped to accomplish?"

"Yes, but—"

"No more buts, Alex. My papers, if you please."

"Of course." Alex turned deliberately, mounted the pulpit, and stood before the Bible. Looking down on the general, Alex smiled and said, "Tell me about your relationship with Elena Popova."

"Elena Popova? I don't know an Elena Popova."

"It's been a while. Think back to your time in Geneva." Alex felt his stomach shrink as he saw recognition dawn.

"Okay. I remember her now. I knew her thirty years ago and haven't seen her since. I know she defected, but that was after our relationship ended. I was back in Siberia before she even met the American."

"It was thirty-three years, to be exact. And I'm not accusing you of defecting, Vasily. I'm accusing you of something altogether different. You see, thirty-three years ago, Elena Popova became my mother."

Karpov stared blankly for a moment, and then his jaw dropped.

"I'd love to discuss the chapters of your life at length, Vasily. Would also like to explain the acoustics of this ancient church, but I fear we won't have the chance. Looks like they're going to demand the first and last word." Alex threw a glance over Karpov's shoulder.

Karpov turned to find himself flanked by a fiery-eyed congregation and its ashen-faced priest.

"They heard every word you said. Every sick, arrogant, radioactive word."

Karpov did not turn back to face Alex. The surging crowd demanded his full and unwavering attention. They were armed only with the candles in their hands and the fire in their hearts, but that was clearly going to be enough.

Alex watched as Karpov's mind tried to catch up to the remarkable reversal of circumstance, but before he could get there, they were on him.

He did not fight. He hardly moved at all. He just surrendered to their blows like a haystack to a hurricane.

His eyes locked with Alex's for a moment as he looked up from the ground. Then the crowd enveloped him.

That flicker in time was all it took for Alex to see that his father recognized the truth. The truth about what he had done. The truth about who he had become. The truth about their relationship.

As the ancient icon of Christ looked down from above, the villagers picked at Karpov's body like a pack of vulturous demons sent from hell to twist and torment his flesh. They burned him with beeswax candles, pummeled him with wrinkled fists, and kicked him until they could kick no more.

It was biblical.

It was animal.

It was his father.

CHAPTER 65

Novosibirsk, Siberia

Anna felt miserable. Not only had they caught Alex because of her, but he had endured days of torture before finally giving her up. She, on the other hand, had betrayed him to Victor in a matter of minutes with nothing but the threat of violence. Anna was disgusted with herself, and it was only going to get worse.

Victor's driver was taking them directly from the helipad to the church to retrieve the list she had hidden there. Once the list was in his hand, Victor would be assured his victory. Then he would deliver her to Karpov, and Anna would be conscripted to defeat. Anna did not know what Karpov had planned for her, but her best guess was—

Anna threw her face between her legs and vomited on the floor of the car. Some sloshed back onto Victor's shoe, and she braced herself for the tooth-jarring slap she expected in reprisal. None came. Instead, Victor just handed her his handkerchief and turned to look out the window. He seemed preoccupied.

It was then that Anna realized that Victor had not actually done anything to harm her. He had burned the dacha, and so thereafter she had taken him at his word, but words were all that had come, words and images. Was he just a brilliant actor, a professional who had mastered his craft, or did he really have a heart of stone?

Anna stole a glance at her watch. It was almost eight thirty. The weekly memorial service would be over now, and soon everyone would leave. Anna did not expect any help from the parishioners, but she was desperate for the sight of a friendly face. She also wanted someone to catch sight of her so that she wouldn't vanish without a trace. Her poor mother would be going out of her mind by now, having returned from the market to find the dacha burned down and her daughter missing. Anna knew her mother would get through it—life in Stalin's shadow had taught her to be tough—but news that her daughter was alive would be balm for her soul.

As she stared out at the snowy landscape whizzing by, a terrible thought struck her. What if something had happened to the list? What if a janitor or priest had discovered it and thrown it away? Would Victor believe her when she told him, "I left it here," or would he need convincing? She shuddered at the thought of what that might entail. He had left little to her imagination.

At last, the car stopped before the church. Anna closed her eyes. *Please . . .*

"Let's go," Victor said, pulling her out his side of the car. When she stood up, he grabbed her by the hair on the back of her neck and pulled her face to within an inch of his. "If you try to run, if you speak to anyone, I'll use the pliers to rip your nose right off your face. Understood?"

Whether Victor was acting or not, Anna was too frightened to speak. She nodded her head feebly.

"Good. Now, take me to the list."

As they approached the portal, Anna understood that something unusual was going on. There was enough commotion within the ever-silent nave to penetrate the massive oak doors. Victor did not seem to notice. He pulled the big brass handle as if he were starting a mower and pushed her inside.

Anna had trouble making sense of the sight that confronted her eyes. The parishioners were mauling around in front of the altar like angry ants on a contested mound. It was like someone had emptied a sack of gold dust on the floor, and everyone was struggling to get his share . . . except for the anguished screaming.

Victor pulled Anna off to the side of the nave so he could safely appraise the situation while their eyes adjusted to the dim lighting. It appeared as though some poor wretch was at the center of the row, and Anna could not help thinking of the stonings that played a part in the history of her religion. Then she and Victor saw it at once, and the sight induced a palpable shock. While the face was unrecognizable beneath the blood and swelling, the shredded uniform was still unmistakable. The poor wretch was Vasily Karpov.

Victor's hand dropped from the back of her neck, and for a moment the two of them continued to stand there, stunned and staring. Then Victor clenched another fistful of her hair and began to drag her back toward the door. As her head twisted, Anna's eyes came to rest on another figure. Standing up in the pulpit, as though presiding over the scene, was Alex.

CHAPTER 66

Novosibirsk, Siberia

Alex snapped out of the spell to the sound of someone screaming his name. He shifted his gaze toward the source of the scream and found that the unbelievable scene was now positively surreal. By what Alex could only assume was yet another act of God, the man who had killed his brother a month before and half a world away was miraculously there before him now, holding the woman who had saved his life.

Jason looked up, and they locked eyes. Then Jason resumed dragging Anna from the church by her long auburn hair.

Alex leapt down from the pulpit and began racing toward the front of the church, ignoring the pain in his feet and the fact that his hands were still cuffed. If Jason had a gun, the fight would be over before it began, but Alex wouldn't be able to live with himself if he let Jason cart Anna away.

It flashed across Alex's mind as he closed the gap that the man he now pursued with a bloodlust in his eyes was his half brother. In fact, the two men in that church were the only direct blood relations he had left. Alex had not found the energy to analyze that news while in

captivity—it was one hurdle too many for his already overtaxed mind—and there was no time to start now.

As Alex rushed at his nemesis from the front of the church, the doors crashed open in the back and a team of soldiers flooded into the nave. Alex's heart sank even as his legs pumped. He would not even get an unfair fight.

The shocking sight of the soldiers caused Jason to slacken his grip. Anna seized the opportunity to bite his arm. As Jason recoiled, Anna kneed him in the stomach and then lunged back—right into a stone pillar. Jason recovered quickly and drew back his arm to punch her, but before he could release the blow, two soldiers picked him up and threw him to the stone floor.

Alex was not sure if they planned to arrest him as well, but he knew that there was no sense in trying to run. He looped his cuffed hands around Anna and pulled her body to his. Anna hugged him back so tightly that it would have been painful even under normal circumstances, but after a week at the Karpov Hilton, her affection was absolutely agonizing. He didn't mind. He tried to run his fingers through her hair but the handcuffs hindered his tender gesture.

A third voice chimed in unexpectedly from behind. "Let me give you a hand with those."

Alex and Anna banged foreheads as they turned to face the speaker. Before them was a thin, elderly man with a crinkled face and a monkish fringe.

"Hello, Alex. So nice to meet you at last."

Alex recognized the distinctive timbre of the diplomat's voice before placing the famous face. For better or worse, the buck was going to stop here. "Minister Sugurov?"

CHAPTER 67

Novosibirsk, Siberia

As the peasants swarmed over him like a pack of dogs on so many bones, Karpov found himself frozen in time. Paralyzed in mind and body. He looked up at Alex as though for the first time—the contour of his jaw, the line of his hair—and knew without question that Alex had spoken the truth.

Karpov was only vaguely aware of the crowd knocking him to the ground. His son's words were crashing over him like a tidal wave, and they drowned out everything else. Time slowed. First he got the feeling that something momentous was coming, then it hit, and he found himself struggling in a sea of disorientation, desperate for air in his lungs and grounding for his feet. Every time he tried to breathe, another wave was upon him:

Alex was his son . . .

He had tortured his own son . . .

Alex was a twin . . .

Frank was also his son . . .

Victor had murdered his own brother . . .

As the conclusions crashed relentlessly down, Karpov felt his defenses washing away, exposing him to the ghosts of the past. Eleven years ago a door had shut with the hiss of a hermetic seal—and locked his soul inside. Karpov understood that now. His son's powerful revelation had broken that seal, and now he lay exposed.

Even as his body lay dying, his soul was struggling to breathe, but the pathway was choked. His sins were piled up like starving beggars at a soup kitchen's door, and the muddle stretched as far as his eye could see. He began to tremble. First in line were six young men, scientists each, with broken ribs and blood-frothed mouths. He remembered. He understood. Six men had lost their lives that momentous day, but seven bodies had surrendered their souls. What had he done? What had he done . . .

CHAPTER 68

Moscow, Russia

Alex was living at the Kremlin dacha known simply as Gorky Eight. His foray into this icon of Soviet luxury had begun exactly one month from the date of Frank's death. Was there anything more elastic than time, he wondered. How many lifetimes had he packed into those thirty days? And it wasn't over yet . . .

Two weeks had passed since the reckoning in the church, and it was now Christmas Eve in America. Alex had ricocheted through a wide range of emotions between those famous walls, coming to grips with what he had learned about his family history . . . and about himself.

With his own fate in the balance and virgin Christmas snow falling all around, Alex found himself feeling particularly charitable. He seized the opportunity to forgive his fathers, both of them.

There were dozens of victims of the Karpov conspiracy, not the least of which was Vasily Karpov himself. Alex understood that Karpov made the sad mistake of believing that the grandest of ends could justify the vilest of means. Although those vile means would haunt Alex for the rest of his life, he drew comfort from the knowledge that Karpov's grandest

ends were exactly that. You could not fundamentally condemn a man for wanting to make his country great again.

As for his half brother Jason—Victor would always be Jason to Alex—he was less charitable. Genes did not a brother make. Jason's circumstances were extreme, Alex granted him that, but his motives were base, and that made all the difference. Perhaps his harsh view would mellow with time, but meanwhile he was content to let the Soviet justice system do with Jason what it would.

Then there was the question of how Alex felt about himself, now that the whole mess turned out to be a family affair. After a lot of back and forth, Alex decided to judge himself as he judged others: by his actions.

He had made good on his vow to Elaine, even if she didn't know it yet. He had fulfilled Andrey's dying request, even if Andrey would never know it. Alex had saved the Kimberlies of the world, those that were, and those that never would be. And, perhaps most importantly to Alex personally, he had lived up to the promise he had made to himself by his brother's grave. Frank would be proud.

That brought Alex to where he was today. Although he was not formally under house arrest at Gorky Eight, he knew he would encounter uncomfortable resistance should he try to leave the Russian Camp David. The same went for phone calls. So Alex decided to do the sensible thing for a change. He treated his time at Gorky Eight as a vacation at a reclusive health spa. That was what he would choose to do anyway, if he were free to choose. He breakfasted on hot *blinis,* ate his weight in Beluga caviar for lunch, and dined on smoky *shashlik* washed down with the finest Georgian wines. He took long, meditative walks along snowy trails, and basted his bones with medicinal balms in the presidential banya. He had no need to stretch his imagination to make confinement bearable this time, and his feet were feeling better, too.

His stay at Gorky Eight also gave Alex the chance to grieve for Frank properly. With the murder solved, the conspiracy that led to it all but wrapped up, and those responsible either dead or in jail, he could finally lay Frank to rest. The snowy trails of the surrounding woods proved to be the perfect place for releasing the rage that had driven him these past weeks, and remembering the love for the man who inspired it.

Minister Sugurov informed him that Anna had been reunited with her mother and that they would be returned home safe and sound after a similar vacation. He spent a lot of time thinking about her. He didn't know if there was a future for them, but he wanted to find out. Absence was making his heart grow fonder.

Of course he didn't know if he had a future. The issues at hand were not of a criminal nature, at least as far as Alex's involvement was concerned. State security was the problem. The government of Russia had to decide how to deal with the remnants and ramifications of the Karpov conspiracy. Like it or not, Alex had to respect the fact that that might not include his freedom.

Minister Sugurov had told him that it would probably take a couple of weeks. That was exactly how long it took before Alex was summoned to Gorky Eight's presidential study. Given the way his fate rested in one great man's hands, Alex felt as though he had been summoned before Pharaoh.

Twenty minutes and a not-unfriendly frisking later, Alex was standing before two dwarfing guards and a massive oak door. He experienced a wave of nausea as the memory of Frick and Frank flashed through his mind, but their image vanished when the guards parted to reveal the presidential seal.

Mikhail Sergeyevich Gorbachev sat before a roaring fire in a high-backed leather armchair. Alex felt a sudden pang for brandy, but, alas, the stereotypical crystal decanter was not a part of the scene. He inhaled deeply, drawing the room's smoky aura down to the bottom of his lungs and calming his nerves. Then the guards closed the doors as the president looked up from his newspaper.

Alex tried to read Gorbachev's expression and body language, but got nothing. No surprise there. The man was a professional diplomat and this was their first meeting.

"Good morning, Mr. Ferris. Please have a seat." Gorbachev motioned to his chair's twin. Alex took this as a good sign.

"Thank you, Mr. President."

"Has your stay been comfortable?"

Alex thought Gorbachev looked tired. He was not here on vacation, nor was he made up for the camera. Still, his eyes conveyed a clarity of thought and a presence of mind that were worth far more than a few strokes from a makeup artist's brush.

"Yes, sir. I thank you for that."

"It is I, we," he gestured around, "who must thank you, Alex. You have done a great service for the people of the Soviet Union."

"Thank you, Mr. President."

"I am sure you understand that what you have uncovered is exceptionally sensitive information. Diplomatically, politically, economically, the knowledge you possess, if leaked, could be disastrous for the Russian people. Do you agree?"

"Yes, sir, I do."

"You are aware, I am sure, how certain of my predecessors would have, shall we say, kept things quiet?"

It was a rhetorical question, but Alex answered anyway. "I believe Comrade Stalin's favorite phrase was, 'No person, no problem.'"

The fire cracked during the ensuing silence, and a glowing ember sprang onto the marble hearth. Gorbachev frowned and nodded slowly but did not comment further. He obviously had their conversation mapped out, and did not plan to deviate from his predetermined course.

"I differ from General Karpov in that I do not believe that good things can grow from evil roots. History has shown us time and again that the easy way out does not make things easy, not in the long run. For that reason, I would like to believe that we, you and I, Alex, can come to an agreement.

"I will tell you what we are going to do. Then you will tell me if you can live with my decisions, if that course of action will satisfy the sense of justice that so obviously drives you." He paused and looked at Alex above the rims of his gilded glasses. "I am sure that it will. Thus agreed, we will shake hands on this as gentlemen. Then we will part, never to speak of the Karpov conspiracy again. To anyone."

"It would be my honor, and my pleasure, Mr. President."

"Excellent. Minister Sugurov had assured me of as much.

"The first issue that I have had to deal with is the fate of Karpov's factories. Although privatized, the factories have reverted to state ownership as a result of the crimes of Karpov and his associates. He acquired them with stolen capital. That leaves the decision of their disposal totally within my control. I have decided that the Soviet Union will keep the factories, their management, and their general manufacturing know-how, given that those are all Russian resources. The stolen intellectual property, however, will all be abandoned."

"You're going to scrap the product lines in their entirety?" Alex asked, forgetting for a moment to whom he was speaking.

Gorbachev did not flinch. "In their entirety. This decision was a difficult one, given that what Russia needs most is a competitive industrial base. But that's why one maintains a belief system, so he has something to stick to when the decisions get tough. And believe me, Alex, this decision was tough—especially when it came to the photovoltaic bricks. You know, nothing remains of the company or the people who invented them. Karpov wiped it from the Earth as though it were never there. When we abandon it, that groundbreaking technology will be lost to the human race, if only temporarily."

Alex was shocked. "If I may say so, Mr. President, your approach is most admirable. I can't say that I truly believe that my president would have the courage to be so . . . virtuous."

Gorbachev's lips tightened with a hint of appreciation, but he did not respond. Instead, he continued.

"The second, and perhaps even more sensitive issue, Alex, is the Peitho Pill. That decision did not require a virtuous man, just a sane one. It is my firm belief that as long as the Peitho Pill exists on this Earth, nobody will truly be safe. Not even those who consider themselves its masters. It's easy to make big decisions when one's children are safe. The Peitho Pill severs sacred alliances: man and country, mother and child. It is the seed of the Devil, and to him it must be returned. All devices, all instructions, all descriptions, all blueprints and records, and any evidence of Peitho that exists anywhere are to be destroyed immediately. Peitho is to be buried, and I will do my best to see to it that it is never resurrected."

"Sir, when you say all evidence . . . ?"

"No, Alex, I am not going to have anybody killed. Peitho will go out the same way she came in. Victor Titov was kind enough to reveal the secret to Peitho's safe removal. Her victims will soon have their devices removed—quietly, unknowingly, while they sleep."

"So they will never know that they're free?"

Gorbachev held up his hand. "They will know, but only after their pill has been surgically removed and the incision has healed. I would like you to play a role in that process, but you can discuss those details later with Minister Sugurov. Meanwhile, I should inform you that there is one exception, of course." Gorbachev raised his eyebrows.

It took Alex a moment before the welcome revelation hit him. "My implant?"

"Gone."

Alex slowly let out his breath. They had drugged and operated on him while he slept. It was a disturbing thought, but better than the alternative. It had occurred to Alex that Gorbachev might choose to leave him Peithoed as a means of ensuring that he kept the Karpov conspiracy a secret.

With the Peitho threat removed, his mind was free to move on to other things. "And what about the device used to paralyze Frank?"

"That would be Medusa. Let us just say that the same strategy applies. She will meet her Perseus."

"So nobody will ever look her in the eye again," Alex added, thinking aloud.

Gorbachev gave another somber nod.

Understanding that his audience was over, Alex got up to leave, humbled, awed, and relieved. But the great man stopped him in his tracks.

"Alex—"

Alex turned around nervously.

"My handshake."

CHAPTER 69

Moscow, Russia

The foreign minister turned from the panoramic view of Moscow to look Alex in the eye. "You understand, Alex—that I had to make sure the state's interests were secure before confiding in you."

"I do understand. Of course I've been very curious these past two weeks, but since you assured me that Anna would be fine, I wasn't distraught. I trust that her condition has not changed?"

"You have my word on that."

"Thank you."

"Now, to bring you up to date. I intend to answer all your questions at this time so that you will never have to ask another one." He paused to make sure this message got through, then continued.

"As you know, Vasily Karpov is dead."

Alex nodded. Apparently no mention of their biological relationship would be made here.

"Victor Titov, aka Jason Stormer, did not get off so easily."

"Lubyanka?"

"Lubyanka. I was there when they logged him in. The warden, Comrade Lebed, is a Peitho survivor. I have no doubt that as we speak Victor is receiving the best they have to offer."

Alex nodded. He would have to examine his thoughts on the fate of his half brother later. Perhaps much later. The realization that he had the blood of a psychopath coursing through his veins was simmering on the back burner of his mind. He did not want to think about it now.

Sugurov removed his glasses and began to clean them with his handkerchief. "So much for what is awkward for you. Now we come to what is awkward for me. Before I tell you that, I should say that when I am done, I hope that we can still be friends. I will understand, however, if you feel that we cannot."

Alex felt his throat turn dry as a sense of foreboding reverberated along his spine.

"Four months ago, the helicopter piloted by my deputy and carrying my chief of staff, crashed in the mountains southeast of Novosibirsk. My deputy, Leo Antsiferov, died in the crash. My chief of staff, Andrey Demerko, walked away."

Alex drew a deep breath as he thought back to the man who had saved his life and the ultimate sacrifice he had made.

"After the crash, Andrey found documents in Leo's briefcase that outlined something horrible. That something is what we now call the Karpov conspiracy.

"We found Victor Titov's fingerprint, but the only name mentioned in the documents was the code name Knyaz. Even without specific names, however, it was clear from those documents that the conspiracy ran very high, so high that even at my level I did not know who could be trusted—who was Knyaz, and who was not. If they had recruited my own deputy . . ." Sugurov shrugged.

"To make matters worse, the fragile yet volatile state of Russian politics combined with the fledgling status of our economy made this the absolute worst time to stir things up. Even without the destabilizing force of the Knyaz, we knew that President Gorbachev was at risk of being toppled at any time. And we knew that if he fell, it would be a tragedy of historic proportions—for our country, and for the world. The bottom line, Alex, was that we were looking at a ticking bomb we could neither attempt to disarm nor afford to ignore."

"So you came to me?"

Sugurov nodded. "If an American were caught meddling in Russian affairs, the scandal would pull the people of Russia together, unite us against a common enemy. Whereas if the government of Russia were discovered conducting a witch hunt among its own, it could blow the country apart."

"Why me?"

"I'm not entirely sure. I left the details and the implementation up to Andrey. He enjoyed my full trust and confidence. Andrey came to me convinced that you were the best man for the job, and I accepted his judgment. Now it's clear that he was right. I doubt there was anyone else who could have done what you did, Alex."

"Still, how did you find me? Was it my CIA file?"

"I'm sure that played a role, but it would have taken more than that. Andrey was not a gambler."

Alex paused. *It didn't really matter how they found him, did it? Not in light of subsequent events.* "But I got involved because of the death of my brother, and it was Jason who killed—" Alex's heart moved into his throat, cutting off his voice.

"It was Jason who killed Frank. He pulled the trigger. But we set Jason up. Andrey broke into Frank's house and sent an e-mail to Jason from Frank's computer. It said. 'I know who you really are. Come by my house tomorrow evening, and we'll see what we can work out.' The next day Jason did what we knew he would do."

Alex looked up at Sugurov, aware that there were tears in his eyes. "And the *puzzler* entry?"

"Andrey planted it. It was insurance. He was afraid you might catch

Jason without learning about the Knyaz, so we had to direct you toward Jason through Elaine. Meanwhile, Andrey kept a watchful eye on you and Jason."

"The loose wire on the car bomb . . ."

"That was Andrey."

Alex nodded his understanding. Sugurov was giving him a lot to think about.

"I won't make excuses for what we did, Alex. As we saw it, there was no other choice."

"Well, I certainly can't question your conviction," Alex said, thinking of Andrey. Then his thoughts shifted to a question that had been eating at him these past two weeks. "You still haven't explained to me how you ended up at the church that night."

"Some time ago an accountant named Luda Orlova stumbled across Karpov's financing scheme—the details of which aren't important." Sugurov's tone on the last part of the sentence indicated he did not want to get into that discussion. "Karpov killed her."

"Her father, already a widower and now further devastated by the loss of his only child, somehow figured out that Karpov was responsible. He went looking for a chance to extract his revenge. He found that opportunity when he found you . . . bringing you breakfast."

"The friendly eye at the peephole?"

"That would be he."

Alex found the wherewithal to smile.

Sugurov put his glasses back on. "I lost track of you after Andrey was killed. Since I couldn't conduct an outright search, I set up a passive search. I called the police and border patrols to request that they inform me immediately of any incidents involving Americans—for diplomatic reasons, you understand. A week later, a call came in from the chief of police in Novosibirsk. He told me of an old man who had gone to the US Consulate to report an American being secretly held by the KGB. I flew to meet Mr. Orlov, got his story, and then came for you."

"Unbelievable. And just in the nick of time." A switch clicked on in Alex's head. "Did you follow us that night in a helicopter?"

"Right again."

"Wow. So much information . . . so many opportunities for things to have gone wrong, terribly wrong." Alex began shaking his head and then stopped to look up at Sugurov. "Tell me, minister, did you ever give up hope?"

"No, Alex, I never did. Guys like Karpov can't go on forever."

EPILOGUE

Crane Beach, Barbados

"When is Anna landing?" Elaine asked.

Alex's cell phone chirped as he looked at his watch. He mouthed "three hours" as he flipped the phone open. "Alex Ferris."

"Please come up to the bar, Alex."

"What?"

"The bar. I'm waiting for you."

". . . Minister Sugurov?"

"Call me Pavel."

Alex gave a shrug to Elaine and did a slow jog across the burning sand and up the cliff-side staircase to The Crane's Nest. Arriving at the picturesque watering hole, he saw that it was not Georgio behind the bar. In his place stood a pale elderly man with the distinguished face of an accomplished diplomat but the sunglasses and faded fishing hat of a beach bum.

"You're blending right in there, Pavel."

Sugurov smiled. "How are you doing, Alex?"

"I suspect you have a pretty good idea how I'm doing, Pavel." Alex had been tripping over Russian agents ever since leaving Gorky Eight, three months earlier. He understood why the surveillance was necessary, but it annoyed him all the same.

"Ah, yes. You understand we just wanted to make sure that you adjusted satisfactorily. No post-traumatic stress disorder or whatnot."

"How kind of you," Alex replied in monotone.

"Now that I see you're doing well, I'm sure the courtesy won't be necessary anymore."

"Thank you."

Sugurov pushed the sunglasses down to the end of his nose and peered over them. "Yes, well, I understand you've got some company arriving this evening?"

"Fancy you should know that. Yes, Anna's flight arrives in three hours." Then the light went on in Alex's head. The fact that Anna's passport application had suddenly been approved was linked to the decision to cancel the surveillance. Alex knew he was lucky to get away with just three months, lucky to have the foreign minister as an ally, but it burned nonetheless.

Sugurov undoubtedly saw the realization dawn on Alex's face, but did not comment. "I'm going back on the same plane."

"Quick trip."

"Just a stopover from New York."

"I'm guessing you have something more to tell me."

Sugurov looked aside and smiled. "I thought you might also like to be among the first to know that Andrey Demerko has been posthumously named Hero of the Soviet Union. The way things are going, he could well be the last. Anyhow, it means that his family will be well provided for."

"I'm glad to hear that." Alex looked down at the sand between his toes. "What about Leo?"

"His untimely death, tragic though it was, probably ultimately saved our nation. Unfortunately, only a few people will ever know the truth, and his family cannot be among them. That revelation will have to wait until the hereafter."

"I figured as much." Alex leaned against a bar stool and gave Sugurov an appraising stare. "You seem to have gotten religion, minister."

Sugurov's face reddened. "Karpov brought us so close to the edge . . ."

"But for the grace of God," Alex finished.

Sugurov removed his sunglasses to focus on Alex with his crystal-clear eyes. "I fear I do have one bit of disturbing news to deliver. Victor Titov has escaped from the Lubyanka."

Alex closed his eyes for a long second, but did not comment.

"We're not exactly sure how he did it—this is a first—but we know he had help."

They were quiet while Alex absorbed the news. Finally Alex asked, "What condition was Victor in when he escaped?"

"He's missing his left eye now. Other than that, the physical damage should heal. Psychologically . . ." Sugurov shrugged.

"I see."

Sugurov nodded toward Elaine down on the beach below. "You certainly travel in style."

It was Alex's turn to blush. "I inherited Frank's stock options. They are paying off nicely now that the sabotage has stopped, so I figured I'd live a little. And I thought it appropriate to share the wealth."

Sugurov nodded his approval. "It was a great idea you had, having Elaine meet personally with the American Peitho victims last month to deliver the good news. Thank you again for ensuring that there was no hint of Russian involvement."

"My pleasure."

"Well, I guess that's it then . . ." Sugurov trailed off and began nodding to himself.

Alex raised his eyebrows.

"It seems you've finally achieved what all of us want but few truly possess, Alex."

"What's that?"

"Freedom."

AUTHOR'S NOTE

Academic City still exists, although it no longer functions as a think tank the way it did during Soviet times. Back then it was full of privilege, but devoid of freedom. Now the opposite is true. The village church is fictitious, although Europe boasts a number of churches that echo like the one described there, as does the US Capitol.

The KGB was abolished by Mikhail Gorbachev on October 24, 1991. At its peak, the Committee for State Security was estimated to have over seven hundred thousand employees, making it the largest organization of its kind in world history.

The politburo, having transferred its powers to the parliament a year earlier, ceased to exist in August 1991. On August 31, 1991 Mikhail Sergeyevich Gorbachev resigned as general secretary of the Communist Party Central Committee. On December 25, 1991, one year after this tale concludes and four days after the Soviet Union itself ceased to exist, Gorbachev resigned as President of the USSR.

Though Gorbachev was immensely popular abroad, his reforms cost him the support of the Russian people. In effect, the people of Russia shot the messenger. Although I am encouraged that the world community chose to honor his sacrifice with the Nobel Peace Prize and *Time* magazine's Man of the Decade award, and am pleased to know that history books give favorable mention of the Gorbachev name, I am disheartened to find that so very few politicians have the decency to choose what is right for tomorrow over what is popular today. Surely that, too, cannot go on forever.

ABOUT THE AUTHOR

Tim began his career in the Green Berets, where he learned Russian and specialized in Soviet counterintelligence. Moving to Moscow in the midst of Perestroika, then Brussels during the formation of the EU, and eventually landing in Silicon Valley as a start-up CEO, he has enjoyed a globetrotting career on the cutting edge of medical technology.

Equally active outside the boardroom, Tim has climbed the peaks of Mount Olympus, hang glided the cliffs of Rio de Janeiro, and parachuted into places undisclosed. He walked the Serengeti with a Maasai warrior, worked medical experiments with an orbiting cosmonaut, and crossed the Atlantic with the Gorbachevs. While none of his adventures were planned to be a thriller writer's research, they certainly help.

Tim lives with his wife, Elena, and their two daughters in the San Francisco Bay Area. Tim earned an MBA from Wharton, and an MA in International Studies from the University of Pennsylvania. He welcomes your feedback. You can learn more about the author at his website, timtigner.com, or at his Amazon author page, amazon.com/author/tigner.

79335386R00191

Made in the USA
Middletown, DE
09 July 2018